ABOUT THE AUTHOR

Edward John Smith known as Eddie to family and friends was born in Rugby in January 1941. He has two older sisters Janet and Ann.

Eddie left school at the age of fifteen and embarked on a five year engineering apprenticeship at Rugby's largest employer, The British Thompson Houston, known as the BTH.

While still working at the BTH he met Betty and they married in December 1962. They were later to have two daughters, Nicola born in 1966 and Andrea in 1968.

In Eddie left the BTH and moved to the Industrial and Ma Division of Bristol Siddeley at Ansty near Coventry. Pu d later by Rolls-Royce, Eddie continued working there un took voluntary redundancy in May 2000 aged 58.

With rly retirement Eddie was able to devote more time to pla golf, and finally fulfilled his dream of writing a book. So thing he had wanted to do for many years but had never found the time. In 2008 he hit upon the idea of Vesuvius 2012.

The inspiration for Vesuvius 2012 came as a result of many holidays in the Italian resort of Sorrento. It was during these holidays that Eddie visited Vesuvius and the remains of the Roman City of Pompeii. This prompted him to research the history of the destruction of Pompeii by Vesuvius in 79 A.D. and hence to write this story.

005028169 0

ACKNOWLEDGEMENTS

To Arima Publishing and particularly Richard Franklin for giving new authors the opportunity to publish their first book.

A big thank you to my wife Betty for her input in helping me to build this story and ensure I told it my way.

Andrea my youngest daughter whose English grammar and literary knowledge kept me focused along the right lines.

For her enthusiasm, support and professional advice, my profound thanks to Ann Richards of Apple Pips Editing Services Kenilworth. (www.applepipsediting.com).

My friend Mike Holden, whose many years experience and knowledge in the art of typesetting etc, has been invaluable in his assistance in laying out the story manuscript.

To Kelvin Hunt of Hunt's Bookshop Rugby, for giving me advice and for supporting all local authors, by allowing us all to promote our books with a book signing session.

And finally to all mine and Betty's friends who have spent many holidays together in Sorrento, for supporting this book and allowing their characters to be part of the story.

Vesuvius 2012

Edward John Smith

Published 2009 by arima publishing

www.arimapublishing.com

ISBN 978 1 84549 405 6

Printed and bound in the United Kingdom

Typeset in Garamond 12/14

Swirl is an imprint of arima publishing.

arima publishing
ASK House, Northgate Avenue
Bury St Edmunds, Suffolk IP32 6BB
t: (+44) 01284 700321
www.arimapublishing.com

Chapter One

Just as the clock in the departure lounge showed 05:30, the public address system at Birmingham International Airport announced, 'Would all passengers flying to Naples on ITAL 5253 make their way to departure gate number 55 please.' Ellis and Beth picked up their hand baggage and moved towards the neon lit sign above entrance 55.

The day was Friday July 7, 2012. This was the seventeenth consecutive year that Ellis and Beth had flown on this exact flight, en route to spend their annual two weeks' holiday in their idyllic coastal resort of Sorrento, in southern Italy.

Little did they realise what they would encounter over the forthcoming days.

It was way back in the year 1995 that they first visited Sorrento.

That first trip was due to the holiday programme annually screened by the BBC. In 1995 the programme was introduced by the very popular presenter Jill Dando (who was later tragically murdered outside her Fulham home in 1999).

In that particular programme, one of the holidays featured was a seven-day coach tour of Italy, followed by a week in Sorrento. Ellis and Beth were so impressed by the content, that they visited the travel agents the following day and booked a similar holiday, for that summer.

That week in Sorrento set a trend that would continue for the next seventeen years.

The public address system blared out again, as they moved towards the check-in desk that was located at the entrance to the aircraft loading stand. At that moment they spotted William and Sandie, two of the people they had become close friends with since first visiting Sorrento many years ago. They were also both retired. William was the same age as Ellis and Beth, whilst Sandie was slightly younger. As they tried to attract their attention William looked round, saw them, and they all acknowledged each other, as they boarded ITAL 5253. Beth remarked how well William and Sandie looked, adding that they looked no different to how she remembered them last year.

As in recent years the aircraft was a Boeing 757, and Ellis and Beth had booked extra leg room seats, 12E and 12D. These were exit seats situated in the middle of the aircraft. Ellis being six feet two inches tall was always troubled when seated in aircraft, coaches, or cinemas. That was why they always booked extra leg room particularly as they were now seventy one years of age. Although Beth was a lot smaller than Ellis she too enjoyed the freedom of the extra leg room.

Both had been retired for some years, Ellis since he was sixty five and Beth since she was 57. Ellis had worked as a foreign correspondent for the television satellite company *Star News*, for many years, whilst Beth had worked as a physiotherapist assistant for the last seven years at the local hospital.

Neither Ellis nor Beth had encountered any problems with retirement. Both had always had many interests away from work. Retirement had in fact worked in their favour as they were able to devote more time to those interests, particularly Beth as she was now able to assist both daughters Jamie and Louise with the grandchildren. Meanwhile in between gardening and renovating Jamie's house, Ellis was also able to spend more time at his local golf club.

Unlike some retired couples Ellis and Beth's relationship did not suffer as a result of the sudden change to their previous day to day routine. In many ways it had improved the relationship as the stresses and strains associated with modern working life had subsided. With both receiving satisfactory pensions from their previous employer plus their state pension, their joint income was sufficient to ensure that they were financially comfortable.

ITAL 5253 flight was due to depart at 06:10. With flight time approximately two hours thirty minutes, and an adjustment for Italian time, they expected to arrive at Naples airport at around 10am local time.

After a wait at baggage handling, they would proceed to Sorrento by taxi to the Hotel Geranio. This was their favourite hotel where they had stayed for the last sixteen years. The 45-

kilometre journey from the airport to the hotel normally took 60 minutes.

As they stepped into the aircraft, they were met by one of the cabin staff. After checking their boarding passes, they were directed towards the middle of the aircraft.

They swiftly located their seats and, after storing their hand baggage in the locker above, they settled into their seats.

Ellis checked his watch; it showed 5.50am which was 20 minutes to take-off time. He turned to Beth, remarking, 'So far so good, wonder how much of a delay there is?'

A few minutes later the aircraft intercom system burst into life, with the following message. 'Good morning ladies and gentlemen, this is your captain Thomas Clarke. Accompanying me this morning is first officer Adam Taylor. I would just like to inform you that we are running a little behind schedule this morning. However, we have been given clearance for 6.20 and very shortly, with the assistance of the cabin staff, we will be securing the aircraft in readiness to be towed off our parking berth.'

Ellis and Beth smiled and simultaneously said, 'That is not a problem.'

Five minutes later they heard a clunk from the front cabin door, as two of the cabin staff pulled the door shut. They then went through a series of checks to ensure the door had been secured correctly. Within minutes, a small judder was felt as the aircraft was detached from its parking berth, and towed backwards by an airport tractor.

Once into its correct position the tractor released itself from the aircraft. At which time the pilot increased the revs of both engines and the aircraft began taxiing towards the take-off runway. Very soon, they were stationary at the end of the runway, the brakes were on and the engines were idling.

Ellis glanced at his watch; it showed 6.18. As he did so, the revs on both engines increased dramatically. The brakes were released, the aircraft raced down the runway, 30 seconds later it gently began to lift off the ground.

The aircraft quickly rose into the sky, as the two Rolls-Royce RB211 engines gradually increased their thrust upwards through 90 per cent to almost full power. Within two minutes from take-off, they were heading into the clouds banking left, and heading towards the Home Counties and then over the English channel towards their destination. Once again they were en route to Sorrento.

Just as Ellis was about to say, 'That's the first third of the journey behind us', Beth leaned over grasped Ellis' hand and with a smile on her face, very quietly said, 'I'm ready for my breakfast.'

Beth smiled again, when Ellis reminded her that they had completed one third of the journey.

She smiled, because Ellis always divided the journey into three parts. The first was arriving at Birmingham Airport, boarding the aircraft, and taking-off. The second was arriving at Naples Airport, collecting the baggage. The final part was the taxi ride into Sorrento, and then arriving at the hotel.

Just then the passengers heard the familiar 'ping pong' sound that indicated seat belts could now be removed and, at the same time, the seat belt sign went off.

As though they had heard Beth, two of the cabin staff appeared at the front end of the aircraft with the breakfast trolley. At this point Ellis leaned back in his seat and reflected on the last four and a half hours.

The journey had begun at two o'clock that morning, when their friend Peter had arrived at their home in Rugby to chauffeur them to Birmingham Airport. This was a journey that Peter had done many times before. Ellis and Beth always enjoyed him taking them, as he was always punctual. The drive in his 2000cc Renault Laguna was always comfortable and secure.

Forty five minutes and 34 miles later, they arrived at the airport. Peter drove into the short-stay car park, which was only a short distance from the departures entrance. Having collected their baggage from the car boot, and loaded it onto a trolley which somebody had earlier abandoned, they said their thanks and farewells to Peter, and headed towards the departures entrance.

Once inside the building, Ellis and Beth made their way over to the check-in desks. These were not open yet, so they positioned themselves at the same desk as last year.

Fifteen minutes later, the desks began to open. They were in luck as they had chosen correctly. Within minutes they were checked in. Soon afterwards they headed upstairs for a coffee before making their way to the departure lounge.

Once in the departure lounge, Ellis visited the newsagents, purchased a *Daily Mail* newspaper, and headed back to where Beth was seated. On the way back, he diverted towards the flight information screens, where he noted that ITAL 5253 was still scheduled to be the third aircraft to take off at 06:10.

As soon as he had reached Beth, she told him that she was going into the duty-free shop that had now opened. This was the same ritual every year, as she purchased perfume for herself and other members of the family.

Ellis smiled to himself as he thought. Yes, she purchases, but with my credit card. Just like the Queen, never carries any money.

Ellis' thoughts were interrupted as the breakfast trolley trundled alongside.

'Breakfast sir?' said a voice, Ellis looked up it was a tall female member of the cabin staff.

'Yes, please,' Ellis replied. At this point Beth leaned over towards the cabin staff, in anticipation of the same question. As she was about to be asked, Beth nodded and answered, 'Yes, please.'

As the trolley was pushed past them, they both began peeling off the silver looking seal that kept the contents of the container in check. When they finally opened it, they were confronted by one sausage, a small omelette, together with a small helping of cubed potatoes; not particularly appetising.

Both managed to eat the majority of the meal, but they were more interested in a drink. Right on cue the tall cabin staff girl appeared, 'Tea or Coffee?' she asked in a low husky voice. Both replied, 'Coffee please.' She smiled, and poured both cups before departing to the people seated behind them.

Shortly afterwards, the cabin staff began collecting the empty breakfast trays. Once finished, they embarked on another trolley trip, offering duty-free goods.

At that point the cabin intercom system sprang into life, 'Good Morning, this is Captain Clarke again, with the latest update on our flight. Currently we are cruising at a height of 37000ft, our speed is 550 mph, and the temperature outside the aircraft is approximately -40 degrees centigrade. With the following wind that is assisting us this morning, our flight time will be approximately two hours fifteen minutes. Our estimated time of arrival is 9:33 local time.'

He continued, 'At this moment we are passing over Geneva. We will then head towards Northern Italy, and from there we will make our way down towards   Naples.'

'Any duty-free goods sir?' another of the cabin staff asked.

Ellis smiled at her, saying, 'No thank you.'

He leaned back into his seat. As he did so he could feel himself relaxing and beginning to look forward to the holiday, particularly the six friends they would be meeting again for the umpteenth time. The 'gang' as they called themselves were known by the waiters at the hotel as the 'English Mafia'.

As his thoughts turned to meeting them once again, Ellis pondered to himself when would be the best time to invite them all to join him and Beth in celebrating their Golden Wedding anniversary.

Suddenly he was jolted back to life as he heard a voice from the cabin intercom system. It was Captain Clarke again, 'We will shortly be making our descent into Naples airport. I hope you have enjoyed your flight and thank you for choosing Ital Holidays. The weather in Naples is currently sunny with blue skies and a temperature of 26 degrees centigrade. Enjoy your holiday.'

He continued, 'I'm sure most of you will have seen the newspaper and television reports this week, regarding recent volcanic activity from within Vesuvius. The latest information we have does indicate that there are still occasional wisps of steam being emitted.'

'The observatory at the foot of Vesuvius is now issuing daily bulletins, and predictions of the situation. Local Naples officials are being briefed daily and the latest comments indicate no cause for alarm.'

As the cabin intercom ceased Ellis' thoughts switched to July 20th 1962 the day Beth and he got married. His mind quickly covered the years from that day to the birth of their two daughters, who were now both in their forties. Jamie the elder by almost three years was divorced with two children, Emily and Matthew, whilst their other daughter Louise had been married to Steve for almost 21 years. They had one child called Paul.

At precisely 9.32am local time, they could feel the brakes being applied as the 757 touched down on to the tarmac at Naples airport. This was followed by a loud roar as the engines were put into reverse thrust. This immediately acted as another braking system. The aircraft began slowing down very quickly. Very soon its speed across the tarmac was reduced to a slow crawl.

It wasn't many minutes before the aircraft found its parking bay, and the pilot turned into it and parked alongside other aircraft. Shortly afterwards, all passengers began to disconnect their seat belts and retrieve their hand baggage from the lockers above their seats.

Within minutes, the large portable exit staircase was manoeuvred into position. As the cabin door was pulled open at the front, rays of sunlight were projected into the cabin. The cabin staff gestured to the passengers to begin leaving the aircraft. Very few needed telling twice.

Ellis collected their hand baggage and walked out of the cabin door and onto the top of the exit staircase. They were met immediately by shafts of sunlight, together with a sudden rise in the ambient temperature. They moved down the staircase and boarded the waiting airport concertina-style bus.

As soon as the bus was fully occupied, it moved off towards the arrivals building, where all would pass through passport control, and onwards to the baggage handling carousel.

The journey took only a few minutes, and very quickly the bus unloaded its occupants outside the arrivals building. Everybody walked inside and immediately was forced to join the queue, which had formed as people waited to go through passport control.

Ellis and Beth reached the control point where two officers in uniform beckoned them forward to hand in their passports. After a quick flick through the pages, they were nodded straight through. Once through, Ellis headed towards a stacked row of baggage trolleys, pulled one out, and he and Beth trundled over to the carousel that identified the Birmingham flight.

When they arrived there, they spotted William and Sandie. They joined them, and spent the next few minutes catching up with the past year's news. 'How is that son of yours doing?' Ellis asked, 'Is he still working abroad?' This was followed by the usual banter as to whose cases would arrive first.

As if on cue William and Sandie's cases suddenly appeared on to the carousel. 'Bad luck,' William said with laughter in his voice, 'we will see you at the hotel later.'

Ellis laughed back. 'Will do, we'll probably see you on the terrace at lunch time.'

Shortly after William and Sandie had left, Ellis' mobile phone bleeped. Ellis laughed, 'Bet you a pound, that's Louise.' He put the phone to his ear, and started to nod. 'We have landed and are waiting for our cases. Yes, I'll text you when we pass the plastic palm tree, bye for now.' He looked at Beth, they both started to laugh. It was by now a standing joke. Every year Louise their youngest daughter would start to text them at about the same time, to see where they were. She had been to Sorrento three times herself and loved to travel the journey with them in her mind.

From here to the hotel they would have at least two more text discussions with her.

It was almost twenty five minutes before their cases came into view. Ellis stacked both cases and their hand luggage onto the trolley; they then set off in the direction of the exit, looking for the holiday rep. They soon spotted her, 'Mr and Mrs Smith,' she exclaimed, 'your taxi is just over there.' She waved her hand at a man standing by a large white Mercedes taxi. She shouted something in Italian. He heard her, raised his hand and came over towards Ellis and Beth.

The rep. said, 'This is your driver, Giuseppe; he will take you to your hotel. Giuseppe, this is Mr and Mrs Smith, you are taking them to the Hotel Geranio Sorrento.' Giuseppe smiled, and beckoned them towards the taxi where he quickly placed their luggage into the boot of the white Mercedes.

Ellis and Beth went into the rear of the taxi, fitted their seat belts, and Ellis in typical style, put both his thumbs up, and laughingly, said to Giuseppe, 'Sorrento here we come.'

Giuseppe lifted his hand, as though he was acknowledging Ellis' comment, started the engine and moved slowly towards the airport exit.

Ellis looked at Beth, and gestured, 'The third and final part of the journey to Sorrento is now commencing.'

Beth laughed, 'Yes, okay, you have made your point. Now put these on and let's look as though we are on holiday.' She handed Ellis a pair of sunglasses. He put them on, looked through the window at the sun shining above, and commented, 'what more could a man want?'

The taxi moved onto the main road and headed towards the outskirts of Naples.

Ellis glanced at his watch. With the correction for local time it now read 10.30.

He turned to Beth, lowered his voice, so that the driver could not hear. 'I wonder what type of driver we have got this year?' he murmured to her. 'Is he a "Fangio" or a "milk-float" driver type?' Beth, put her finger to her mouth, 'Ssh', she said, 'he might hear you.'

Ellis nodded, he turned to Giuseppe, and speaking slowly asked him if he spoke any English? 'Just a leetle, Mr Smeeth,' he replied.

So far so good, thought Ellis, and replied, 'Whereabouts do you live?'

Giuseppe answered, 'I leeve near Sorrento.'

'Very nice,' said Ellis. 'We envy you.'

At that point, Beth nudged Ellis, saying, 'Leave him alone and let him concentrate on his driving. You talk too much.'

'Ok,' replied Ellis, 'point taken.'

They had now reached the motorway, which would take them to the winding coast road. This was the moment they would find out Giuseppe's driver type.

After five minutes of driving, it was evident that Giuseppe fitted neither of their categories as his driving appeared exemplary. He drove at an acceptable speed, did not 'tailgate', neither did he hog the outside lane. Ellis and Beth breathed a sigh of relief, as in previous years they had not always felt comfortable with their driver.

It wasn't very long before they came off the motorway, and joined the dual carriageway. Very soon, this came to an end, the road narrowed to a single carriageway and soon they were proceeding along the coast road. This would eventually lead to Sorrento.

As they turned and headed left along the coast road, they spotted Vesuvius some 1281 metres high. She was standing with a backdrop of a sunny clear blue sky. Sitting close by was Mount Somme from where Vesuvius had originated from, some 18,000 years ago. Ellis spotted a plume of steam coming from the crater and commented to Beth, 'Now you see it for real, it does seem scary. I just wonder if this is the year, she wakes up.'

Ellis pointed to Vesuvius, and asked Giuseppe, 'Do you think everything is all right with Vesuvius?'

Giuseppe replied, 'I do not know, Meester Smeeth, some people think Vesuvius is starting to get angry.'

Ellis answered, 'I hope not, otherwise we'll all be in trouble.'

It all went quiet; the taxi sped on along the winding road heading through the first of three tunnels en route to Sorrento.

They started to climb upwards; the road stretched ahead of them, as they turned a corner, there in front of them was the Bay of Naples. Beyond the bay was once again Vesuvius, looking towards them with that plume still being emitted from its crater.

That time Vesuvius was on the right hand side. However, as they continued on their journey, it appeared on the left and then on the right again. This was caused by the configuration of the winding road.

Very soon, they reached the first of the favourite bathing spots for the local people. This one was called Bikini Beach, and sitting on its own in the middle of the small bay, was a green plastic palm tree. Ellis laughed out loud, and said, 'I'd better text Louise and let her know where we are.' He took out his mobile phone and sent a quick message, informing her that the palm tree was fine and well.

Beth also laughed, saying as she did, 'You're both as silly as one another.'

Before Ellis put the phone down, it beeped twice. It was Louise again, her text message saying, 'You will be at your hotel soon, "Ciao" for now.'

As they passed through Bikini Beach, the local traders were putting the finishing touches to their fruit and food stalls, in anticipation of a good monetary return for the day. With the sun high in the clear blue sky, and a temperature already reaching 26 degrees centigrade, they stood every chance of a good day.

Having now climbed to the highest point on their journey, they started a gradual descent. As they did, they could see where the road a few miles on, curved dramatically around to the right, leading into the small resort of Sant'Agnello, just two kilometres from Sorrento.

Ellis and Beth glanced at one another, both faces beaming, as Beth with a cheeky smile enquired, 'It's still here then?' Ellis just pulled a face, refusing to reply.

The taxi was now rolling down the hillside as though being pulled by a strong magnetic force. In no time at all, they had reached ground level, and were soon on the outskirts of Sant'Agnello. Giuseppe turned off the main road, and turned down towards the narrower back roads. Before long, he reached the junction where a large notice board displayed all the names of the hotels in that area.

Halfway down the board was the Hotel Geranio. As they turned another corner, they could see the entrance to their hotel, just a hundred metres or so away.

As their taxi pulled up outside the hotel entrance, Ellis checked his watch. It showed 11.30. Not bad, he thought, about five hours from Birmingham to the hotel.

They both alighted from the taxi just as Giuseppe took the entire luggage from the boot. Ellis walked over to him, shook him by the hand. He thanked him, with the mandatory 'Grazie'. At the same time he slipped a ten euro note into his hand. Giuseppe smiled and thanked them. He threw in 'Ciao' for good measure.

Giuseppe moved to pick up the suitcases but, before he could, the small hotel porter nicknamed Oddjob, arrived with a sack barrow. He loaded them, and quickly set off to the hotel entrance.

As soon as he went through the main entrance, followed closely by Ellis and Beth, they were spotted by Beppe Marcello, one of the owners of the hotel. He moved quickly towards them, arms outstretched, saying, 'Mr and Mrs Smeeth, how are you?' He embraced each in turn giving them the traditional kiss on both cheeks. As he finished, Perla, his cousin the other joint owner appeared from the office. She too embraced both Ellis and Beth.

'You both look very well,' Beppe exclaimed.

Ellis replied, 'And you look well too. We both hope to look and feel better after two weeks of your weather and fine food.'

'I'm sure you will,' replied Beppe. 'Go and book in; we will see you later.'

As they moved to the reception desk, Gino, the Chief Concierge, beamed at them, saying, 'Welcome Mr and Mrs Smeeth, so nice to see you once again.'

He handed them the obligatory form for them to fill in. On completion he handed Ellis the room key. 'There you are Mr Smeeth; we have saved you your favourite room number 505. We hope you enjoy your holiday.'

Gino raised his hand, and Oddjob beckoned them to follow him. He boarded the lift, whilst Ellis and Beth did their usual thing which was to walk down the wrought iron, twisting staircase, which would lead them to their room.

Once downstairs, they walked across the small open area, into the first corridor, then straight on, two right turns and they were outside their room. Already inside was Oddjob waiting for them. Ellis thanked him and gave him a small euro note tip. Oddjob smiled, returning the thanks with a 'Grazie'.

Once inside Ellis went over to the curtains, at the end of the room. He pulled them to the side using the hanging cord. He then opened the glass door, and stepped through onto the balcony. Once there he looked out across the Bay of Naples where Vesuvius was sitting proudly on top of the skyline. The plume of steam was still very visible. Ellis looked at it for a few moments, thinking to himself, that plume looks larger and denser than it did earlier today.

As his thoughts started to subside, Beth came out onto the balcony. 'I'll unpack some of our clothes so they become less creased,' she said, 'then we'll go for lunch.'

'That will be fine,' Ellis replied. 'In fact that's a good idea. I'll have a beer whilst I am waiting.' Ellis went inside opened the mini-bar, picked up a bottle of 'Nastro Azzurro' beer, flipped the top off, and went back out onto the balcony. He sat down in the wicker type basket chair, and poured the contents of the bottle into a glass.

He sat there quietly, watching the plume of steam, pushing upwards into the sky. He was mesmerised by it; he felt his eyes closing, but could do nothing about it.

Then suddenly a voice said, 'I'm ready for lunch if you are.' It was Beth, speaking as she appeared on the balcony. She had changed into a pair of shorts and a halter top; her sunglasses were perched on top of her head. 'Give me two minutes,' yawned Ellis, as he pulled himself out of the chair and disappeared into the bathroom.

'Whilst you're getting ready, I'll give the girls a ring, to let them know we've arrived,' said Beth.

'Good idea,' replied Ellis. Beth rang Louise first and managed to get connected straightaway. The call only lasted two minutes, before she put the receiver down and dialled Jamie's number. Again she was connected first time, as Ellis heard Beth say, 'Hi Jamie, its mum. Just a quick call to let you know we have arrived. We are about to go for lunch.'

After a few more pleasantries, the call was finished.

'Right let's go and eat,' Ellis called. At that point Beth joined him, picked up her handbag with the door key, and followed Ellis out of the room.

Chapter Two

As they arrived on the terrace where lunch was served, Carlos the terrace bar manager had his back to them. He was dressed as always in his cream jacket, white shirt and black trousers. All the creases were immaculately pressed. The sun was glistening on his shaven head. Ellis turned to Beth. He winked, and said mischievously, 'I don't think the service is as good as last year.'

Carlos turned around quickly, with a hurt look on his face, which soon changed to a broad smile when he recognised Ellis and Beth.

'Oh it's you.' He laughed, and hugged and kissed both of them saying, 'you do this to me every year, and I always fall for it.'

Still laughing, he escorted then to a table, enquiring as to their health and well-being. As they sat down, Carlos gave them a menu and Ellis and Beth quickly made their choice of meal.

'One small beer, an orange without ice, to start with,' indicated Ellis. 'I will have the ham omelette.'

Beth looked at Carlos, smiled and said, 'I'll have my usual please.'

Carlos smiled back, 'That will be the tomato salad, if my memory serves me well.'

Beth looked, and nodded. 'Your memory is still good.'

Whilst they were sitting there, William and Sandie appeared. As if by magic, Dene and Paula, their other friends from Southampton, came onto the terrace via the American Bar, so it was hugs and kisses once again. So now there were six of them. By Monday, when Bernice and Phillip arrived, the 'gang' would be complete. The full complement of eight would be together again as they had been at this time last year.

Before they could start a conversation with Dene and Paula, the terrace floor started to shake, making the glasses on the tables wobble. At that moment Carlos came onto the terrace with a very worried look on his face. Ellis commented, 'What is that?' Carlos shrugged his shoulders and said, 'I do not know for sure, but it has happened a few times in the past few days. Nobody is saying anything, but we think it is to do with Vesuvius.' At this point he turned and pointed across the Bay of Naples.

As quickly as the shaking started, it finished. Ellis and Beth returned to their table, and were joined alongside by Dene and Paula. They were soon discussing their respective flights, and taxi rides to the hotel, what their rooms were like, and catching up on family news.

The arrival of the food slowed down the immediate question and answer session. Soon all were eating their respective meals. Ellis commented to Beth, that his omelette was still as good as ever. Whilst talking, he leant over and obtained a forkful of Beth's tomato salad. He received a stern look for his action and Dene, who had witnessed this, urged Beth to take stronger action. She declined but issued Ellis with a playful warning about his future conduct.

As he sipped his beer, Ellis looked across the bay to Vesuvius; he was slightly concerned by what he saw. The plume from the crater was undoubtedly larger and thicker in width, than when he had sat on the balcony a short time ago. He turned and mentioned this to the others. Both William and Dene agreed with Ellis. Carlos came over and asked if there was a problem. Ellis explained that the plume of steam/smoke had increased since their arrival.

Carlos looked puzzled. 'You are right,' he said. 'I am going to make further enquiries.' With that he disappeared, back through the bar.

Some people at the other tables were now pointing across the bay. They appeared to be in agreement that the plume was expanding.

As Ellis and Beth finished their lunch, Carlos appeared again. He walked towards them, with a worried look on his face. Speaking slowly and forcefully, he said, 'The newscaster on the Italian news network *TG5* has just announced that the Vesuvius Observatory has issued an "attention" alert warning.'

'What does that mean?' enquired Ellis.

Carlos replied, "An 'attention" alert is the first phase of a national emergency plan that is made up of three phases. The first is the "attention" which follows any significant change in the behaviour of Vesuvius; this is followed by a "pre-alarm" phase. Should the situation deteriorate further, and experts are convinced an eruption is almost certain, the "alarm phase" will be declared. That means the area in the immediate vicinity of Vesuvius will be evacuated.'

Carlos continued: '*TG5* network believes the local government of Naples will convene this afternoon, to assess the situation. In the event that they conclude there is a possibility of an eruption, they will put their evacuation procedures on standby, pending further evidence from the Observatory.'

William heard his words and said jokingly, 'Hey, Ellis, you might be back on television yet.'

'Crikey,' replied Ellis, 'I hope for once you're wrong, William.'

Nobody seemed to have an appetite for any more food or drink, so they began to drift away from the terrace. They all headed back to their rooms.

Once back in their room, Ellis switched the television on. He flicked on the news channel, just as the newscaster was announcing that the volcano, Vesuvius, was showing signs of abnormal activity. He then went on to outline the same course of action that Carlos had explained to them ten minutes ago.

Beth frowned as she asked Ellis, 'Do you think this could be serious?'

Ellis replied, 'At this stage, I don't think so. If it was, I think the authorities, would be doing more than just convening a meeting later on this afternoon. We'll have to wait and see. I think I'll lie on the bed for a while. I feel quite tired.'

With that he lay on the bed. Within minutes he was snoring as though he didn't have a care in the world.

Beth looked across at him. Smiling to herself, she thought, 'Whilst he's asleep, he won't be worrying.' She looked at her watch; the time was 2.45pm.

Almost two hours later Ellis woke up. He asked, have I been asleep long?'

'Nearly two hours,' Beth replied. 'I was about to wake you up. Would you like a cup of tea?'

'Yes, please, that would be nice,' yawned Ellis. 'I'll drink that, and then I think I'll have a shave and shower. I can then relax a little more before we go to dinner.'

'That fits nicely with my plans,' Beth remarked. 'I'll use the bathroom after you, once ready we can go for dinner at 7 o'clock.'

'That suits me fine,' said Ellis.

As he came out of the bathroom, Ellis adjusted his bathrobe, indicating to Beth at the same time, that he had finished. 'Thanks,' she said, 'I'm ready for a good long soak, after such a long, tiring day.'

Ellis switched on the television, changed the channel and walked across to the mini bar. He looked inside and selected a small bottle of Gordon's Gin and tonic water. Pity there's no lemon or ice, he thought, still never mind I'll soon remedy that tomorrow.

He sat down on the small settee, made himself comfortable, and poured his drink.

As he did so, Charles Small, the news presenter, started to read out the 'Breaking News' headline that was scrolling along the bottom of the screen:

BASED ON INFORMATION RECEIVED FROM THE VESUVIUS OBSERVATORY EARLIER TODAY THE LOCAL GOVERNMENT OF NAPLES ARE INITIATING PHASE ONE OF THEIR EVACUATION PROCEDURES.

***

Charles Small then went on to explain the happenings and comments that had taken place throughout the day.

He paused for a few seconds to say that, according to a statement issued over the wires by Reuters a few minutes ago, the authorities in Naples were only initiating the first part of the evacuating procedure as a precaution.

The statement went on to say that, although there had been signs of abnormal activity within Vesuvius during the last twenty four hours, there was no firm evidence, to indicate an eruption was imminent.

He continued, 'We'll move on, however, if we receive any further information we will of course update you.'

At that point Beth came out of the bathroom. 'What was that all about?'

'Just clarification of the Vesuvius situation,' Ellis answered. 'The Naples authorities are only initiating their procedures as a precaution.'

'Let's hope that's all it's for!' replied Beth.

Ellis moved from the settee as it was time to dress for dinner. Beth was just finishing her makeup, and was about to dress.

Soon they were both ready so they left their room and headed upstairs to the dining room. They were met at the entrance by the maitre d' Angioletto who directed them to their table.

On the way to their table, all the waiters smiled and greeted them with 'Buona Sera' (good evening). This was followed by, 'How are you? It is nice to see you again.' It was all spoken in broken English, in a way only the Italians can say it.

They were met at the table by head waiter, Giraldo. 'Owe are you both?' he asked.

'Very well,' they both replied.

Giraldo gestured to them. 'Please be seated, I hope you enjoy your stay.' With that he handed them both a menu.

When he returned a few minutes later, they were ready to order.

'Madame, what would you like to order?'

Beth replied, 'I will have the Tagliatelle Emiffiana style, to start with, followed by the Lamb Fornaia.'

'And you sir.'

'I will also have the Tagliatelle and then the 'Gilt-head' escalope with almonds,' Ellis replied. "May we also have a bottle of Greco de Tuffo and a bottle of still water, please?"

'Of course,' nodded Giraldo, 'and your room number sir?'

'505' replied Ellis.

Minutes later the meal and wine arrived. Ellis went through the process of sampling the wine, before nodding and giving the waiter his approval. The waiter, who served the wine, was not one they had seen in previous years. However, when the starter arrived, it was served by Augusto. He was of medium stature, dark haired, wearing modern rectangle glasses. Augusto had been at the hotel since their very first visit. He was just one of three Augusto's working in the dining room. To avoid confusion the other waiters had nicknames for each of them. He beamed when he saw them. 'Owe are you?'

They both replied together, 'Very well.'

The food and wine, as usual, were both excellent. Soon both had empty plates. When it came to ordering a dessert, they both decided upon ice-cream. Once they had finished their meal, they left the table and retired downstairs to the terrace bar, overlooking the Bay of Naples. They were greeted by Carlos. He took their order for two cappuccinos and one brandy. They settled into their chairs, both of them simultaneously, looked across the bay towards Vesuvius. In the glow of the sunset, it stood out on top of the mountain, its plume of steam, still gushing from the crater.

Whilst they were both contemplating the possible scenarios, Carlos arrived with their drinks. He placed the drinks on the table, and then pointed towards Vesuvius. 'Everybody is saying, everything is okay, do not worry. What do you think, Mr Smeeth?'

Ellis looked straight at Carlos, 'I do not know what to think. If Vesuvius is going to behave badly, I hope she waits until our holiday is over.'

Whilst they sat there, Ellis and Beth contemplated what they would do that evening. They both agreed to take a quick visit into town, come back via the Piazza Tasso, and to pop into the Fauno Bar for a night cap.

As soon as they had finished their drinks, they said farewell to Carlos and made their way towards the hotel exit. Entering the reception they spotted a familiar face behind the desk, it was Cirino another of the hotel staff. 'Mr and Mrs Smeeth how nice to see you again.' He said in an excited voice. 'Did you arrive this morning?' 'Yes we did,' replied Ellis. They spent the next ten minutes talking to Cirino before heading out of the hotel, towards the town centre.

On arrival, they decided they would first peruse the small cobbled back street, (fondly known as the 'drain'). This ran parallel with the Corso Italia, the main street running through the heart of the town.

Once in the 'drain', they knew they were in Sorrento, as they were met immediately by the smell of leather. Twenty paces in, they came across the first of several shops that sold leather goods. Both inside and outside the shop, there were leather handbags, belts, purses, etc on display, all at very reasonable prices. They wandered slowly down the cobbled street, pausing occasionally to window shop. Soon they came upon the small square, where people were sitting at tables under large umbrellas. Some were eating, others just drinking, all were enjoying the Neapolitan music that was being played by a local, on his electronic keyboard.

Just after the square, there was another small street, which turned left and led on to the Corso Italia. They decided to take this route, and then make their way back towards the Piazza Tasso.

After one or two stops, while Beth looked at what the local boutiques had to offer, they entered Piazza Tasso. Just across the piazza, they could see the Fauno Bar. They both looked at one another. 'Shall we?' exclaimed Ellis.

'Yes why not' laughed Beth.

Within minutes, they were seated close to the roadside.

This they liked, as it gave them a perfect view for people watching. One of the many waiters soon came to the table. After clearing the table and changing the table cloth he took their orders for a beer and orange juice. The order was quickly processed. As they drank, they watched the crowds of people wandering past in all directions.

Beth turned to Ellis, 'It's like we've never been away.'

Just as they were finishing their drinks, there was a sudden juddering. The tables began to shake; glasses and bottles were falling over. Some fell off the table, shattering, as they fell onto the floor. There was a shout of concern from some people. Others got up from their tables immediately. All looked bewildered, and some were frightened.

Ellis and Beth were as startled as everybody else. As they started to rise from their seats, the shaking ceased. Within seconds, everything was back to normal, just as it was prior to the incident.

The waiters emerged from the inner entrance of the bar, some carried brushes and pans, and others had buckets. Within minutes they had cleared all the broken glass, and other debris, that had fallen onto the floor.

By now everybody was discussing the incident; the people in the square were in deep conversation with the local police. The waiters were gesticulating, and talking loudly with those people who were still at the tables.

General consensus seemed to be that a small earth tremor or even an earthquake had occurred. Ellis heard somebody ask? 'What effect might this have on Vesuvius?'

Beth heard too. 'What do you think?' she asked Ellis.

Ellis replied, 'I'm not sure, although usually when there is volcanic activity, it is preceded by an earthquake.'

'I'd like to go back to the hotel,' Beth exclaimed.

'Me to,' Ellis agreed. They quickly settled their bill, and started making their way back.

As they started to pass another bar, known by them as Toni's Bar, Toni himself saw them, and immediately waved and came over to them. He hugged and kissed them both on their cheeks, enquiring at the same time if they were all right. They said they were, and explained that after that tremor they were going back to the hotel. Ellis asked him what he had heard. Toni shrugged his shoulders and said he had heard nothing different to what the television had been saying.

With that they exchanged goodbyes, and Ellis and Beth set off again, walking briskly as they went. They reached the hotel in less than fifteen minutes, and made their way straight to the terrace bar.

As they approached, they could see William and Sandie seated at a table with another couple. They soon realised that the couple with their backs to them were Dene and Paula. They stopped by the table. As they did so, Carlos saw them, and brought two chairs over and placed them by the table. Ellis thanked him. As they sat down, Ellis said, 'Well, did the earth move for you?' They all laughed.

'What did you make of it?' William asked. Ellis explained what had happened at the Fauno Bar, adding that great concern was shown, particularly by the locals.

'My concern is that tremors or earthquakes usually precede volcanic activity,' Ellis concluded.

Dene agreed, and added that if the tremors continued, then there would be cause for concern. With that, it was decided to have a night-cap, and then to retire.

Once the night-caps had all been consumed, they all bid each other good night, and made their way to their respective rooms.

On reaching their room, Ellis turned on the television, to see if there was any further news on the tremor that evening, or particularly any comments on Vesuvius' activity. On switching through the channels, Ellis stopped just as the evening presenter, announced they were going over to Naples for an update.

The Italian reporter, speaking in broken English, referred to the tremor earlier that evening. He also commented that it was the second one that day. When asked by the television presenter what the local government officials were saying, he replied,

'They are currently meeting in the municipal buildings, in the centre of Naples.'

He then moved on to discuss Vesuvius. He explained that, whilst the grey plume of steam being emitted had definitely increased in density, the scientists at the observatory had concluded that it did not necessarily mean any type of eruption was imminent.

At this point Ellis switched off the television, saying as he did so. 'There is not a lot we can do about it tonight. Let's hope that when we get up in the morning, Vesuvius has settled down.'

'I'll go along with that,' Beth responded.

Little did they know what events would unfold later that evening.

Chapter Three

It was about 2.30am on Saturday morning, twenty four hours since they had left for Birmingham Airport. Suddenly, the bed in room 505 started to shake violently. Beth woke up and shouted, 'What's happening?' Ellis was so startled that he tumbled out of bed.

'Bloody hell,' Ellis shouted, 'let me put the lights on.' He stumbled across the room, forgetting there was a light switch by the bedside. He flicked on the light switch. Thankfully it worked and the ceiling lights came on.

The room was still shaking. He noticed the standard lamp in the corner of the room was swaying side to side. Small items on the dressing table were jumping about. The pictures on the wall were hanging at funny angles.

'Jesus!' he uttered, 'what's going on? Are you okay Beth?'

'Yes, I'm okay but scared, what's happening.'

'I don't know yet,' Ellis replied. 'That's some earth tremor; let's have a look outside.'

With the room still shaking, Ellis made his way across the room to the curtains. He pulled them back to reveal the balcony door. As he opened the door, the shaking appeared to be subsiding.

'What the hell is that?' he exclaimed. 'Goodness gracious look at that. Beth, come and look,' Ellis shouted. 'Vesuvius is erupting.'

'Oh no,' groaned Beth, 'are you sure?'

'Sure as I'll ever be,' replied Ellis.

Beth ran out onto the balcony.

What she saw horrified her. Against the horizon in the distance, she could see what looked like large, intense, grey cloud spiralling high into the atmosphere. From the crater of Vesuvius there occasionally appeared a slight orange glow. This helped to illuminate the cloud above and made it easier to follow its pattern into the sky.

'What do we do now?' Beth asked.

Ellis thought for a moment, replying, 'I think we should put some clothes on. Get our passports, money, and a bottle of water, put them in your handbag and go upstairs. We can then find out what the situation is.'

'Yes, good idea', agreed Beth, 'let's do it.'

Within minutes they were making their way up the winding staircase. As they walked through the reception area, the night porter Benigno pointed towards the terrace bar, saying. 'Everybody has gone that way.' Ellis acknowledged the comment, and both he and Beth walked through the lounge onto the terrace. There were already many people there. Most of them were standing, a few were seated, and all were looking out towards Vesuvius. The one thing they all had in common was the worried look on their faces.

As they made their way further onto the terrace, more people arrived. Amongst them were Dene and Paula. They went over to them. Dene smiled at them, with that cheeky grin of his, saying at the same time, 'That's what I call a good firework display.'

'Stop it, Dene,' pleaded Paula. 'This might be more serious than we think.' Dene apologised, adding, 'Yes, it might very well be.'

They were in the middle of discussing the situation when William and Sandie made an appearance. 'Sorry, we are late,' muttered William. 'Someone couldn't get their hair to look right.' He glanced towards Sandie as he said it.

'Careful, William,' Sandie retorted.

'What's the latest you've heard?' Ellis asked William.'

'Well,' sighed William, 'whilst I was waiting for Sandie, I looked at the various television news reports. None of the satellite networks were operating properly. I assume the volcanic eruption has polluted the atmosphere. The satellites do not work satisfactorily in these conditions.'

'However, I looked at the *Italian News* channel. Although I couldn't understand what they were saying, there was a translation text in three languages, running across the bottom of the screen. Fortunately, English was one of them.'

'Apparently,' William said, 'the Observatory cannot explain why they did not foresee this eruption. They stated that, "Although it is a mild one, it offers no real threat." However the *Italian News* was critical. They said that seismic behaviour, and changes in gas pressure are one of the first indications of potential eruptions. I think there will be some searching questions asked tomorrow.'

William continued, 'It seems that the next 24 hours will be the crucial time. Meanwhile, the authorities in Naples are urging people living around Vesuvius to move out of the vicinity, as a precaution. They will be making a further statement in the morning.'

'Not really a lot we can do tonight then,' Ellis commented.

They all agreed.

As they spoke, Beppe the owner appeared at the doorway. His tanned face adorned by his black moustache was accompanied by a very stern and worried look. Everybody sensed he was troubled by what he was about to tell them. He looked around at everybody, and in a stern voice made the following statement: 'I am like all of you very worried by what has happened this evening. I do not have a great deal of information; however, I will share it with you.'

Beppe went on to describe what the *Italian TV News* was saying. It was similar in content to what William had just told them. He continued, saying that if anybody wanted to stay in the lounge for the rest of the evening, he would ensure that there were adequate refreshments for all. For those who decided to go back to their rooms, he would instruct the night porter to sound the fire alarms, if the situation deteriorated.

'Right, I'm for bed,' said Ellis.

'Me too,' replied the others, including Beth. They all muttered, 'Goodnight,' and set off to their rooms.

Once back in theirs, Ellis and Beth got back into bed. The time was just approaching 3.50am. Both just lay there making occasional comments to each other. Neither thought they would sleep. However, both were wrong, within a short time they were fast asleep.

Chapter Four

Beth was the first to awake, just after 5.35am. She lay there for a few moments before getting up. She looked across at Ellis who was still asleep. She moved quietly across the room towards the curtains. She wanted to see what Vesuvius was up to, if anything. Very quietly, Beth moved the curtains partially aside.

Although not fully daylight yet, she could just see an outline of Vesuvius. She went to the dressing table and put on her spectacles. Once back at the window, she could now see a large, dense, grey cloud spiralling upwards from the top of Vesuvius. Her eyes wandered to the slopes below Vesuvius. The light was not sufficient to see clearly. Beth wondered what if anything was happening on those slopes. She sighed, saying to herself. 'All I wanted was a nice peaceful holiday. No chance of that now.'

As she moved towards the bathroom, Ellis woke up. He saw her and asked, 'Is everything okay? How's Vesuvius this morning?'

Beth replied, 'Not quite as aggressive, as last night. Let's hope she goes back to sleep for another sixty years.'

Ellis snorted at Beth's comment, and said, 'Would you like a cup of tea? I'm going to put the kettle on.'

'Yes, please,' she replied. 'I'm just going to the bathroom. I'll be ready in five minutes.'

Ellis got out of bed, went across the room and plugged in the small portable kettle. He then went to the terrace door and looked out towards Vesuvius. After pausing for thought for a few moments, he said to himself, 'Yes it would be a good idea if you went back to sleep.'

Whilst waiting for the kettle to boil, Ellis switched on the television. Using the remote control he changed the station to *Star News*, to see if there was still any atmospheric interference. To his delight, both the sound and picture quality were excellent. That's a good sign, he thought.

He listened intently as the newscaster discussed Vesuvius with an Italian news reporter in Naples. The outcome of the discussion was not particularly helpful. It seemed that further investigations using the data collated by the Observatory, over the last 48 hours, were to take place today. Meanwhile, people in the immediate vicinity of Vesuvius were again being urged to move away on a temporary basis. At that point, steam was just starting to curl upwards from the kettle's spout. Ellis went over and started to make two cups..

After they had finished their cups of tea, they relaxed for a while, before showering and dressing. Although still early, they decided to go for breakfast. They both agreed an early start might be beneficial as they had no idea what the day had in store for them.

On arrival, they went through the dining room to the terrace beyond, to see if it was comfortable to sit and eat outside. Apart from the thick dense plume still being emitted from Vesuvius, the sky was blue and the sun was shining.

Fortunately, any breeze that was about that morning, was directing the plume towards Naples. This, together with the distance from the hotel to Vesuvius which was estimated at 20 kilometres, was preventing any ash or debris reaching their part of the Sorrento coastline.

They decided to eat outside, and sat down next to the terrace perimeter fence.

As they did so, Augusto came through the dining room door and headed towards them. He smiled as he approached, greeting them with 'Buon Giorno', (good morning) 'How are you?'

Ellis replied, 'Well we survived last night, so we cannot grumble but tonight may be a different story.'

Beth ordered tea for two. As Augusto left, they rose from the table and went through to the self service breakfast bar. Ellis favoured a bowl of fresh fruit salad, followed by toast and apricot preserve. Beth had her usual helping of prunes, and two croissants. They finished eating at 8.15. They had decided over breakfast that they would walk into Sorrento, have a wander around, and then visit the Fauno Bar for a cup of cappuccino.

On the way back through the dining room, they met William and Sandie. They exchanged pleasantries, and arranged to see them by the pool a little later.

After visiting their room, Ellis and Beth walked upstairs to the reception area. They stopped briefly at the desk for Ellis to collect his *Daily Mail*, and a quick chat with Gino, who was on the early shift that morning. Once outside, they turned right, and headed towards the town.

As they walked past the tennis club, they could see a figure on the upstairs level, waving at them. It was Maura, the club stewardess. They waved back to her. Ellis looked up and shouted, 'How are you? We will visit you tomorrow for lunch.'

She waved back, 'I see you tomorrow.'

They walked on with purposeful strides. Soon they reached Piazza Tasso. At that point, they both decided that a cappuccino would be the best course of action before exploring the town. With that decision made, they walked straight for the tables at the front of the Fauno bar and sat down.

Shortly after their cappuccinos arrived, the waiters went into a huddle, and began talking loudly and quickly in a very excitable manner.

Beth looked at Ellis, 'I wonder what that is all about?'

Suddenly, a loud wailing sound echoed around the square.

At that point, the waiters broke off their huddle, and began gesticulating and shouting to each other. Somebody, from one of the other tables called out, 'What's that noise for? Is there a problem?'

A waiter spoke up, 'The noise is from a siren that is sounded only in emergencies. We are not sure what the problem is, although we think it has something to do with Vesuvius.'

Ellis and Beth exchanged worried glances. Ellis said, 'I think we should return now to the hotel.' She nodded. With that, Ellis placed some euros on the table, raised his hand towards the waiters, saying 'Ciao', and they both left, moving swiftly across the square, and then into a side road that would lead them directly back to the hotel.

The siren continued to wail incessantly. As they hurried along, it reminded Ellis of the London air-raid sirens used during the Second World War. Suddenly, they were both thrown off balance, as they felt a tremor beneath their feet. They stumbled, and both raised their arms as though to protect themselves. Beth fell towards Ellis; he stretched out and took hold of her at the same time. This prevented her from falling onto the pavement. Just as they regained their balance, the tremor stopped as quickly as it had started. Beth somewhat shaken, released her hold on Ellis.

'That was frightening', she exclaimed. 'Let's get a move on, and get back to the hotel.'

They moved quickly, lengthening their stride, as they walked. Soon they had the entrance gates to the hotel in their sight. Once through the entrance, they relaxed a little, shortening their stride. As they entered the hotel lobby, Gino saw them, 'Mr and Mrs Smeeth, please go through to the lounge. Mr Beppe is going to speak to you all in a few moments.'

On entering the lounge, they were met with people everywhere. Some sitting, some standing, most in groups huddled together, most were talking in whispers. Not only was the lounge full, but the patio doors to the terrace were fully open. Many people were outside also, using the terrace as an overspill area.

Beth saw Dene and Paula, deep in conversation with William and Sandie, plus another couple who were regulars at the Geranio. They wandered over, and joined the group.

'What's this all about?' enquired Ellis.

William replied, 'I think Beppe is going to inform us all about the latest situation regarding Vesuvius. I have also heard that the holiday rep. will have something to say.'

At that moment Beppe appeared, followed by Gavin, the holiday rep. for the area.

'Ladies and Gentlemen, may I 'ave your attention for a few moments?' Beppe called out. 'We 'ave all been aware during the last 24 hours that all is not well. Vesuvius has shown signs of seismic activity and, preceding this, there have been a number of earth tremors. That siren you can now hear was first sounded 45 minutes ago. It has been sounded by the Sorrento Council Authorities in order to warn the population of Sorrento and all those other inhabitants nearby, that further major activity from Vesuvius is very likely in the near future.

'At this moment, nobody is absolutely sure when or if, this might occur. However, I have been informed that the scientists and volcanologists at the Vesuvius Observatory have been made aware of a large fission opening up deep down below the heart of the volcano. This has allowed volumes of gas under pressure to be released upwards, towards the surface. This is why we are now seeing increased activity from within the crater.'

Beppe lowered his voice as he said, 'With the possibility of a major eruption, Gavin and I have been discussing the situation. We are of the opinion that if anybody wishes to terminate their holiday immediately, then Gavin will try and make arrangements for you to be evacuated, from the Sorrento region as soon as possible.'

He continued. 'However, the evacuation may not necessarily be a flight home. As you will appreciate, demand will more than likely outstrip the availability of aircraft.

'What Gavin will do, once he has the number of people interested in being evacuated, is to contact his company's headquarters to establish what the alternatives are. Once Gavin knows how many people are involved, he will be able to organise some transport. This could result in people only being moved a few miles further south, to be outside the capability of debris from a volcanic eruption reaching them.

'Those of you, who wish to stay, can do so. A further meeting will be held with you to establish what the hotel is planning to do. For the remainder, Gavin will take your names and other details, immediately after I have finished. You do not need to tell him now, as he will be here till 5 o'clock. This will give you time to discuss the options.'

In concluding the meeting, Beppe went on to say that, 'Whatever option you choose will not be binding on you. At this moment these arrangements are purely precautionary. Thank you all very much, for your co-operation. We will of course keep you informed of any further developments.'

With that, Beppe had a quick word with Gavin and left the lounge.

There was silence, for what seemed to be at least 30 seconds. This was suddenly broken as the people gathered there realised what had just been said. Then, as if on cue, the babble of nearly 200 people all trying to converse at once lifted the decibel level considerably.

Dene was the first to speak. 'So Paula,' he said, turning towards her 'what do you want to do?'

Paula replied, 'I'm not sure. I need time to think about it.'

'What about you?' Dene asked looking towards William and Sandie. 'I think the same as Paula,' answered Sandie. William agreed.

Beth looked at Ellis, 'I think I know what you are going to say.'

'Tell me?' Ellis asked, smiling at her.

'I think you will want to stay,' she replied.

'Possibly, but not definitely,' replied Ellis. 'Yes, I want to stay. However, I need to talk to Beppe and find out some more facts before we commit ourselves. Once we have that we can make a decision.'

As they left the lounge to return to their rooms, they agreed to meet later by the pool. On the way back, Ellis went to see Beppe. Unfortunately, straight after the meeting he had disappeared through the gates on his scooter.

Back in their room, Ellis and Beth discussed the situation at some length.

Neither of them was sure what to do, although they both agreed that if their safety was in any way compromised, then they would not hesitate to evacuate the hotel to a safer place.

Whilst they were discussing this, Ellis remarked to Beth, 'I can't hear the siren any more, can you?'

'I haven't heard it for a while,' Beth replied. 'I think it must have stopped some time ago'.

'Perhaps that's good news,' Ellis said.

During the discussion Ellis suggested that he contacted his old news editor's office back in London. He wanted to inform them that the local authorities appeared to becoming very concerned with the recent increase in seismic activity within the area. Beth agreed.

With that Ellis began scanning his mobile phone until he came across the number he was looking for. He selected it and pressed the call button. At this point Beth walked though to the balcony. As she went through the door, Ellis started to speak to someone. Beth smiled to herself, shook her head and stood against the balcony rail and looked across to Vesuvius.

Ten minutes later Ellis appeared on the balcony with a large smile on his face.

'It looks like you've had some success,' said Beth.

'Yes', smirked Ellis, 'I spoke to the News Editor himself and told him of the situation. He is going to suggest that they get a team over here pronto. He's taken my phone number in case anything transpires in the next 24 hours.'

'Okay, let's go to the pool now and see what the others are doing today,' suggested Beth.

With that they wandered down to the pool. The others were already there discussing whether to stay in the hotel or go elsewhere.

Chapter Five

Little known outside of Naples is the location of the Vesuvius Observatory. To those who know, it can be seen situated on the western slopes of Vesuvius. It rests on a knoll, which puts it out of range of ejecta. It is positioned so that lava from an eruption is channelled around the Observatory, over and through it. It is the oldest such institution in Italy, and is still very active for important research in geophysics and volcanology.

The Observatory is responsible for monitoring the volcano upon which it rests, as well as looking after other geological happenings in the area.

To ensure that observation is continuous, around the clock shift pattern is deployed. This system ensures that there is always two staff on duty at the Observatory. They are responsible for checking seismic development of volcano's in that area. It is their duty to communicate to the authorities any significant phenomena observed by the seismic monitoring system.

For the people who live in the immediate vicinity, (estimated at hundreds of thousands), described as the 'Red Zone', this is good news, since in the event of an eruption, they would need as much time as possible to evacuate the area.

That Saturday morning (July 8), there were four personnel manning the Observatory. Normally at the weekend, only two were deemed to be required. However, with current activity being at an abnormally high level, the alert rating had been raised to Amber 3. When this is reached the sirens are sounded to warn the population within a 30 kilometre radius. They are within one upgrade of serious seismic activity.

This was the reason for the sirens being sounded earlier that day.

If the situation deteriorated further, the next alert upgrade would be to Red 1. This level triggers evacuation procedures, and puts the military and civil defence units on standby.

Local authorities within the Campania area have all adopted their own emergency action plans. These have been assembled over the years, and are updated periodically. Whilst they are based mainly on their own local requirements, information received from other worldwide disasters, assists in preparing for all eventualities.

During the last seven days, the scientists and volcanologists at the observatory had seen many variations in seismic activity, and fluctuations in gas pressure. The last 48 hours had been the most unpredictable.

Whilst it has always been believed that the Observatory, would be able to give the authorities seven days' notice of a major problem, recent events had contradicted this.

That Saturday morning, the four staff on duty went about their duties as normal. They were all seated in front of numerous screens; these screens were receiving data from the various sensors and telemetering systems installed in and around Vesuvius. Other sites around the region were also being monitored by this Observatory.

Just after 09:20 that morning a junior scientist Pepe Salvadori, was preparing to monitor gases being emitted from **fumaroles**[1]. These are effectively vent holes, and are to be found on the slopes of the volcano. There are many ways to monitor the escaping gases. That morning a helicopter was measuring both the **Carbon Dioxide Gas (Co2) and Sulphur Dioxide Gas (So2)** concentrations being emitted from the fumaroles. This method is known as **'Cospec Measurements'**. The data is collected by the use of spectrometers. These are mounted directly onto helicopters, and the concentrations are catalogued and monitored on a daily or weekly basis.

The gases that Pepe Salvadori would be examining that morning were the results from those that had been collated over the previous days. They had been examined in the geochemical laboratory in Naples and then the results were forwarded to the Vesuvius Observatory. It was normal procedure to do this every 48 hours.

---

[1] Fumaroles – these are vent holes found around the slopes of a volcano. Normally, they have a yellow coloured cloud flowing from the vent opening. This yellow cloud is normally sulphur vapour escaping.

At the Observatory the results would be fed into computers, along with other data, to help scientists build an accurate picture of the volcano's activity. The data is then analysed against a standard model of variations to volcanic activity. Any deviations that are outside acceptable levels are immediately transcribed to produce another model. This model identifies any potential problems. Should the data being analysed remain at that level, the model is programmed to produce the worst case scenario on seismic activity.

With all the latest information available, Pepe loaded the disks into the computer and selected the standard model scenario for analysis. This done he moved away to complete another task. The initial results would take about 30 minutes. He glanced at the clock on the laboratory wall; it showed 09:50.

At 10.15 Pepe started to move towards the printer in anticipation of the initial findings of the standard model analysis. As he did so, an alarm buzzer suddenly shrilled loudly on the computer console. In addition to the buzzer, a number of coloured lights began flashing vigorously. Pepe moved swiftly to the console. He immediately spotted that the computer had switched from the standard model analysis, to a worst case seismic activity scenario.

As Pepe stared at the screens intently, his other colleagues had joined him. There was much finger pointing and gesticulating at the screens from all of them. The more they spoke, the faster the chatter and anxiety became.

At this point Pepe and his immediate supervisor Benito Silvestre pored over figures being displayed on an adjacent screen. It was obvious to the other two members of the staff, that there was real concern. They looked at one another; Pepe's face showed immediately that there was a severe problem.

After a few minutes of heated debate, the supervisor turned to Pepe, saying, 'We must call the First Director of the Observatory, and then inform all relevant personnel, as detailed in the "First Stage Alert Warning Procedures".'

As he was saying that, the supervisor moved across and pressed the red button on the telephone numeric pad. Straight away he could hear the ringing tone, as it connected almost immediately to the First Director's telephone.

The telephone was soon picked up. As soon as he heard the voice the observatory supervisor responded. 'Signor, we have indications of a worst case seismic activity scenario.' The response was immediate from the First Director. The other staff that was listening to the conversation realised, as soon as the supervisor said 'Ciao' and put the receiver down, that the First Director was on his way.

The supervisor instructed the remaining three staff to inform all relevant observatory personnel of the problem. He would make all necessary contact with the outside authorities before the First Director arrived.

Chapter Six

It was just after 11 o'clock when Ellis and Beth arrived at the pool. Marco, the pool attendant, had already positioned their deck chairs for them. The rest of their group were already there, standing by William and Sandie's sun beds. Ellis and Beth walked over to join them. 'Anything to report?' Ellis asked. They all shook their heads.

'Nothing to report,' replied Dene.

William asked Ellis, 'Have you made up your mind what you are going to do if Vesuvius threatens us?'

'Yes we have,' replied Ellis.' If there is any immediate danger, we will evacuate to wherever is safe. If Vesuvius erupts, but does not affect the hotel, we will stay.'

'That's exactly what we thought,' William said. Dene and Paula nodded in agreement.

'Right,' Ellis asked, 'who's for a cappuccino?' Everybody responded in the positive. Ellis called Marco over and placed the order. Ten minutes later Marco arrived with the cappuccinos. He served everybody, and with a satisfied smile on his face he nodded and said, 'Please enjoy.'

They had just finished their drinks, as the time was approaching midday, when suddenly there was violent shaking and juddering all around the pool. It was another earth tremor, probably the worst one yet. Cups and saucers were sent flying from the tables and footstools. Two umbrellas were sent toppling, even though they were fitted to their cast iron supports. People started to pick up their belongings and move away from the pool. Some were running, some were panicking.

Chapter Seven

Back at the Observatory, shortly after 11.30, the First Director, hurried through the door into the Observatory. He went straight to his supervisor who was studying the latest computer analysis. Together they pondered over the information that was being printed out. After a few minutes two other members of staff were asked to join them. Together the four of them moved towards a different computer screen where they spent five minutes discussing the data with agitated voices and fingers pointing at the screen.

Whilst the four of them were remonstrating, a red light started to flash on another console. This was followed almost immediately by a loud bleeping as a warning alarm began sounding. Both the supervisor and First Director moved swiftly towards the console in question. Within seconds of reaching it, they both came to the same conclusion; an eruption was imminent.

With his face now ashen coloured the First Director rushed over to the telephone and hurriedly pressed the red button. As he did so, he shouted instructions to the supervisor, glancing at the wall clock at the same time. The clock showed 12:05.

Before the supervisor could carry out the instructions, the Observatory began to shake violently. This was followed quickly by a very loud klaxon sounding, accompanied by warning lights flashing on all the consoles. The ceiling lights began to flicker and shortly afterwards the room went completely dark.

At 12:05 precisely a series of deafening explosions were heard from the vicinity of Vesuvius. Then a huge, black cloud soared out from the summit of the volcano. It raised high into the atmosphere, creating a huge column. This huge column was soon to create a pyroclastic flow [2] that was to be the cause of one of Italy's worst disasters, in living memory.

---

[2] **Pyroclastic flow** – a fluidized mixture of solid to semi-solid fragments and hot expanding gases that flow down the flank of the volcanic edifice. These features are heavier-than air emulsions that move like a snow avalanche except that they are fiercely hot, contain toxic gases, and move at phenomenal, hurricane-force speeds, often over 100km/hour. They are the most deadly of all volcanic phenomena. A pyroclastic flow has been known to travel beyond 60 km from its source.

Another series of explosions was heard. These coincided with more earth tremors. This was followed by another huge column soaring out of the crater, partially obscuring the sunlight. The sky went very dark.

By now those people still in the vicinity of the pool were moving swiftly in all directions, not knowing quite what to do.

Ellis and Beth picked up their belongings and hurried through to the terrace bar. As they reached the perimeter fence, they were joined by some of the hotel staff. Oddjob was amongst them, pointing towards Vesuvius. His right arm was waving; he was shouting something to the rest of the staff. It was difficult to hear what he was saying, although Ellis thought he heard him mention Naples.

It was very difficult to see clearly across the bay. Although in the past few minutes, the sky appeared to be clearing sufficiently to view the outline of Vesuvius. Ellis strained to see what was happening. At that moment Carlos appeared and handed Ellis a pair of binoculars so he was able to get a good view of Vesuvius.

Suddenly the air was filled with the shrieking of many sirens. They were far louder, more eerie and frightening than previously. Clearly, the situation was now dangerous, and the authorities were now desperately trying to warn everybody of an impending disaster.

Just as Ellis was using the binoculars to follow the coastline towards Naples, there was another earth tremor and huge explosion. Ellis immediately swung back to view Vesuvius. What he saw concerned him. Spewing out of the crater was another huge column. This time it was wider than the first one; it was growing taller by the second.

Ellis watched it grow - within minutes it appeared to be many kilometres into the sky. It was accompanied by a huge, grey cloud, which he thought probably consisted of ash and debris. The second he thought this, he wished he hadn't.

Before he could dismiss those thoughts from his mind, it happened. As quick as it rose into the sky, the cloud column started to collapse at a great rate of knots. 'Oh no!' exclaimed Ellis.

'What's the matter?' asked Beth.

'I think we might be going to witness a pyroclastic flow.'

'Is that bad?' Beth asked.

Ellis replied, 'Yes I'm afraid it is.'

Carlos looked at Beth with a startled look on his face. He turned around facing other guests, gesticulating and murmuring that things were bad.

Ellis put the binoculars to his eyes again, and focused on the activity of the collapsing column. It appeared to have reached the rim of the crater at this point. Ellis could not see which way it was flowing. He looked again; this time he could see what appeared to be a large dust storm moving away to the north east from Vesuvius.

He called Carlos over, to ask him to identify exactly where the Naples coastline started and finished. Carlos pointed out two landmarks to Ellis and said, 'In-between the two you have Naples.'

Ellis looked again. What he saw horrified and frightened him. Moving at great speed down the side of Vesuvius was this huge grey cloud. It appeared to be tumbling over and over, like an avalanche. This was different though. Its speed was awesome, its height colossal, and there was this greyish like froth, bubbling along on top of the cloud.

As it raced down, and along the tapering terrain, Ellis turned his view further to the left, and then he adjusted his view back towards the right. He sighed deeply, turning around he said to Carlos, handing him the binoculars. 'I hope I am wrong, but have a look and tell me if that fast moving grey object is moving towards Naples.'

Carlos looked for about 30 seconds. 'That is definitely moving towards Naples, Mr Smeeth,' he said, with a look of dismay in his eyes. Carlos continued, 'Naples is 9 kilometres away, surely that cannot reach.'

Ellis replied, 'Sorry, Carlos, if it is what I think it is, then it can reach with kilometres to spare.'

Carlos threw his arms in the air, 'Mamma Mia,' he uttered. 'What is to become of us? I will go and look at the television to see what is happening in Naples.'

By now more and more people had crowded onto the terrace. Some had binoculars; all were looking across the bay towards Vesuvius. One rather large Englishman with a loud North-East accent was gazing intently towards the far coastline. 'Nae lass, that avalanche cloud is going nae way near Naples. Whoever thinks it is needs a geography lesson I tell ea.'

Ellis looked at Beth and those people near to him, and just shrugged his shoulders without any comment.

Suddenly, Carlos came running out through the terrace patio doors, in a very agitated state, shouting, 'You are right, Mr Smeeth, the volcanic avalanche has just hit Naples. It is burying everything in its path. The newscaster believes there will be high population casualties, and severe structural damage.'

Carlos went on, almost sobbing by now. 'He mentioned pyroclastic flow, like you,' said Mr Smeeth. 'Does that mean it will be very bad?'

Ellis looked at Carlos saying, 'If the full force hits Naples, then yes, it will be very bad. There could be as many as a hundred thousand casualties. It could even be a lot more than that.' Carlos looked towards the Geordie, as he spoke those words.

At that point, the cruise ship that was anchored in the bay below them started sounding its own siren in earnest. It was continuously sounding for about 30 seconds then it paused for a brief moment before starting again. This pattern continued, presumably a prearranged signal for those passengers who were on shore.

Four empty tenders were hurriedly being despatched towards the harbour. They must have been going to collect those passengers who had been taken into Sorrento, earlier that morning.

As they gazed out across towards Vesuvius, Ellis looked at his watch; it was just approaching 1.45pm. He thought for a moment, Saturday afternoon, just over 24 hours since we arrived. What a lot has happened.

Just then Carlos appeared, telling everyone that there would not be any sit down lunches served today. Instead a running finger buffet would be made available to those who wanted something to eat. Drinks would also be available. He also mentioned that the television in the far corner of the bar was now receiving terrestrial programmes from the Italian stations. News updates on Vesuvius and Naples were just starting to filter through. All satellite channels were currently unavailable, due to the volcanic ash covering the immediate area.

Ellis and Beth decided to take up the lunch offer. They moved into the bar to get the latest update on the eruption. They met Dene and Paula coming the other way, and told them of their plans.

Dene mentioned to Ellis that the latest news was not very good. He had just been talking to his son via the hotel's telephone land line. His son was watching the *BBC 24* hour news programme back in England. They were reporting that a massive pyroclastic flow had hit Naples at around lunchtime. Initial reports were sketchy but observers were saying that a major disaster was about to unfold.

They all moved to a table near to the television set. It was showing current views of Vesuvius. The commentary was in Italian, but it was aided by a text in English, that was running across the bottom of the screen. The area around the television was soon very crowded, as people filtered in from the terrace patio. There was a deathly hush as everyone strained to see and understand, what was being said.

Carlos then appeared, announcing that the buffet lunch was now available. A table had been set up in the far corner of the bar area. Almost everybody turned to acknowledge him. They all added 'thank you' then they turned back to watch the television.

The streamer text that was running along the bottom of the television screen, was now explaining in English what was being shown.

The pictures of Vesuvius were horrifying, but spectacular. The column cloud had now disappeared. This had been replaced with a large grey plume, which was billowing ash and debris into the atmosphere. Most of it was being directed towards Naples by a stiff breeze that was now blowing. Also being emitted from the crater, was what appeared to be hot water and debris that was giving off clouds of steam, as it moved quickly down the side of the mountain. Any vegetation in its way was immediately engulfed and destroyed by the intense heat of the flow.

Beth nudged Ellis saying, 'I am going to get some food. Would you like some?'

'Yes please,' replied Ellis. 'If you see Carlos, ask him for some drinks if he is free,' Beth nodded.

Shortly afterwards Beth returned with two plates of food. The television coverage of Vesuvius was interrupted, by an Italian news reader. With the help of English text, he was confirming in a very sombre voice, that a large area of Naples had been engulfed by a pyroclastic flow. He said that the Naples local government had announced a state of emergency, and that the city would be placed under the control of the local Chief of Police. He would have all the emergency services, plus all branches of the military, reporting directly to him. He added that further detail would be made available to the general public and media as soon as the information became available.

The television camera switched to another presenter who informed viewers that pictures of the centre of Naples were now available. The picture changed from the studio to a live aerial shot (presumably being viewed from a helicopter). The scenes were beyond belief. The whole of one area for as far as the naked eye could see, was covered grey. The devastation had to be seen to be believed. Of the taller buildings, none seemed to have escaped the force of the avalanche that had swept through this area of Naples. All that was left looked like partly finished constructions. Some brick or concrete walls remained in place. The roofs were no longer there; they had been destroyed, leaving just a large hole in their place. There was not a window to be seen anywhere.

Two storey dwellings and other small buildings were non-existent. The only sign of cars appeared to be where a number of them were piled on top of one another. One or two coaches could just be seen below the surface of the grey, murky substance. But like the cars, they appeared to be mounted on top of something.

The whole scene looked like a city, after it had been bombed mercilessly, throughout the night during the Second World War.

The people in the bar were viewing every camera shot they were being shown in silence. This was then broken by somebody remarking, 'Where are all the people? We haven't seen anybody yet?'

Once again there was complete silence. Everybody who sat or stood watching the television pictures were left speechless.

Carlos had now arrived with the drinks, Beth had ordered. As he placed them on the table, he glanced at the television screen. His eyes opened wide. He tried to speak, but no words came out. He lifted his hands onto his head, his eyes were filling. He could no longer contain himself as tears began to roll down both cheeks.

Nobody said anything as Carlos turned and walked away, apologising as he went.

It was at this moment that the coverage of Naples from the helicopter ceased. The Italian news reader had now reappeared on the screen. He announced that they would show more coverage from the helicopter, as soon as they were able to do so.

At this point the Italian news network continued showing the events that had occurred, earlier that day. First they showed the eruption of Vesuvius, minutes after it happened. This was followed by the first pictures of the centre of Naples, shortly after it was engulfed by the pyroclastic flow. Although having already seen the eruption in real life, the gathered assembly were still transfixed by those pictures.

Beth asked Ellis, 'What shall we do now?'

'Let's go back to our room, assess the situation and then see what plans if any, the hotel or tour operator has in mind,' he said. As they rose to leave, the English text on the television screen indicated that there would be an official statement from an Italian Government official later that afternoon.

Chapter Eight

Once back in their room Ellis turned the television on. He flicked through all the news channels. The Italian news on the terrestrial network was the only one available.

As he looked at the screen, he wondered why the network appeared to be only repeating footage from earlier that day. With all that had happened he assumed that there would be numerous other situations to report.

Ellis wandered over to the mini-bar and selected a beer for himself. He took his beer and walked through to the balcony. He sat down on one of the wicker chairs and sat looking out towards Vesuvius. The grey plume of smoke and ash was still pouring out of the crater high into the atmosphere. It was still moving towards Naples, aided by a strong breeze, although Ellis suspected that the force and density of the plume was probably less than before.

The stream of water and debris that he had seen earlier was no longer evident. Ellis stood up to try and see just how far it had travelled. It made no difference as the distance was too far to see. By now he could see that it had passed the bottom of the slopes. He wished he had some binoculars. He began to wonder what had happened to all those properties which had been constructed without planning permission, near to and on the slopes leading to Vesuvius? Again his thoughts went back to the television coverage. Why had there not yet been any comment or film coverage on the immediate area around Vesuvius? Something, at the back of his mind, told him all was not well.

Ellis sat back in his chair, sipping his beer and staring across the bay and wondered what was really happening. His mind conjured up many different scenarios, including reconstruction of the Pompeii disaster of 79 A.D. His thought pattern continued. If this eruption was in any way similar to that of 79 A.D or even worse, the less documented event of 1780 BC, (*Bronze age eruption*), then the whole of Naples and the densely populated area around Vesuvius were all at risk. Ellis calculated that this would place something like three million people in that category.

It was at that moment that Ellis suddenly realised that they should ring their daughters back home in Rugby. They would have heard the news and would be wondering if everything was okay.

Ellis rose from his chair, went into the room and picked up his mobile phone. As he did so, he shouted to Beth that he was phoning Louise. From the bathroom came Beth's voice. 'Good idea, with all that's gone on it slipped my mind to ring.'

Ellis immediately selected Louise's number from the menu. As he pressed the ring button, a message appeared on the screen, 'No Networks Available'. All he could hear from the phone was a loud buzzing noise.

He called to Beth, 'Mobile phone networks are unobtainable. I'll try the land line.'

Ellis walked over to the bedside table, picked up the phone and dialled for an outside line. He was successful. After dialling Louise's number, he could hear the phone ringing.

'It's ringing,' he shouted to Beth. 'Good,' she replied. 'I'll be there in a minute.'

Suddenly from the phone came a click and a voice said, 'Hello.'

Ellis replied, 'Hi Louise.'

'Thank goodness you've called as we were starting to get worried. Even though the problems appear to be all at Naples, we know how close you are. I've tried your mobile many times but it would not connect,' said Louise.

'We are okay,' Ellis replied, although as you can imagine we're very concerned with the events of the last 24 hours. What can you tell us from your end as there is only one Italian news station operating at the moment?'

'There are problems for *Star* and *BBC 24 News*. All news via a satellite, are still having reception trouble in the Naples area, due to the ash and pollution in the atmosphere,' replied Louise. 'We have been told that a large area of Naples has been devastated by the effect of the eruption. It's not yet confirmed Dad, but our news stations are reporting that a pyroclastic flow of immense power did strike Naples earlier today.'

At that point Beth came out of the bathroom, and put her hand up, indicating she would like to talk to Louise. Ellis made this point to Louise, and handed the phone to Beth. With that he left them chatting to one another, and walked out on to the balcony.

Ten minutes later he heard Beth say goodbye to Louise. After she put the phone down she came out onto the balcony. At this point Ellis asked her, 'Are you going to ring Jamie?'

'Yes, I'll do it now,' replied Beth.

Whilst Ellis sat outside looking at Vesuvius and pondering what might happen next, he could hear Beth talking to Jamie. He lay back in his chair and listened to what she was saying. He could hear his name being mentioned a few times along with consoling words to Jamie. They spent a good ten minutes talking before Beth ended the conversation with, 'Dad sends his love to you and the children. We'll ring again, bye for now.'

The time was now just after 5 o'clock on that Saturday afternoon of July 8. Ellis called to Beth. 'That statement by the Italian Government will be on shortly. I'll see what stations are operating on the television.'

He switched on the television and, with the aid of the remote control; he flicked through the numerous channels. Most were blank; suddenly on the screen as large as life appeared Charles Small the *Star News* presenter. The picture was slightly hazy, but Ellis had no problem with that.

As Ellis adjusted the volume, Charles Small was just explaining to viewers, the problems satellite channels have when atmospheric conditions change. He outlined that severe weather conditions were often the main cause of transmission problems. He continued his statement by saying, 'that the current problem had been caused by the millions of tonnes of ash and debris, ejected into the atmosphere by the eruption of Vesuvius.'

Whilst he was talking, a 'Breaking News' streamer began moving across the bottom of the screen.

Ellis waited and then read to himself, the following message as it began to appear:

STAR NEWS SOURCES HAVE LEARNED THAT THE ERUPTION THAT OCCURRED FROM THE VOLCANO VESUVIUS AT 12:05 TODAY WAS SIMILAR TO THE ONE THAT BURIED THE ROMAN CITY OF POMPEII IN 79 A.D. IT HAS SINCE BEEN DEFINED AS A PYROCLASTIC FLOW.

***

As he finished reading the message, Charles Small suddenly ceased talking, then he paused for a moment and announced, 'we are now going straight to Rome for a statement by an official of the Italian Government.'

The picture changed immediately, from the television studio to what looked like a Press Conference room inside the Italian Parliament. Seated on raised staging at the front of the room were three officials. The one seated in the centre was clearly the Italian Prime Minister. The other two were identified by a *Star* reporter as the equivalent of the UK Home Secretary, and Defence Secretary.

With an English translation being transmitted ten seconds behind. The Italian Prime Minister began his statement; he gave detail of the events as they had occurred earlier that day. He began by confirming that the initial eruption of Vesuvius had begun with a huge column being thrust many kilometres into the atmosphere. Shortly afterwards the column collapsed downwards, under masses of debris and pumice. This action caused a pyroclastic flow, which in turn generated a massive avalanche down the eastern sides of the slopes of Vesuvius. With a downward slope speed in excess of 100 kilometres per hour, it descended on Naples in minutes. He paused to catch his breath, evidently feeling the calamity of what he was reading, and then continued to give further details. Towards the end of his statement, his voice became softer and less audible, as he gave estimates of the number of fatalities. Clearly he was being overwhelmed by the figures he was reading out.

Ellis listened intently, as he said: **'There will be many thousands of casualties, maybe as many as two hundred**

thousand.' At this point he was clearly overcome by emotion. He quickly finished his statement, rose from his chair and bowed to the seated press personnel, before turning and departing from the room.

Ellis sat there, in silence, listening to the horror story that was unfolding. He held his head in his hands and said nothing.

Beth came out of the bathroom, having now finished washing her hair.

'What did he say?' Beth asked.

'He indicated that the situation is worse than what *Star News* were reporting' Ellis stated.

'What do you mean?' asked Beth.

Ellis looked up, with a bemused expression. 'A large proportion of Naples is buried under metres of ash and rubble. Nobody had time to flee the avalanche of hot ash and rubble, which swept down upon them. The area is a total disaster. The Italian Government has declared a "State of Emergency", and they are forecasting massive fatalities. They have appealed to the rest of Europe for help.'

They both sat there, listening to the television for another 30 minutes.

Neither of them spoke as more details emerged. After a few moments' silence, Ellis spoke, 'Although I'm not very hungry, we might as well get ready for dinner.' Beth nodded quietly in agreement.

As they walked into the dining room that Saturday evening, Giraldo escorted them to their table alongside the terrace windows. The atmosphere in the dining room was much muted. The background noise was barely audible. It seemed that people were whispering, as though they were frightened to talk normally.

From their table they had an excellent view of Vesuvius. They could clearly see the grey plume of smoke and ash billowing into the sky. Although now there was no power in the plume, as it seemed to drift aimlessly towards Naples. It was as if it knew that the damage had been done earlier.

Although neither of their appetites had returned they both ordered their starter and main course. While they waited for their meals, they discussed the news in sombre tones with a couple at an adjoining table. They all fell silent when their meals arrived.

It wasn't long before Ellis and Beth had finished their meal. They excused themselves and headed towards the terrace bar. On arrival they met Carlos. As soon as he spotted them his eyes misted over. He came straight over to them, threw his arms around them both, saying at the same time. 'What is happening to my fellow Italians in Naples? What can we do to help them, Mr Smeeth?'

Even Ellis' eyes started to fill up. Choking back the tears he put his arm around Carlos. He looked straight into his eyes saying as he did. 'Carlos, I guarantee you, that as we speak, the British Government will be meeting representatives from all the relief and rescue organisations. By tomorrow morning they will put in place their first relief package, and by evening it will be happening.'

Carlos wiped away his tears with a handkerchief. As he did so, he asked, 'But how can we help?'

Ellis replied, 'As soon as I see Beppe, I will discuss what we can all do to help. I am sure that even this far from Naples we can organise something.' Other guests nearby hearing what Ellis said, all nodded in approval.

With that assurance, Carlos perked up. He finished wiping his eyes, and then asked Ellis if it was two cappuccinos and a brandy. Ellis nodded in reply.

Soon Carlos arrived with their drinks. As he placed them on the table, he started to apologise for his earlier tears. Ellis assured him that there was no need to be sorry for anything he said or did. 'You are a proud and true citizen of your country,' Ellis said. 'I wish more people in my country were as patriotic as you are.'

On hearing these words, Carlos smiled. He looked at Beth, saying, 'Your husband is also a proud man. He and I are two of a kind; thank you both very much.'

Whilst drinking their cappuccinos, they decided it would be sensible to stay in, and around the hotel that evening. Ellis suggested they could maybe go over to the tennis club to see Maura. If on the way they saw Beppe, Ellis said he would like to ask him if the guests could help in any way.

No sooner had they finished their drinks, when Beppe appeared on the terrace. As he walked towards them, Ellis beckoned to him. As he arrived at the table, Ellis pulled a chair out for him. Beppe sat down. Ellis then asked him if he had any more news from Naples. Beppe replied saying, 'The situation now appears to be worse than the authorities first thought. The fatalities amongst the population are forecast to be very high.'

Ellis asked Beppe if he had any plans to assist the people of Naples. He explained further that they and many of the guests were offering their services.

Beppe explained that once he had met with other business dignitaries later that evening, he would have a better idea of what help was needed. He thanked Ellis for his concern, and promised to convene a meeting with all the guests tomorrow.

As Beppe left, William, Sandie, Dene and Paula came from the bar on to the terrace. Ellis called them over and briefed them on what he and Beppe had been discussing.

Whilst they were talking, Carlos came across to the table, apologised for interrupting and asked Ellis if he could spare a moment.

Ellis left the table and followed Carlos into the bar. He directed Ellis towards a table where there was a man sitting by himself.

As they approached, the man rose from his seat, Carlos stepped forward and said to Ellis. 'This gentleman is from *Star News*. He has just arrived with his colleague to cover the Vesuvius eruption. Unfortunately, his colleague has developed a stomach upset and is not well enough to carry out his reporting duties. He understood that you were staying here and he asked me to contact you.'

The man held his hand out to Ellis, and introduced himself as Mark Rogers. He explained that he and Frank Brady, the *Star News* presenter, had just arrived in Sorrento. Mark continued by outlining the course of events that followed Ellis' telephone call to the *Star News* Editor about the Vesuvius situation. Shortly after the conversation he and Frank were told to get to Sorrento as soon as possible. Because of potential problems with Vesuvius they flew directly to Nice, and then boarded a ferry to Southern Italy. From there they hired a car and came along the coast to Sorrento. Mark smiled as he said, 'As it turned out it was the right decision.'

Mark continued to explain that he was a camera and sound technician. He could set up his equipment to record pictures of Vesuvius, and transmit them back to the London studio. Unfortunately with Frank ill there could be no commentary, or interviews with live witnesses to the events of the last 24 hours.

Mark looked at Ellis saying, 'I was hoping that with your previous experience you might be able to help out. What do you say? Will you come out of retirement and help us out?'

Ellis smiled and said, 'Tell you what Mark; I'll do better than that. If *Star* will allow me, I'll do a live, eye witness coverage of what has happened to-date, plus live interviews with guests and the hotel owner, if he will co-operate.'

'Are you sure? Let me check with the studio first', he said, as he pulled his mobile phone from his pocket.

'What experience have you had?' joked Mark.

'None really', smiled Ellis. 'But don't worry I'll not let you down.'

Mark nodded, 'Okay, leave it with me and I'll get back to you.'

Ellis went back to his table. As he sat down, Beth asked, 'What was that all about?'

Ellis explained what the situation was with Mark and Frank from *Star News*. At this point he did not tell them that he had offered to take Frank's place. He continued to stretch the story for a little while longer, until Beth asked how they would get another presenter in time. Ellis smiled but said nothing.

As soon as Beth saw that smile she knew, 'You've offered your services haven't you?'

'As a matter of fact I have,' said Ellis. Those round the table all burst out laughing.

Beth stared at Ellis saying, 'What did he say?'

'He's phoning the studio now to clear it with the News Editor.'

This development caused a stir around the table. For the next few minutes Ellis had to take the butt of comments and jokes, until Mark arrived and walked over to Ellis and shook him by the hand.

'Welcome back to *Star News*, Ellis. Subject to a successful trial run in 15 minutes, you will be reporting live on the 10 o'clock news.'

Amidst applause and some 'Mickey-taking', Ellis raised both arms into the air, before kissing Beth on both cheeks saying, 'The rebirth of a star.'

At this point Mark intervened, telling him that they needed to go and prepare for his trial commentary. Ellis rose from the table and followed Mark up the short flight of steps to the swimming pool.

Whilst setting up his equipment, Mark explained although it was dark he was going to use Vesuvius as the backdrop to his commentary. He wanted Ellis to stand with his back to the perimeter fence and tell viewers what he and Beth had experienced over the past 24 hours. Mark advised him to turn towards Vesuvius expressing his comments by pointing and raising his arms as necessary.

By now Mark had the equipment in position. Two very powerful arc lights lit up that side of the swimming pool as though it was daylight. His camera and sound boom were all securely fixed. Ellis stood out in the lights looking slightly pensive.

Everything was now set up. Mark complete with earphones was now talking to the studio. He lifted two fingers to indicate two minutes to transmission.

By now a number of people had gathered in and around the swimming pool, waiting for Ellis to utter his first few words. Ellis looked around, licking his lips as he did. He spotted Beth and the rest of the 'gang'. They were all smiling and mimicking him doing a commentary. At that point he thought to himself, what am I doing this for?

As he turned back towards Mark he saw Beppe emerge from the corner entry of the swimming pool. Before he could look elsewhere, Mark called, '30 seconds to transmission.'

This is it; no going back now! Ellis thought.

Suddenly he heard Mark counting down, 'ten, nine eight' Crikey, thought Ellis, I'm on. 'Three, two, one, action!' shouted Mark.

Ellis took a deep breath. You could have heard a pin drop, as all around him went silent.

'Good Evening.' The words seem to crackle from his mouth, as he started his introduction. 'At noon earlier today here at the "Hotel Geranio" and all along the surrounding Sorrento coastline I and many people witnessed a massive volcanic eruption. You will all know by now that the eruption was emitted from the Volcano Vesuvius. It is believed to be a similar eruption to the one that devastated the Roman City of Pompeii in 79 A.D.'

Ellis continued for five to six minutes. Everything and everybody was still and quiet; they were listening intently to every word Ellis spoke. Some seemed to be nodding their heads in approval; others just gazed straight at him.

Mark raised his hand and mouthed a message to Ellis. He turned his hand in a circular motion indicating it was time to finish.

Ellis again turned towards Vesuvius; he pointed and made a final comment about the people of Naples. He then signed off with, 'Good Night from Ellis Smith for *Star News*, here in Sorrento.'

There was a moment's pause, before everybody around the pool in unison started to clap and cheer. Even Mark joined in, and as he walked towards Ellis he was heard to say, 'It's like you've never been away. Well done.'

Ellis looked slightly embarrassed. He turned to the people and raised a hand saying, 'Thank you' at the same time.

Whilst Ellis went to see Beth and the rest of the 'gang', Mark was on his mobile phone talking to the studio. A few minutes later he joined them smiling from ear to ear. 'Well, Ellis, or do I have to call you Mr Smith now. I've spoken to the News Editor back in the studio and he is delighted with your performance. So much so, that he wants you to go live on the 10 o'clock news. Are you up for it?' Mark smiled.

Ellis looked around, grimaced a bit, and said, 'doesn't seem that I have any choice does it?'

'Not really,' they all echoed.

'Okay,' Mark said. 'It's 9.15 so we've only got 45 minutes to sort out your programme. We need to get on with it straightaway.'

Ellis suggested that they retire to the lounge. Mark agreed. En route he picked up his portable autocue programmer.

Once in the lounge they ordered two cappuccinos, and got down to organising the content for the 10 o'clock news. Whilst they were talking, Beppe came across to them, 'Mr Smeeth, I understand that you wish to see me?'

'Yes,' Ellis replied, 'tomorrow morning if required, would you let me interview you live for *Star News?*'

Beppe paused for a moment, 'Of course, Mr Smeeth, that will be fine. I should have more information about what the people of Sorrento will be doing to help the people of Naples.'

Mark looked up and shook Beppe by the hand, saying, 'That will be excellent. We can use that to launch our appeal to the British public, for funds and material requirements.'

Ellis nodded in agreement. Beppe clasped both their hands and solemnly said, 'Thank you both very much.' As he turned and walked away, they both detected tears on his cheeks. Ellis said thoughtfully, 'It can only get worse.' Mark nodded in agreement.

It was now 9.30. Mark had loaded the opening script into his mobile autocue. They had both agreed that Ellis should use the same opening as that used for the trial presentation. After that, Charles Small would question Ellis on the latest situation. Ellis would then ad-lib his way through the thoughts of the British holidaymakers, and possible comments about the local population.

Ellis had fifteen minutes before he was on air. He excused himself from Mark and sought to find Beth for a few quiet minutes, before embarking on a historic moment in his life.

He soon found her outside on the terrace, sitting with their friends and a few other guests who had all congregated together. As he approached, he was met with a few wisecracks and some light-hearted banter.

'How goes it?' somebody asked.

'Okay,' replied Ellis, 'just having a five minute break before transmission.'

Beth got out of her chair and together they walked to the far end of the terrace. They spent a few minutes discussing his forthcoming television debut. As they parted, Mark raised his hand, beckoning Ellis to the swimming pool area; this is it, thought Ellis. There's no going back now.

Once there Mark fitted him out with a small body microphone and an earpiece. He then proceeded to debrief Ellis on the procedure up to, and including his live report. 'At 9.59pm, you will hear a member of the news staff say, "sixty seconds to transmission". There will then be a 10 second warning, followed by 3, 2, 1, run the introduction.'

Ellis listened intently to everything Mark said, as he continued to take him through the opening few minutes of the programme.

Finally Mark concluded with, 'You will then hear Charles Small mention you by name, then you will be counted in to start your report. Always be aware that at any moment he might interrupt you either to ask you a question or to give the viewers the latest information.'

Ellis moved again to the perimeter fence, with his back to the Bay of Naples and, in the distance, Vesuvius. He stood there waiting for his cue. Almost immediately, the prompt came through his earpiece, 60 seconds to transmission. He braced himself and focused on to the mobile autocue that Mark had fixed to the camera tripod. The 10 second warning seemed to erupt in his ear. He took a deep breath just as Charles Small began to read the news headlines. Then he heard his name mentioned as Charles Small explained to the viewers that Frank Brady had been sidelined with a stomach complaint. He went on to say that at the last minute a replacement had been found. With that he heard, 'And now we go over to Ellis Smith in Sorrento.'

In his left ear he heard, 'Cue 3 seconds, 2, 1, you're on.'

Ellis did not hesitate. He went straight into his opening introduction. His first comment was to identify that he was at the Hotel Geranio, situated in Sorrento looking out over the Bay of Naples, towards Vesuvius.

Once he had cleared the opening statement, he was soon into his rhythm. He went back to yesterday and the earth tremors that had occurred since then. He detailed the unsteadiness that had caused cafe tables and chairs to fall over, including fruit, vegetables, and bottles of wine plus other items that were displayed on the pavement.

He explained the look of bewilderment in people's eyes when they first experienced the movement beneath their feet.

He continued with a graphic description of the steam and smoke, which had gradually increased its velocity from the crater of Vesuvius, since the 24 hours they had arrived from England. He also emphasised the increase in ash that had started to gently fall over Sorrento despite the gentle breeze moving towards Naples.

Ellis was by now building up to the eruption. Mark who was listening to every word heard the studio director say, 'Good stuff Ellis, now give them the eruption.' He had no sooner finished that comment when Ellis pointed towards Vesuvius as he said, 'At 12.05pm local time earlier today without any warning, a series of deafening explosions was heard from the vicinity of Vesuvius.'

Ellis continued to describe the events that followed those explosions.

As he finished his summary, Charles Small came on air.

He questioned Ellis about the latest situation, particularly the latest estimate of fatalities. Ellis explained that they had had no further official information since the Italian Prime Minister's statement earlier that afternoon Even the Italian news channels were void of new information, although some were still not back on air.

At this point, Ellis said to Charles Small. 'We have heard unofficially, that a news blackout is in progress at this moment. It is understood from an inside source, that the City of Naples, and outlying districts have been totally devastated. It is expected that the infrastructure and inhabitants of the affected area will reveal horrendous fatalities.'

Charles Small interrupted Ellis at this moment, to ask him, 'If what you have just told us is true, what is the purpose of the secrecy?'

Ellis responded quickly, 'It is understood that the Italian Government and the local authorities, are preparing another statement which will include an emergency plan of action. It is believed the reason for the delay in information is to prevent widespread panic. Our source believes all will be revealed early tomorrow morning or maybe before.'

'Okay, Ellis,' Charles's voice said into his earpiece, 'we will leave it there for now.'

Ellis looked across as Mark pulled his hand across his throat, clearly indicating transmission had finished.

Ellis pulled out his earpiece and walked towards Mark who greeted him with a handshake.

'Where did all that stuff about the Italian Government and "our source" come from?'

'Sorry about that,' Ellis replied. 'I was speaking to Beppe just before we went on air. He was telling me all about the devastation and casualty estimates. The government is in turmoil at the moment. They are just buying time until they have a coherent plan. As I said, they expect to announce it tomorrow.'

Mark commented, 'Well done; anyway that will give them something back at the studio to work on. Right, I think we are finished for the night. I'll check with London and get back to you.'

Ellis removed his body microphone, excused himself from Mark and headed off to find Beth. He found her at a table by herself with two cappuccinos and a small brandy waiting.

'I thought you would be ready for a drink,' she smiled.

'You read my mind,' replied Ellis.

'That seemed to go well,' she said.

'Yes it did. I feel really good about it. Mark was pleased. He is just checking if we have finished for the night.'

Beth responded with, 'I hope so.'

'Me too,' added Ellis.

A few minutes later Mark joined them. He confirmed that they had finished for the evening, adding that they were on again at 9 o'clock local time tomorrow morning.

He continued by telling them that the reaction in the studio to tonight's report was excellent. They were intrigued to know how he got the information about the government stalling for time. They were now attempting to follow up this information with the network's own people in Italy.

By the time Mark had finished, it was getting late. They bade him goodnight and set off for their room. On the way they saw Carlos, who came across saying as he did, 'I saw you, Mr Smeeth, on television. You were very good, but I knew you would be.'

After that they reached their room without any more interruptions.

It wasn't long before they were in bed, and fast asleep.

Chapter Nine - Eruption plus 1

Ellis was the first to rise on Sunday morning on July 9. As he awoke, he needed to go to the bathroom. He got out of bed slowly trying not to disturb Beth. Just as he reached the end of the bed, Beth turned over and woke up.

'What are you up to?' she asked.

'Just off to the bathroom,' came back the reply.

On his way back, he opened the balcony door and walked outside to view Vesuvius. It was dawn but there was enough daylight to see Vesuvius through the early morning haze. From his vantage point Ellis could see there was still a large grey cloud drifting over and upwards towards Naples. However it was clear that it did not contain the velocity of yesterday's emissions.

After a few minutes, Ellis went back into the room. 'How is it looking this morning?' Beth enquired.

'A lot less volatile,' he replied.

'Thank goodness for that! I'll make a cup of tea.' As she plugged the kettle in, Ellis switched on the television, and found the *Star News* channel. Raymond Kelly was reading out a statement from *Reuters News Agency*.

Ellis turned the sound up and listened intently, to the statement: 'At 6.15 this morning the Italian Government released a video recording showing the aftermath of the avalanche that had engulfed the City of Naples at 12.15pm on Saturday afternoon.

'This video recording was filmed from an aircraft of the Italian Air force, 60 minutes after the eruption of Vesuvius occurred.'

Beth came over and sat next to Ellis on the sofa. Neither spoke as they watched the scene of destruction as it was unfolded during the next 15 minutes.

The scenes they viewed yesterday were only of two to three minutes duration. What they had seen had left most people speechless. What they were about to witness would leave them mentally scarred for a long time.

The scenes recorded from the aircraft started from the point where the hot, thick cloud of ash and gas had slipped down the mountainside, incinerating everything in its path. The temperatures inside the cloud probably reached in excess of 200 degrees centigrade. On reaching the bottom of the mountain slope the pyroclastic flow then proceeded on its way to Naples. It left a trail of devastation unlike anything Ellis and Beth had ever seen before.

As the aircraft moved towards Naples, the ground below reminded Ellis of a landscape picture of the moon. Everywhere the aircraft camera pointed, it seemed to show exactly the same picture. An unrecognisable landscape covered by steaming gases and ash.

What really stood out for Ellis was the lack of any definition to the landscape. The whole area was practically the same. Where the avalanche of debris, ash and gases had travelled was now just a blank, grey expanse of virtually nothing.

Buildings, trees, and any tall constructions were non-existent. Ellis assumed that whatever was there before now lay underneath the redefined grey surface that they were looking at.

Gradually the definition of the pictures they were looking at started to change. Clearly they were beginning to enter the outskirts of the City of Naples. What they were seeing was a repeat of the three minutes shown on television yesterday afternoon. However, with the aircraft manoeuvring such that a 360 degree panoramic view was shown, the magnitude of the devastation was clear for all to see. Everywhere the camera searched, the pictures were the same. Buildings destroyed partial sight of cars, lorries, and buses all strewn about. Some were partially buried, others piled on top of one another. Piles of rubble were evident; and the roads had completely disappeared.

By now the aircraft appeared to be in the centre of Naples. As it continued its flight path along the edge of the Bay of Naples, the scenes were just as catastrophic as those they had been witnessing for the last fifteen minutes. At this point the video ended as the aircraft banked away. For a moment the screen went blank, before Raymond Kelly reappeared, unable to disguise the horror on his face.

It was at least ten minutes before either Ellis or Beth spoke. Ellis broke the silence by saying, 'Let's have that cup of tea, and I think whilst we are doing that we should plan our day ahead.'

Whilst drinking their tea, they decided they would go for an early breakfast, and then look for Mark and Beppe, so they could check the contents for the 9 o'clock news slot, if still required.

They finished their tea, and showered and dressed for breakfast. They were the first hotel guests down to breakfast and were able to sit at their usual table outside on the terrace.

Whilst they were eating, Mark appeared. As he arrived at their table, Ellis asked, 'Am I on air today?'

'Yes, indeed you are,' Mark replied. 'Also I have just seen Beppe, and he is ready for you to interview him.'

Ellis and Mark agreed to meet in the lounge after breakfast.

When Mark did so, he was accompanied by Beppe.

All three sat down and Mark outlined how he thought they should fill the 10-minute slot they had been given.

He suggested Ellis spend two to three minutes updating the viewers on the latest local situation. This would be followed by an interview with Beppe. Mark suggested that Ellis let Beppe describe his feelings, leading on to identify what actions, if any, the people of Sorrento would be taking. Whilst Mark outlined his plans to Beppe, Ellis checked out the script and prompts on the autocue. All seemed okay and in the correct order.

With just five minutes to transmission they made their way to their allocated positions.

It wasn't long before Ellis heard the familiar prompt through his earpiece, '60 seconds to transmission.' This was followed by the sombre voice of Kathy Broome stating, 'Since the eruption of Vesuvius yesterday afternoon, the City of Naples has been engulfed by a pyroclastic flow that occurred as a result of the eruption. Viewers by now will have probably seen our early bulletin that showed the damage and destruction this has caused. To bring you right up to date with the latest situation, we are going over to our reporter in Sorrento.'

Ellis heard the countdown clearly '3, 2, 1, action!'

Without any hesitation Ellis began to summarise local reaction to the scenes of destruction. Most of the television news channels had been showing those pictures non-stop since the early hours of Sunday morning.

Whilst Ellis was giving his summary, Mark focused the camera towards Vesuvius. As he listened to Ellis describing the events in detail, he adjusted the camera to give a slow moving view down the side of the mountain. He followed this up with a panoramic view across the bay towards Naples.

Ellis took a little longer than the three minutes they had planned. However, Mark could tell from the studio reaction that it had set the right tone for what was to follow. Now Mark gave the signal for Ellis to introduce Beppe Marcello the joint owner of the Hotel Geranio.

Once Ellis had introduced Beppe to the viewers, he began by asking him the history of the family hotel, and how long they had lived in the area.

It was the perfect question to set the interview in motion. This question immediately put Beppe at ease, as he could talk quite freely about a subject he was very passionate about; his family and their hotel. His passion soon took over as he described the history of the hotel. Starting from the day it was built, he went on through the years, detailing all the modifications and changes to the building. He detailed the constructional changes and modifications to the building. He described in detail how his parents ran the hotel on a day to day basis, including the years of involvement he and the rest of the family had from an early age, to the present day. He talked about his involvement with the local community of Sorrento and the surrounding district. Like all Italians he was deeply passionate about his country and people.

It soon became clear to everybody watching that Beppe was starting to get very emotional, particularly when Ellis asked him for the local community's reaction to the current situation in Naples.

Although he was starting to find it a little difficult, Beppe began by reiterating that what had happened to Naples and the surrounding area was a disaster of the highest magnitude. He stated that help from throughout Europe and the rest of the world was needed immediately. He urged that the Italian Government now take overall control, and put their contingency plans in motion.

At this point Ellis asked Beppe if the local authorities had any plans of their own. Beppe replied that they had, and continued that most of the hotels in the area would be preparing a casualty type field hospital within their grounds. He confirmed that the large lounge within the Hotel Geranio would be stripped of all its furniture and fittings later that day. It would then be converted into a reception centre where children who had become separated from their family during the destruction of Naples, and had sustained minor injuries, could be assessed and treated accordingly. Depending on their condition, they would then be transferred to other medical centres for further treatment, or to reception areas to be cared for until repatriated with their family or relatives.

Beppe looked straight into the camera. He paused and with tears in his eyes he made an emotional plea to anybody and everybody, including all governments to help the people of Italy to overcome this dreadful catastrophe.

There was complete silence for what seemed like an eternity, and then Beppe bowed slightly to the camera and said in a low voice. 'From myself and the people of Italy, Molte Grazie' (thank you).

As he finished, he moved towards Ellis and shook him by the hand. The two or three dozen people who were watching the broadcast applauded, many of them had tears in their eyes.

Ellis heard a voice in London give him 20 seconds to finish the broadcast. He did so with the familiar, 'This is Ellis Smith for *Star News*, Sorrento, Italy.'

It was now approaching 9.30am on that Sunday morning, as Mark and Ellis were discussing the reaction to the Beppe interview. Before they had finished, a familiar figure approached them from the other side of the pool.

'Good morning Mark and hello to you Ellis.' Ellis looked at him, and smiled. It was Frank Brady.

'Are you feeling better?' asked Ellis.

'Much better,' came back the reply.

Mark intervened. 'I meant to mention it earlier,' he said, looking at Ellis.

'Looks like I'm out of a job now,' laughed Ellis.

Frank suggested that they went to the terrace bar for a coffee. Now that he was fit for work again they could discuss the situation. Both Ellis and Mark agreed.

Once seated and having been served by Carlos, Frank proceeded to outline a proposal *Star News*, were putting forward for consideration.

He then went on to explain that not only was he and *Star News* extremely pleased with the reports that Ellis had transmitted so far. The viewing public had let it be known how much they had enjoyed them. Already following this morning's 9 o'clock interview with Beppe, there had been a positive reaction from the public. Thousands of e-mails, and telephone calls had been received, most of them enquiring how they could physically help. Others wanted to donate money, clothes, etc. As a result of these offers, *Star News* was to open an exclusive web site, detailing what the public and the business sector could do to assist.

Just at that moment Beth arrived, 'I was just wondering what you were getting up to!'

Ellis introduced Frank to Beth. Then Frank explained that he would now be fronting the *Star News* coverage of the Naples disaster. However, if Ellis agreed, they would like him to be available for any special reports they might want to cover.

Ellis looked towards Beth, who nodded in response.

'Yes, that's fine,' Ellis said. 'Whilst we are here, I'll be only too pleased to help out.'

They both agreed that Mark would contact Ellis as and when he was required. With that Ellis and Beth decided they would seek out the 'gang' and see what else was going on. As they made their way into the pool area, they could see that William and Sandie were already sitting in their favourite spot. They parked their belongings on their deck chairs and wandered over to speak to them.

On arrival, William said, 'I have some news for you. It looks as though Bernice and Phillip will be with us after all. They have spent the last week in Ischia, and are booked in here tomorrow for a week.' William continued, 'I gather they will be travelling over on a Seacat ferry straight into Marina Piccolo.'

As he finished speaking Dene and Paula arrived. William repeated the information to them about Bernice and Phillip. Dene then mentioned that the hotel staff had started to clear the lounge of all of the furniture and fixtures. This also included all the art and antique collections. Apparently Beppe's objective was to have in position by that evening the minimum requirements necessary to establish a workable casualty area. Dene explained further that an Irish nurse, who was on her honeymoon at the 'Geranio', had been asked by Beppe if she would help to supervise the preparation of the casualty area.

Whilst they were still discussing this latest development, Oddjob appeared and began distributing what looked like a sheet of paper to everybody. Once in their hands everybody began digesting the content.

Ellis began reading it. It was a communication from the local authorities of Sorrento, it was written in English and it read:

To the residents and visitors to Sorrento. Following the terrible disaster that occurred yesterday, the City of Naples, and the surrounding district, have all been subjected to the most destructive natural forces that the area of Campania has ever witnessed.

The aftermath of the Vesuvius eruption, has left those areas affected by the eruption totally devastated.

The devastation is so massive that at this moment it is difficult to estimate accurately what the final number of fatalities and casualties might be. However, the local

Government officials of Naples, who have been accounted for, are predicting a number in excess of one hundred thousand.

I must warn everybody, that this is only a provisional estimate.

As Mayor of Sorrento, I am appealing to everybody within this area to assist the people of Sorrento, in helping those who have been affected by this disaster.

For those of you who are visitors to Sorrento, and wish to offer your services please register your interest with your hotel reception. Or visit the mobile help office, which will be in situ in Piazza Tasso later today.

I know from the bottom of my heart that everybody will endeavour to help this community. I therefore offer you all my thanks in advance of your assistance.

Signed: Mayor of Sorrento   Dated: Sunday 9th July 2012

As Ellis finished reading the letter, he looked up and glanced around at the 30 or 40 people who were all engrossed in the letter. Hardly anybody was speaking.

At that moment Beth spoke, 'I'm going to reception, anybody else coming?'

'Yes, Yes.' Many voices spoke at once. Somebody then suggested that the ladies went to get the info for the rest. Once the ladies departed William, Ellis, and Dene continued to discuss the situation. It wasn't long before the ladies returned. On their return everybody moved off with their other half, to where their chairs and lounges were situated.

On reaching theirs, Beth began to give Ellis details of what was being planned for the Geranio. It was quite a simple plan, but after listening to everything Beth said, Ellis agreed it would be effective.

The idea was that, once the lounge area had been transformed, it would initially operate as an assessment and medical treatment unit for young children. Until such time that more medical staff could be found, it would be supervised by Shona O'Neill a qualified nurse from Ireland, who was staying at the hotel. She would require many volunteers to assist her. Beth stated that they had all offered their services and those of their husbands. Ellis nodded.

Having listened to what was being planned, Ellis decided to visit the lounge area and see what progress was being made. On reaching the lounge, Ellis could see that Beppe was inside fixing a large sheet of white paper to the wall. As he walked in Beppe beckoned him over, saying at the same time. 'Ah, Mr Smeeth, come and 'ave a look at this and I will explain to you.'

Ellis went across and studied what looked like a building plan layout.

Beppe started to explain to Ellis what each square or circle meant. He started by identifying a casualty station near Naples. From here people needing initial treatment would be diagnosed and then moved to the appropriate site for their injuries to be treated. He explained that serious injuries would be taken by helicopter, ambulance or ferries, to the nearest suitable or available hospital. Clearly with the number of casualties many hospitals further afield would have to be facilitated.

As far as children with injuries classified as minor or non life threatening were concerned, their destination would be the Hotel Geranio and other designated Sorrento hotels. They would be transported when possible by helicopter to the football pitch opposite the hotel. Alternatively they would be transported by sea to Marina Piccola, and then by road to the hotel.

Ellis was so engrossed in what Beppe was telling him, that he did not notice that Beth had arrived by his side.

'I've just been speaking too many of the other guests,' said Beth. 'They are all volunteering to assist in the casualty unit if required.'

Beppe nodded. 'That is good news; I will let you know when the unit will start to operate.'

Ellis and Beth acknowledged Beppe's comments and bade him goodbye. They reminded him to inform them as soon as everything was ready to commence.

As they walked back across the terrace, they could see Frank getting ready for his first presentation on *Star News* since his recovery. They walked through to the swimming pool area and chose a vantage point where they could see and hear Frank on a TV monitor that was situated nearby.

At 11 o'clock presenter Joanne Birch began reading the *Star News* headlines. The first one was about the devastation of Naples. As Joanne spoke, pictures not seen before were being shown. These pictures had scenes of people appearing to scavenge amongst the huge piles of rubble that were everywhere. People were trying to pull or lift debris from these piles. It appeared that they were trying to rescue people who were probably buried underneath.

Whilst these pictures were being transmitted, a 'Breaking News' streamer started to move along the bottom of the screen:

REUTERS NEWS AGENCY: REPORTS THAT A SOURCE FROM WITHIN THE ITALIAN GOVERNMENT IS SAYING THAT FATALITIES WILL BE IN EXCESS OF 100,000.

***

At this point Joanne was describing the reaction to this disaster from around the world. She went on to identify what aid other countries had promised, and in particular what the UK Government had said. She read out a short statement from the Prime Minister, who was currently on holiday somewhere in Southern Italy. His statement identified that the government's emergency 'COBR' committee (Cabinet Office Briefing Room), had been alerted. It would have its first meeting later that afternoon. He would be flying back to London to chair the meeting.

He continued with the news that the various volunteer organisations throughout the United Kingdom, like the Red Cross, Salvation Army, etc, were already on red alert. Large transportation planes had already been despatched to the various sites around the UK. These would be loaded with the necessary supplies that are stored throughout the UK, in readiness for any disaster area throughout the world.

The statement concluded with the Prime Minister offering his Government's condolences to the people of Italy. He assured them that they would receive all possible help from the people of the United Kingdom.

Joanne Birch now turned her attention to the present situation. She began by mentioning that Frank Brady had now fully recovered from his illness. He was still in Sorrento and they were now going over to him for the latest news from that area.

Ellis and Beth watched with interest as Frank came into view, and began his introduction. He started by thanking Ellis for standing in for him during his illness. He continued by outlining the plans of the local community, particularly those Beppe had earlier briefed him on. Ellis and Beth listened to him for a further five minutes before moving to their spot beside the pool.

On arrival they agreed they would spend the rest of the morning there. Beth suggested that they have lunch at around 1 o'clock. She added, 'Let's go to the tennis club and see Maura.'

'Good idea', said Ellis.

It wasn't long before the others arrived at the pool. Dene and Paula sat alongside Ellis and Beth, whilst William and Sandie stayed in their usual spot about 10 metres away.

Once they were all seated. Ellis asked Dene and Paula how they had settled into their retirement. Dene smiled back that after two years he was totally relaxed about it. Paula added that she too was very much enjoying it particularly as their new grandson, who was now three years old gave her another perspective to focus on.

They continued to discuss the last year's events for another 20 minutes before they had exhausted all their stories.

As Dene stood up to stretch his legs, he commented that the day was very hot with an exceptionally clear sky. The ash haze that had dominated the skyline over the past 20 hours or so was receding very quickly over Sorrento and nearby areas.

Towards Naples, and beyond there was clearly still a fuzzy haze that spread as far as the naked eye could see. This was being added to by the ash etc, which was still being emitted by the plume of smoke and steam from the crater of Vesuvius. It was further aided by the breeze that was again flowing from land out to sea across the Bay of Naples.

As they waited for their drinks to arrive, Ellis and Dene discussed the casualty figures that had been headlined in the early morning news; whilst Beth decided to cool off in the pool before going for lunch. Soon after Beth had finished, she announced they were going for lunch at the tennis club.

After a lazy afternoon by the pool, they decided to go back to the room and prepare for dinner. As they walked through the reception area they noticed the porters carrying mattresses into the lounge. 'It looks like they have started preparing the lounge for the casualty centre,' Ellis remarked.

'Yes, I think we might be in business tomorrow,' replied Beth.

Dinner that evening was a quiet affair. Both enjoyed the meal. Ellis started with a pasta dish called Tubettoni with sword-fish and tomatoes, whilst Beth went for the Potato and noodle soup. This was followed up by Scorpion-fish fillets, Sicilian- style for Ellis, and a Pork steak, Milanese-style for Beth. Once they had eaten this, they only had room for ice cream. Even Ellis could not find room for a piece of the pastry chef's cream filled gateaux.

After their meal, they retired to the terrace bar. As they sat down, Carlos came over and took their order for two cappuccinos. It wasn't long before he returned with two cups of the frothy white liquid. As he served them, he asked them what their plans were for the rest of the holiday. Beth explained they were hoping that tomorrow the transformation of the lounge would be completed.

If so they would be offering their services to help in any way they could.

Carlos nodded, saying, 'I expected you to say that. I am very thankful of you both for helping my country.'

'That is no problem,' replied Ellis. 'It is the very least we can do.'

With a wave of his hand Carlos took his leave moving across to greet other guests who were coming onto the terrace.

Ellis and Beth spent the evening on the terrace bar, with the rest of the 'gang' before retiring to their room at around eleven o'clock. As they made their way to room 505, Beth indicated to Ellis that once they had got themselves a nightcap she wanted to discuss Jamie and the children with him.

Whilst she made herself a coffee, Beth told Ellis that what she was about to discuss with him was as a result of a conversation she had had with Jamie prior to the holiday about Jamie's future.

During the conversation Beth said that Jamie herself had raised the issue as both she and Louise were concerned with how their parents would cope over the next few years now that they were both in their seventies.

Ellis smiled at this telling Beth he did not envisage any problems adding 'but if age begins to get the better of us, we can go and live with her or Louise.'

At that they both burst out laughing. Beth continued that Jamie had suggested if their house had been larger she and the children could have moved in so that if at some stage either or both of them needed care and attention, she would be on hand to help them.

Beth continued that she had been surprised by this suggestion as they were both fully aware of how much Jamie loved her house.

There was silence for a few moments as Ellis took this information in and then Beth asked him what he thought. Ellis agreed that their three bedroom house was not large enough, something they had experienced first- hand when Jamie and the children had moved in for six weeks after the divorce during the transition period between moving houses. He could not see a way that a permanent move could work when they would be living on top of one another.

Beth agreed but suggested that such a move could solve some of Jamie's problems particularly, being a one parent family. 'It would also mean,' she said smiling at the same time, 'that Jamie would have built in child minders.' Ellis nodded and smiled in agreement.

As they climbed into bed, Ellis had clearly been pondering the situation. 'The only way this could work,' he suggested, 'would be if we sold both houses and purchased a larger one. 'Would you consider doing that?' asked Beth. 'I'm not sure,' he replied.

'In any case, 'I'm not convinced Jamie would agree to that, and we need to consider how Louise would feel about it too.' With the time approaching midnight they agreed to discuss the subject again tomorrow.

Chapter Ten - Eruption plus 2

Ellis and Beth rose from their bed on Monday morning, at 6.30. Ellis made them both a cup of tea, and he and Beth drank it as they sat and watched the early *Star News* programme. It was as usual being presented by Raymond Kelly, who was explaining some statistics which had been released by the Italian Government earlier that morning.

Although not unexpected, the information he was reading out was very depressing. 3000 people had already been confirmed dead, where the pyroclastic flow first struck, on the outskirts of Naples. He explained that these figures were estimates provided by the first rescue service to have reached the scene. In addition to those dead a further 1500 people were injured in one form or another.

As these figures were being shown in more detail across the screen, Raymond Kelly explained that due to the damage or destruction of hospitals, those injured were being transported further afield to wherever any form of medical centre was available. Those whose injuries were not life threatening were to be treated at one of many temporary field hospital/casualty centres that were hurriedly being assembled all around the outskirts of Naples and surrounding towns.

Raymond Kelly continued to summarise the current situation, and then interrupted himself to give the latest predictions of fatalities etc., that were being released by *Reuters News Agency*. *Reuters* claimed that estimates to be released by government officials later, would show that at least 100,000 fatalities should be expected. These figures were apparently released to ministers at the Italian Government's Emergency Cabinet meeting last night in Rome.

Ellis looked at Beth and suggested, 'Let's get ready and go for breakfast. I think there will be a lot of work to do upstairs today.' Beth agreed.

Later, whilst they were eating they started to discuss the day before them. Ellis suggested that straight after breakfast, they should visit the lounge turned medical centre to see if Shona the Irish nurse was available.

Beth nodded in agreement. She looked at Ellis paused and then asked him if he had thought any more about their conversation regarding Jamie last night. 'Yes I have,' he said. 'As a matter of fact I was awake last night for some time thinking about it.' 'Did you come to any conclusion?' Beth asked. 'Not any final conclusion,' Ellis replied. He then went on to explain that although he wasn't totally against the idea, he could see no point in pursuing it if Jamie's comments were made in a moment of idealism.

Beth looked at him rather sheepishly saying as she did, 'Actually that point was mentioned during the conversation and Jamie did not rule it out.'

Ellis said nothing for a full minute; Beth wondered what he was going to say. She was pleasantly surprised when he announced in a slightly stern voice that it was something for him to think about during the holiday. However, '*think*' did not necessarily mean '*yes*'. Beth smiled to herself. She was more than happy for Ellis to think about things. At least he had not completely dismissed the idea.

As Ellis was about to make further comments, he stopped and sighed, 'Oh, guess who we have forgotten.'

Beth looked at Ellis, with a startled expression on her face. 'Who?' she said in a slightly raised voice.

'Phillip and Bernice', Ellis exclaimed, with a hint of laughter in his voice.

'Crikey', responded Beth. 'I'd forgotten all about them. What are we going to do?'

Ellis replied. 'We will mention it to William and Sandie, and see if they can find out what time they are expected.'

'Good idea,' said Beth.

When William and Sandie arrived a little while later, Ellis asked if there was any news about Phillip and Bernice. William smiled as he said. 'Job done, we have just been to reception and spoken to Cirino. Phillip and Bernice are coming over today, they should arrive before lunch.'

'That's good,' Beth replied. 'After breakfast we're going to see if Shona O'Neill is around, to see what she has planned.'

'Let us know if you find anything out,' Sandie asked.

'Will do,' replied Beth.

After they had finished their breakfast, they walked upstairs and headed for the lounge. As they walked through the door they were amazed to see what transformation had taken place in the last 24 hours. All the walls were bare, no sign of a painting anywhere. Every antique that had been displayed throughout the lounge had disappeared. However, the biggest change was the disappearance of all the furniture. No grand piano, no casual tables, no settees or armchairs etc. All had been replaced overnight with single metal frame beds, some cupboards and tables with two computers waiting to be used. In addition there were countless boxes of all sizes, all clearly marked as medical supplies. Ellis wandered passed the boxes, pausing for a few seconds to read the contents: labels. Syringes, swabs, medical instruments, bandages of all shapes and sizes, plus bottles of general antiseptic and small plastic containers of hand wash antiseptic. Protective clothing, face masks, fine surgical gloves were also there in abundance; nothing had been forgotten. The array of boxes seemed endless. There was even a portable x-ray machine in a wooden box, propped up against the wall.

Beth was across the other side of the lounge, looking at the sheets, blankets, pillows and towels that were piled high on the floor all in their polythene wrappings.

As Ellis made his way across the room, Shona entered the lounge from the terrace entrance. Both Ellis and Beth moved towards her, Ellis offered his hand and said, 'My name is Ellis Smith and this is my wife Beth. I hope you don't mind us looking around. We were waiting to see you. We and other people are keen to find out what you had in mind for those who want to be of assistance.'

Shona's reply was very positive. 'Not at all. I'm glad of all the interest there is. I'm going to need all the help I can get.'

'I'm pleased you're here,' she said. 'I am going to hold a meeting here in the lounge at 11 o'clock for everybody that is interested in helping. I will explain everything at that time; meanwhile I would be grateful if you could both spread the word.

In addition I am going to put some posters up around the hotel advertising this meeting.'

'That sounds like a good idea,' replied Ellis. 'Leave it to us and we'll rally the troops.'

'Thanks very much,' said Shona with a smile. 'You are both as enthusiastic as I was told you would be.'

With that Ellis and Beth left the lounge and went down to their room to collect their belongings for the pool. On the way back from their room, Ellis picked up his *Daily Mail* from reception. Cirino was first on duty that morning and greeted them both with 'Buon Giorno, how are you both this morning?'

'We're okay,' Ellis replied. 'We will feel better when we are able to help.'

'I understand what you mean,' commented Cirino. He continued, 'I think your help will be needed shortly Mr Smeeth.'

'We hope so,' Ellis replied, as they moved towards the door that led to the swimming pool. As they arrived at the pool entrance, Marco was in the process of removing the rope barrier, which he put there whilst preparing the pool each morning.

They walked onto the pool side, and placed their bags alongside their deck chairs that he had already positioned for them.

William and Sandie were not far behind them. Ellis told them of the 11 o'clock meeting in the lounge with Shona and mentioned that she had asked them to pass the word around. 'That's okay,' William said, with a nod of his head. 'We'll spread the word.'

'As soon as there are more people around the pool, I'll make an announcement about it,' said Ellis.

Thirty minutes later Ellis looked around the pool. By this time it was fairly well occupied. He leant over towards Beth saying, 'I think it's time to inform these people about the meeting. What do you think?'

Beth looked around, 'Yes, I should go for it.'

'Okay,' replied Ellis.

With that Ellis stood up and walked across in front of the steps leading into the pool. He took from his pocket a whistle that he had borrowed from Carlos earlier that morning. He put the whistle to his lips and blew three long blasts on it, similar to those that a football referee does at the end of a game. The result was quite electrifying. The buzz that had been apparent round the pool just prior to the whistle sounding had now ceased. Everybody was looking at Ellis.

Ellis raised both arms in the air, and speaking in a loud voice made the following statement. 'Ladies and Gentlemen, could I have your attention for a few moments. I will try and speak slowly and clearly, so those of you whose first language is not English, may be able to understand what I am saying.'

At that point he stopped speaking as two helicopters flew low over the hotel heading towards Naples. The deafening noise of the engines and the loud whirring of the rotor blades, made it impossible for anybody speaking to be heard. The increase in air and water traffic since late yesterday afternoon was very apparent.

'At 11 o'clock this morning a fully qualified nurse named Shona O'Neill will be holding a meeting in the lounge area. The lounge has now been adapted in the last 24 hours into a casualty reception unit. Shona, who holds a position as a senior sister in the Dublin University Hospital, has been asked by the joint owners of this hotel, Beppe Marcello and his cousin Perla to organise and be in charge of this unit.

'The unit is to be used initially for injured children. Shona needs many volunteers to help her run it. If anybody is interested, please go along to her meeting later. Finally, it is not necessary that you have any medical training. Many types of skills are going to be required. The skill that will most probably be needed is love and affection. Thank you all very much for your attention.'

With that Ellis turned and headed back to where Beth was standing. 'How was that?'

'Fine, just fine,' replied Beth.

As they both stood there they felt a sudden tremor beneath their feet. Before either could speak, it stopped.

Beth looked at Ellis, saying at the same time, 'Surely it's not going to happen again.'

'Don't panic yet,' said Ellis. 'Small tremors and aftershocks are a common occurrence after eruptions and earthquakes. The problem is that if they continue they can be enough to initiate an eruption.'

Fifteen minutes later there had been no further tremors so Ellis and Beth decided to make their way towards the lounge where they found a large number of people had already gathered. As they looked around they could see Shona by the patio doors, asking people to move from the lounge area onto the terrace.

Within ten minutes the whole terrace area was full.

Without a moment's hesitation, Shona walked up the steps onto the staging.

She held her hands in the air, the assembled crowd hushed immediately as she began to speak, 'Thank you all very much for being here this morning. I am very grateful that you have come to listen to what I have to say.' Shona spoke with authority, as her Southern Irish accent emphasised what she was saying.

'I think most of you are now aware why we have converted the lounge over the past 24 hours, into a medical ward. For those of you who are not aware let me confirm to you, that as from tomorrow morning, this ward will be receiving children who have sustained injuries from the Vesuvius eruption.

'The type of injuries that we will be receiving will be non-life threatening. Minor burns, lacerations, severe bruising, possibly broken bones, and no doubt there will be trauma cases.

'My position here is to organise a medical unit that can cope with all of those injuries I have mentioned, and possibly others as well.'

There was silence as Shona continued. 'I will be getting further medical support, as and when people become available. However, until then, I and any volunteers will have to manage as best as we can.'

'In order to get this unit up and running by tomorrow morning, I need volunteers to step forward and be ready to assist in any way they can. I will assess those of you who want to help, and discuss with you individually where I think your skills would best be suited.

'Once I have finished what I have to say, I would like those of you who wish to help to remain behind.'

Shona continued by outlining what skills would be required. She detailed the type of medical skills that would be an asset to her. She was particularly looking for those people who had nursing or dental experience, were first aiders, or anybody that had worked within a hospital or other medical environment.

'Finally,' Shona said, 'even if you have no experience in any of the areas I have just mentioned. I still need other skills to ensure the unit is run efficiently so please speak to me if you wish to be considered. I have no more to say. Would those who wish to be considered, please stay in the lounge. I will be back shortly.'

With that Shona left the raised staging, and disappeared, through the lounge but within ten minutes she returned with her arms full of envelope files and two box files. She walked through and placed them on the desk at the far side of the lounge. By now the number of people in the lounge all standing around had swollen to about 40 or 50 in all.

Shona beckoned them all forward and said, 'Would you first of all split yourselves into three groups? The group on my left will be those of you who have any medical qualifications, on my right anybody with any medical experience. The remainder, who just want to help in any way they can, please make your way over to the desk on the other side of the room'.

Ellis looked at Beth. 'You belong in the queue for those who have worked in a medical environment. I'm just a qualified basic helper, so I'm across the other side of the room,' he said laughing.

'Right, let's go and see what's needed,' replied Beth.

Once Ellis reached the designated area, he looked back across the room. He was pleased to see that their friends, William, Sandie, Dene and Paula had arrived.

At that point Shona walked to the centre of the room, and clapped her hands, 'May I have your attention again for one moment please?'

She continued, 'As there are so many of you, I am giving each area a number of these cards. Please take one and fill in your name and room number then very briefly write what experience you have which may be of assistance to me.

'Please put your card in the box by the door. I will assess each one and get back to you as soon as I can later today. To make it easier for me to locate you, would you tell reception where you will be within the hotel complex. Thank you all very much.'

Ellis walked to the table, picked up a card and went across to Beth.

'Let's fill these in and then go for lunch,' he suggested. Beth nodded her approval.

With that they went into the reception area, sat down by a table and spent 10 minutes filling in forms. Ellis picked both of them up and went in search of the box that Shona mentioned. He found it located just inside the door adjacent to the reception area. He posted both cards through the slot in the top of the box and made his way back to the reception area.

Beth was there waiting for him. 'Shall we go for lunch now?'

'Yes, okay,' Ellis replied. 'And before we go, let's tell Cirino where we will be for the rest of the afternoon.'

Ellis walked across to the reception desk and gave Cirino their location. He wrote their information down on a pad he had in front of him. Ellis could see that already he had a number of names written down. They bid farewell to Cirino, and made their way through the bar onto the terrace. Carlos spotted them and raised his hand to them, gesturing for them to come over to him.

As they reached the table, a sudden shudder shook the whole of the terrace. A wine stand toppled over, some glasses and bottles fell off the tables, scattering slivers of glass everywhere as they struck the concrete floor. Those umbrellas in the open position, swayed violently, as though struck by a sudden gust of wind. Worse followed as Dario the young waiter who was carrying a large silver tray lost his footing and fell. He rolled over and fell onto the terrace. The large tray and its contents flew in all directions; the tray striking a table before settling on the floor. Everybody on the terrace was trying to hold onto something, or where there was nothing available, they held onto each other.

Just as somebody started shouting, the shuddering stopped.

There was complete silence for about thirty seconds, as everybody looked around at each other. Nobody spoke for that time; it was as though they thought any noise might start it up again. It was Carlos who spoke first; he went across to Dario and asked him if he was all right. 'Let me help you up,' Carlos said with a concerned look on his face.

That was the signal for everybody to begin speaking. As he got up from the floor, Dario started to walk. After a few steps it was clear that the only damage he had suffered were a few bruises and his own professional pride. Fortunately, nobody else sustained any injuries, even though the broken glass had showered in all directions. Within 20 minutes the terrace was back to normal. Luigi, the part time waiter just back from college, had swept up all the broken glass, the spoiled food and other debris. Everybody was still looking a little pensive, when some 'wag' with a Scottish accent from the far end of the terrace shouted, 'Is there any chance of lunch?' The whole terrace erupted in laughter, as Carlos turned around to see who it was. His face soon broke into a large smile when he saw who it was.

'Normal service will be resumed as soon as possible.' He added, 'For my friends.' He turned around and looked towards the person who had just made that remark, and said, 'You will 'ave to wait a while.' He smiled again as he said it.

The person he referred to raised a glass towards Carlos saying as he did, 'Touché.'

'Right,' commented Ellis, 'let's eat.' With that they sat down, and Carlos came across and handed them both a menu.

They were about to order when who should appear on the terrace but Phillip and Bernice, accompanied by William and Sandie. Big hugs and kisses followed, as each one of them showed their delight in seeing one another again; the first time for 12 months.

As they sat at the next table, Dene and Paula appeared so it was big hugs and kisses again. Just then Carlos arrived and began preparing the table on the other side of Ellis and Beth. 'Tell you what,' Ellis said. 'If we swap places with you William, then you four can sit between Dene and us. We can all talk to Phillip and Bernice then.'

'Good idea,' they all said in unison.

Table by table, Carlos took their orders.

Beth decided on a cheese and tomato toasty, whilst Ellis went for the Chicken l'orange with a side order of French fries. A glass of fresh orange juice and a small bottle of 'Geranio' red wine accompanied their meals.

Once all tables had ordered the conversation continued. Phillip and Bernice were the first to speak. They explained that an elderly aunt, who she looked after with the help of a carer, had agreed between them that she and Phillip should take a fortnight's holiday this year. After much deliberation they accepted the offer and decided to split the holiday, one week in Ischia the other in Sorrento.

Bernice continued that when they saw the Vesuvius eruptions they had considered ringing Ellis and Beth. 'We wondered what was happening, and how you all were. Phillip was watching television; I was in the bathroom, when Ellis pops up on *Star News*. Phillip could not believe it. He was shouting and laughing at the same time, as he called for me to come and see Ellis. Our eyes were glued to the television screen. It was the most surreal thing we have ever seen but we didn't know you had come out of retirement. Phillip and I thought you were very good.'

'Thanks, Bernice;' replied Ellis, 'I didn't know either until Saturday.'

Bernice looked at William. 'So what's happening now?' Bernice enquired.

William continued the story, telling Bernice and Phillip what Beppe's plans were, and how the lounge had been transformed overnight into a casualty unit. He further mentioned the nurse in charge was called Shona.

As Bernice and Phillip asked further questions, they were told about the volunteers that Shona required to help run the unit. Beth mentioned that they had all filled in forms, giving details of any experience that might be useful for Shona to evaluate.

As they continued to give details, their lunch and drinks began to arrive.

They agreed to continue after they had eaten.

After they had finished lunch, the discussion on the events to date continued, with Dene asking Phillip and Bernice where they were when that tremor occurred just before they came to lunch.

Bernice said that they were still in their room, when it happened. 'I thought for one moment that the hotel was going to fall down!' she exclaimed. 'We also felt those from the other day.'

She further explained that when the first tremor happened in Ischia, they were in one of the spa hotels. All the people in the complex at that time quickly evacuated the spas and pools, and congregated in the large gardens at the back of the hotel. Once it had all settled down, everybody continued with what they were doing before.

Ellis continued on with the topic of tremors, telling Phillip and Bernice their experiences at the Fauno Bar and the subsequent walk back to the 'Geranio'.

Once he had finished, Phillip chirped up. 'Anyway, Ellis what's all this *Star News* reporter malarkey then?' They all laughed. For the next ten minutes or so, Ellis went to great lengths to explain to Phillip and Bernice how it all came about.

He would have continued on, but with more people coming onto the terrace for lunch they decided to vacate their tables.

'I'll tell you the rest later,' Ellis said with a laugh.

'He's not joking,' William retorted. 'It's a bit like that programme *Mastermind*. I've started so I'll finish.' Bernice shrieked with laughter at that comment. Before anybody could make any further comments, another tremor occurred.

This one lasted a good 30 seconds, and the force of it shook the terrace floor considerably.

The result was again to send plates of food, glasses, cutlery and wine, flying off the tables. People hung onto one another for balance; one or two people stumbled over. Like the others it soon stopped. However, this one had been more forceful than some of the others.

As the 'gang' sorted themselves out, Dene spoke with an alarming sound to his voice. 'Those tremors seem to have woken Vesuvius up again.'

Everybody turned and looked across the Bay of Naples. What they saw was cause for alarm. A large dark cloud was now billowing out, from the vicinity of where the original crater was. This was accompanied by the appearance of an orange stream of lava spilling out over the side, and beginning to move very slowly down the side of what was left of the mountain.

'Oh no!' Beth was heard to say, with a touch of despair in her voice.

At that moment Carlos appeared from the bar onto the terrace. His facial expression as he saw that Vesuvius was active again, could only be described as one of horror and amazement. He lifted both arms into the air, shaking his head in disbelief and saying. 'Why is this happening to us?' With that he turned around and disappeared quickly in the direction of the television. Everybody on the terrace continued to look towards Vesuvius.

All eyes were transfixed on the slow stream of orange lava as it continued on its journey down the side of the mountain. Dene commented that if the rate of progression did not accelerate, and even if the flow continued for some time, the authorities would have time to minimise the effect, by diverting it away from those areas of population, or buildings of significance. They all stood against the perimeter fence of the terrace watching the flow of lava for 15 minutes or so, before deciding to return to the pool side for the rest of the afternoon.

As they started to walk away, Carlos appeared from within the bar. He spotted them, and walked across. As he reached them, he proceeded to tell them what the television newscaster had been saying.

'They are saying that the lava flow is as a result of the many aftershocks that have recently occurred,' explained Carlos. 'The aftershocks have opened up a fission, deep inside Vesuvius. The scientist's 'ave assured the authorities that this will not result in another 'ow you say' pyroclastic flow. Furthermore, the scientists cannot say for certain ow long this flow will last. They say it might be a day or two, or could be as long as one or two weeks.'

With that Carlos raised his arms in the air, shrugging his shoulders at the same time muttering something in Italian. He smiled at the 'gang', then turned and walked away. With the time approaching 3 o'clock, they decided to go back to the pool. As they approached the pool entrance, Shona appeared.

'Mr and Mrs Smith have you a few minutes to spare please?' she asked.

'Yes, that's no problem,' Ellis replied.

They both followed Shona into the now completed, casualty reception unit. Once there she beckoned towards the desk at the far end of the room. As they sat down, Shona picked up a pile of the cards she had distributed earlier. She selected those previously filled out by of Ellis and Beth.

Over the next half an hour Shona discussed how she wanted the unit to operate. She started from when the first child casualties arrived for assessment, to when they were discharged. Once assessed and treated, Shona then explained the different types of action that would be open to them.

The first action would be that once the child needed no further treatment, they could go back to their parents or guardians. If, at that point, neither were available they would go to another holding area. If they need further medical treatment at a general or specialist hospital, then that would have to be arranged. 'We need an Italian speaking person for this role,' Shona added.

She continued that records needed to be kept and updated from the moment the child was received, to when they were discharged. Shona then went on to explain that they had a computer with the appropriate database programme already installed, for this situation. What she now needed was somebody to be in charge of this operation. She looked at Ellis and Beth saying, 'I think that you two would be ideally suited for this task.'

They both looked at each other and then nodded to Shona to accept her offer.

Beth added that she would also like to be hands on with the children, if and when there was a lull in the computing work. Ellis then proposed that they would operate the database system between them. Then whenever necessary and subject to their availability they would assist elsewhere.

Shona was delighted with this suggestion, and after summarising their positions she said they should report to her after breakfast tomorrow morning. 'Thank you very much,' she said. 'I will go and find some more of the volunteers.'

On their way back to the pool, Ellis and Beth diverted to the terrace to have another look at Vesuvius. On arriving they could see Carlos with his binoculars scanning the landscape across the Bay of Naples. The orange lava was still slowly finding its way down the mountainside. As he took the binoculars away from his eyes, he turned and saw them. Still looking concerned he said, 'It eeze still flowing Mr Smeeth, although very gently. I hope it eeze not doing much damage to the people over there.'

Ellis replied, 'I think they will have had sufficient warning. Do not worry, Carlos, I'm sure they will have moved to a safer place.'

Before they departed, Ellis explained to Carlos what they had discussed with Shona. This brought a smile to his face.

'See you later,' they said in unison.

As they entered the pool from the terrace entrance, Ellis and Beth spotted the rest of the 'gang' following Shona towards the casualty unit.

'It'll be interesting to see what jobs they end up with,' laughed Beth. Ellis also started to laugh.

'What's tickling your fancy?' asked Beth.

Ellis burst out laughing again. 'I wonder which one will get bedpan duty?'

That remark did it, Beth burst into laughter again; this time tears were running down her face. It was fully one minute before she composed herself. 'Stop it,' uttered Beth. 'Come on, let's go and sit down before I fall over.'

With that they wandered over to their pool-side deck chairs. Once there they spent a few minutes discussing the earlier meeting they had with Shona.

As their discussion progressed, Beth started to plan what she would do. It wasn't long before she was beginning to get into the fine detail.

'How does the database work?' she asked Ellis.

Ellis briefly explained with the aid of a piece of paper and a pencil. However, before he could continue the rest of the 'gang' arrived. They all congregated where Ellis and Beth were sitting. Within a minute they all started to discuss what duties they had signed up for.

Sandie, Paula, and Bernice identified a number of tasks they would be undertaking. Amongst them were making up new beds, setting up and maintaining a clean linen cupboard. Additionally, where necessary, they would serve food and drinks to the patients. Also they would assist those people whose injuries were such that they needed help to eat or drink.

Dene, William and Phillip had more ranging responsibilities. They would fetch and carry as and when required from within the hotel, or from other hotels or suppliers, using a van that Beppe had put at their disposal. They might also be called upon to assist with any other manual tasks that were required within the unit. They spent some time discussing the tasks that lay in front of them. In particular children who had been separated from their parents, before being rescued from the debris in isolation.

As the time approached 5 o'clock, Ellis and Beth decided to head back to their room and prepare for the evening. On arrival at their room whilst Beth sorted out her evening clothes Ellis tuned in to *Star News* to for an update on the latest Vesuvius eruption.

The news about the eruption was as Carlos had said earlier; recent aftershocks had caused the lava flow. The news reader concluded by saying that volcanologists were currently satisfied that the eruption would not get any worse, providing the aftershocks remained at around the same level. As this report on this latest eruption was being presented by Joanne Birch, a 'Breaking News' streamer was running across the bottom of the screen.

It was from the *Reuters News Agency* it read:

THE LATEST CONFIRMED NUMBER OF FATALITIES HAS NOW RISEN TO 25,000 PEOPLE

***

Chapter Eleven - Eruption plus 3

Beth was the first to rise on Tuesday morning. Ellis still half asleep heard her fill the kettle and plug it in.

'Cup of tea?' she asked. 'That will do nicely,' Ellis replied with a stifled yawn to his voice.

After she had made the tea, Beth announced that she was going to read her book on the balcony for half an hour.

'How is Vesuvius this morning?' Ellis enquired.

'About the same as yesterday' came back the reply.

'I'll get an update from *Star News* in a minute,' yawned Ellis.

With that he threw back the sheets and clambered out of bed, as Beth opened the doors to the balcony and went through. Ellis picked up the remote control and switched the television on to *Star News*. As the picture came on, he was confronted by the same view of Vesuvius as could be seen from where Beth was now sitting. He thought how surreal this was, realising as he said it to himself that the *Star News* team were now staying at the 'Geranio'. He increased the volume just as Frank Brady was informing viewers of the latest situation.

He spoke for about five minutes. Frank indicated that the lava flow had decreased slightly in the last 24 hours. At this stage the news reader back in the UK studio asked him if he had heard any revision to the latest fatalities figure of 25,000 given yesterday. Frank said he had heard of no revision to that number. The news reader continued that an Italian Government Official had unofficially told a *Star News* reporter, that yesterday's figure would be revised dramatically upwards in the next few hours. Frank responded by saying that he would speak to his sources to try and confirm that comment. With that he ended his report. The picture changed back to the news reader in the studio.

Ellis went through to the balcony and updated Beth on what he had just heard, particularly the report that the fatality numbers may be considerably increased later today.

'I guess our first day in the casualty unit is going to be a busy one,' Beth said.

As they walked onto the breakfast terrace they saw Shona sitting at a table at the far end of the terrace. She spotted them and beckoned them over. On reaching her table she asked them if they could start working after they had finished breakfast. She explained that everything was beginning to move at a fast pace now. The central medical control station, which was based just outside Naples, was sending ten children to the 'Geranio' later that morning. Both Ellis and Beth confirmed they could. Ellis added. 'Just give us time to grab some breakfast and we'll be there soon after.'

'Excellent,' replied Shona. 'As soon as I have finished this cup of coffee, I'll be at the unit.'

'Okay. We'll see you there,' nodded Beth.

As soon as they had finished breakfast, Beth and Ellis made their way to the casualty unit. Shona welcomed them and ushered them across to the desk where a computer and printer were set up. 'I was hoping you would be early. I wanted to show you the database programme that is now installed and waiting to be used.'

As they sat down around the desk, Shona leaned across and switched on the computer. Whilst waiting for it to warm up, she explained that their first patients were due to arrive very shortly. The latest information indicated about ten children were already on their way.

Within two minutes the computer screen indicated that it had fully 'booted up' and was ready for use.

'Okay, here we go. Let's see if it works,' said Shona. She looked down at a typed sheet of A4 paper that had a list of instructions printed on it.

'First click on the icon identified as "Casualty Database",' she read out. This she did, straightaway the computer screen changed to a format that Ellis immediately recognised. It was a simple format that showed a number of headings down the left hand side. Ellis read out each field as they appeared on the database. As he did so, Shona read out from her instruction sheet a brief résumé of what was required against each heading.

IDENTITY No:	Each patient to be given an identity number. Beginning at 001.
FULL NAME:	Full name to be shown. If name not known put unknown.
AGE:	If child does not know. Estimate and show as Est.
ADDRESS:	Full address. Or area found.
INJURY:	After assessment give details of injury etc.
DISCHARGE:	When discharged give details of medical treatment.
TRANSFER:	If patient transferred elsewhere for further treatment or discharged identify where to.
NEXT OF KIN:	As much information as possible. Parents, Relatives, or Friends.
GENERAL:	Any other information to ensure correct identification of patient.

'That seems straight forward enough. I feel quite encouraged by that,' said Beth.

They all agreed. Shona then picked up a bag containing plastic name tags and some pre-printed forms. Turning to Ellis and Beth, she explained that when a patient arrived they would be assigned a number. This number would accompany the patient's name (if known) on the name tag. The number and name would then be written on the pre printed form and handed over for transferring to the database. The patient would have the name tag fitted around their wrist as first choice, or ankle or elsewhere if injuries obstructed its fitting.

Shona continued, 'Whoever is manning the database will be given an update on the patient from time to time. This must be entered on to the database immediately, as this information may be all that the authorities have to enable them to assist people whose children have gone missing in the aftermath of the eruption. At this stage we do not know who we will be receiving, or what mental condition they will be in.'

Shona concluded by saying. 'In order to help us, we will be getting an Italian medical assistant who also speaks very good English. She will be your link between you and the medical staff. When she arrives, I will introduce you, and inform her of her duties.

'Okay, it's now a quarter past nine. We only have 45 minutes before the first patients are due to arrived. I'll leave you to practise and familiarise yourself with the database. Best of luck.'

Ellis and Beth looked at one another. At the same time they both shrugged their shoulders. 'Let's get to it,' said an excited Beth. With that she sat down at the desk, made herself comfortable and began to arrange the contents of the desk into a tidy state.

Whilst she was doing that, Ellis switched on the printer, ensuring at the same time that the paper and ink cartridges were in their correct place. Once that was done, he walked across to the stationary cupboard, and selected a number of pens, pencils, two A4 notepads, and a large box folder. He arrived back at the desk just as Beth had satisfied herself that the desk was now tidy, everything was in place, and they were ready to begin work.

As they finished getting themselves organised, two workmen arrived to fit a flat screen television to the wall behind the screens where Shona sat. They positioned it so that it was not visible by the children in the ward. Within five minutes they had finished. They left it switched on; it appeared to be the *Italian News Channel TG5*, which had live pictures of rescue work underway in what looked like the suburbs of Naples. The volunteers fell silent as they looked at the unbelievable scenes. The silence lasted a good minute, before people, some shaking their heads in disbelief, turned away and continued with what they were doing.

As Ellis looked at his watch, the time was just approaching 10 o'clock. As if on cue the sound of a wailing siren began to get louder and louder.

Ellis looked at Beth saying, 'I think we are in business. That sounds like it's coming here.' Ellis had no sooner finished speaking, when he caught the reflection of a blue whirling light coming through the door that led to the reception area. They gazed at the door in anticipation. As they did, it opened and a nurse walked in.

'That must be the Italian nurse Shona was telling us about,' Beth said in a low voice.

The nurse was greeted by Shona and taken immediately across the room to the desk where Shona had been sitting. A few minutes later, both doors opened and two paramedics came through the door carrying a stretcher. Both Ellis and Beth strained to see who was on the stretcher. It was very difficult to see exactly who it was, as a face was obscured by an oxygen mask. However, they soon realised that it was a child, as the blanket on their side of the stretcher had become partially detached. Hanging out was a bandaged arm; they could both see a small hand firmly grasping a soft toy bear.

As the stretcher passed them by, there was more evidence of surface injuries to the forehead and scalp; fortunately they appeared to be mostly superficial.

As the paramedics carried the stretcher towards the area of the room where two cubicles had been erected, using a double frame tent and curtains, more paramedics came through the door. One was carrying a small girl who was clearly in distress.

Another came in pushing a wheel chair. In it was a boy who looked about seven years of age. His head was bandaged, and his right arm was positioned across his chest held in place by a blue sling. He looked dazed and bewildered, and made no sound. As he passed Ellis and Beth, his eyes turned towards them. Ellis glanced at Beth, her eyes showed signs of watering. Ellis said nothing and turned his eyes towards the door again.

He was anticipating more patients. However, there were no more, those three were the only ones at present. Others were to follow a little while later.

Ellis and Beth sat there waiting whilst the three children's injuries were being assessed. Twenty minutes later Shona and the Italian nurse walked across to them.

On arrival at their desk Shona introduced them to the nurse whose name was Carla. Shona explained to her, that she would be the link between the medical staff and both of them. She asked Ellis to briefly show Carla the database so she would understand what sort of information was needed.

Ellis quickly brought the database on line, and summarised each field. As he did so, Carla nodded and gave Ellis the first casualty form, which was for the little girl.

As Ellis passed it over to Beth, he glanced at the contents. He noticed that the space for the patient's name was blank. There was an estimated age of five years identified, but with the exception of her injury details, all other sections were blank.

As Beth started to input the scant details onto the computer, Ellis looked over her shoulder to see what injuries had been diagnosed. The report read severe lacerations to the forehead and scalp. Left arm also badly lacerated, possible fracture, with evidence of overall body bruising. Treatment required x-ray of left arm, to clean wounds and stitch if necessary. Treat lacerations to forehead and scalp. Check all body bruising and x-ray all severe painful areas.

Identity No: 01 was the first field to be filled in. Followed by; unknown for name; estimated age of five years. The only other information on the form was medical.

Beth typed in all the medical assessment notes as written in the report. She added a note to say that this field would be updated as further information became available. At this point Beth turned to Ellis saying. 'They have not included a data field for date of admissions or the day the patient was discharged. Ellis acknowledged that this was a good point. He suggested that two new data fields should be inserted. He also suggested that after every amendment to these records the date of that amendment should also be included. Beth nodded her head in agreement. She turned back to the computer and began modifying the changes they had just agreed. As she finished them, Shona appeared. Beth guided her through the first patient's record, explaining the changes they had just made.

Before Shona disappeared, Beth asked her that when patients' names were not known, should they be given one for identification purposes only. Shona thought this was an excellent idea and agreed they should implement it. When asked what type of names they should use, Shona replied. 'Use British names; it will be easier for you to remember them.'

'What are we going to call patient number one?' Ellis asked?

'Well,' replied Beth, 'why don't we go in alphabetical order, obviously starting at A?'

'I agree,' responded Ellis.

Beth pondered for a few seconds, 'Okay, let's start with Ann.'

Whilst waiting for the second assessment, Ellis complimented Beth on how well she had grasped the workings of the database. 'However, you have forgotten one very important step.'

'What is that?' asked Beth?

He replied, 'You have forgotten to save your work'.

'Okay, clever clogs, show me how you do that,' Beth replied.

He leant across, saying as he did, 'Watch carefully, I will show you this only once.'

As he moved away, he received a playful clip on the side of his head from Beth. Before he could retaliate, Carla appeared with the second assessment form. This was for the second patient they had received. Beth took the form from her and immediately began to input the information into the computer.

Identity No: 02, name not known, Beth added Alan. Age estimated at seven years, no address or area found. Treatment required, x-ray right arm, check head lacerations, examine body bruises fully, and x-ray any painful areas. Within five minutes the second casualty's details were all on the computer.

As Beth turned around to speak to Ellis, she could hear more wailing sirens in the distance. Within 30 seconds the blue flashing lights were once again reflecting through the door. The incessant wailing of the sirens stopped abruptly as the ambulance came to a halt at the reception entrance. They said nothing as they both looked towards the door, anticipating the next patients. Within two minutes the doors were flung open, two paramedics came into view pushing a trolley. Shortly afterwards the doors opened again as another casualty was wheeled in.

The next 30 minutes saw a marked increase in the sound of wailing sirens, and flashing blue lights. At least five more ambulances arrived. When they had all discharged their patients, the number in the casualty unit had risen to 18. Ellis and Beth watched as one by one, children of all ages were brought into the unit. Some were carried in on stretchers, two more were in wheelchairs, and there was also some walking wounded. Most of the children's clothes were torn and dishevelled, some had bandaged heads. They looked around as they came through the door, some had fear in their eyes, others just stared, and a few were sobbing.

As Carla came over with a number of forms, Ellis indicated to Beth that he was going outside for a moment. She raised her hand saying, 'Okay.' Ellis left to go to the terrace. On his way, he had to go through the bar where he saw Carlos watching television. Ellis walked across, nodded to Carlos, and looked at the screen. An Italian newsreader was talking; across the bottom of the screen was a transcript of what he was saying.

Ellis followed the script as it went across the screen. It said:

THE UNITED KINDOM PRIME MINISTER, IS FLYING FROM LONDON TO ROME LATER THIS AFTERNOON FOR A MEETING WITH THE ITALIAN PRIME MINISTER. IT IS EXPECTED THAT HE WILL OUTLINE THE ASSISTANCE THAT THE UK GOVERNMENT WILL BE MAKING AVAILABLE. IT IS ALSO BEING REPORTED THAT HE MAY VISIT ONE OF THE AREAS HIT BY THE AVALANCHE. DETAILS WILL BE RELEASED LATER.

***

Carlos turned to Ellis asking him. 'What help do you think he will offer, Mr Smeeth?'

Ellis said, 'In addition to what has already been sent, I think he will announce a lot of help from the armed forces, particularly the Royal Navy. I suspect there will be additional medical, clothing, and water and food supplies, plus a large amount of money will be made available for the Italian people.'

Carlos smiled as he said, 'You are very optimistic, Mr Smeeth, I will watch with interest this evening.'

Ellis bade Carlos goodbye, walked outside onto the terrace. As he descended the terrace steps, he looked across to Vesuvius. The sky above the Bay of Naples was clear and blue. However, once across the other side of the bay it changed. The sky above the mountain where Vesuvius was perched was no longer clear and blue. It darkened considerably as smoke and steam was still being emitted in a spiral shape leaning towards Naples. There was no force behind the emissions and, although the orange lava was still making its slow journey down the mountainside, it too had lost some of its earlier pace and volume.

Ellis leant on the perimeter fence, spending a few minutes looking and thinking about what had happened, and what he had witnessed in the last three days. His thoughts turned to the people of Naples and the surrounding areas. He wondered how they would recover from such a devastating experience. At that point his thoughts were interrupted by Beppe calling over to him. 'Mr Smeeth, can I have a word with you?'

'Of course,' Ellis replied, 'what can I do for you?'

Beppe's eyes lit up, his excitement was obvious. His voice trembled as he said, 'what I am about to tell you must go no further than you and your friends.' Ellis nodded to acknowledge what Beppe had said.

'I have been informed by the Mayor of Sorrento, that following his meeting with the Italian Prime Minister tomorrow morning, your Prime Minister will see from a helicopter the destruction of Naples. He has also requested a television interview from the location where *Star News* first broke the news of Vesuvius erupting to the rest of the world. That means, Mr Smeeth (Beppe beamed as he said it), he will be coming to my hotel. I am told that his helicopter will land on the football pitch across the road.

'He will then come to the Hotel Geranio and be interviewed by *Star News*. I am also informed that he might want to speak with you. What do you think to that, Mr Smeeth?' He beamed even more.

'That's wonderful news, Beppe. This visit will be shown throughout the world. We must make sure that he visits the casualty unit. When people see those children with bandaged heads and limbs, they will send donations before any appeal for funds is made.'

'I will speak to the Mayor,' responded an excited Beppe.

With that they shook hands, and both went their separate ways. Beppe headed back towards the terrace bar, whilst Ellis walked back towards the hotel entrance.

As he approached the entrance, a white van being driven by Dene came down the slope and pulled up outside. Both doors opened simultaneously, William jumped out first. Ellis said with a smile, 'Sorry, guys, we don't need any bread or milk, our supplier has just made today's delivery.' They both smiled.

'What's in the van?' Ellis enquired.

'More blankets and sheets, a selection of night gowns for the children and boxes of medical supplies,' said William.

'Do you need any help?' Ellis asked.

'Yes, please,' was the response.

With that Ellis slid open the side door. Inside were two sack barrows. He lifted one out and held it whilst Dene loaded some boxes on. 'Right, be back in a minute', said Ellis. As he approached the entrance doors, they opened automatically. He walked through pushing the barrow in front of him. Once inside he turned left into the casualty unit.

It had been about forty five minutes since he had left the unit. He was quite taken aback by the change in that time. The obvious difference was the number of occupied beds and the sound of children crying. He looked around. Half of the beds were now occupied, as were both the assessment cubicles. Around a few of the beds there were some adults. Ellis surmised these were either parents or relatives.

As he looked to the far end of the room, he spotted Sandie and Paula. They waved him across. He pushed the barrow towards them. 'Just in time,' said Sandie. 'We have run out of bedding at the moment.' Paula showed Ellis where to put the bedding. Ellis followed and stacked the boxes against the wall, whilst the blankets and sheets went into the linen cupboard. Once he had finished he set off back to the van. As he made his way across the unit, he saw Beth beckoning him over.

Ellis passed the barrow to Dene and went across to see what Beth wanted. On arrival at her desk, Beth explained to him that she needed some help updating the computer database. She went on to say that a buffet lunch was available in the breakfast room for anybody wanting to eat. Beth suggested to Ellis that if they could input the outstanding information first then he could go for lunch.

Ellis agreed. By 1 o'clock they had finished inputting the outstanding patient's details. As Ellis set off for lunch, Beth asked him to bring her back a plate of salad and a bread roll with some butter.

Whilst waiting for Ellis to return, Beth spent some time tidying her work station, which had become somewhat untidy as a result of the hectic last two hours. Once she had finished that she ran off a paper copy of the latest updated patient register. She had just completed it when Beppe's cousin Perla walked into the unit. She smiled as she spotted Beth, and walked towards her.

On reaching her she kissed Beth on both side of her cheeks, saying as she did what a wonderful job everybody was doing. As she looked around the room, Beth noticed immediately how the expression on Perla's face quickly changed. When she first entered the unit, although she had shown signs of concern, she was also smiling and there was a look of gratification on her face.

Perla said nothing; she stood there as if transfixed. Beth watched as her facial expression changed yet again. Perla turned to Beth, her eyes were beginning to moisten and she slowly shook her head. She tried to speak, but initially nothing but a croak came from her mouth.

After a second or two, she composed herself saying, 'Mrs Smeeth, I would like to walk around the unit if I may. Would you accompany me?'

'Certainly,' Beth replied, her voice also faltering as she recognised the maternal instincts of Perla.

Before they moved away from her desk, Beth picked up the patients' register.

As they approached the first bed, Beth told Perla that this patient was the first of eighteen they had received that Monday morning. With the aid of the register Beth was able to inform Perla of the type of injuries that had been confirmed, and the treatment required. In addition the register identified what further investigations were required to confirm other injuries. As they moved from bed to bed, Perla had words of comfort for many of the occupants. Where in some cases there was a parent or relative sitting by the bedside, she also spoke to them.

They spent about 30 minutes moving slowly around the unit. When they had finished, Perla went across to Shona and Carla. As she embraced them both, she could not hide her emotions any longer. Tears flowed down her cheeks she raised her hands in the air saying between the tears. 'Molte Grazie, Molte Grazie, (thanks very much) you are all so good and kind.'

As they moved towards Beth's work station Ellis came through the door carrying a tray. He walked towards them saying as he did. 'How's that for service?' as he placed the tray on the side desk.

They both smiled. Perla squeezed Beths's hands and thanked her for showing her the unit. 'I must go now and start preparing for tomorrow's visit.' Her voice lowered as she said it, 'Ciao for now.' With that she walked away towards the reception entrance.

'What was that all about?' Ellis enquired.

'I'll tell you later,' said Beth.

Later that afternoon the unit received eight more patients. That left only four beds available, until such time other patients were discharged, or transferred to another medical unit for further treatment.

As the afternoon drew to a close, Shona paid them a visit. 'How have you found the first day?' she enquired. Beth replied that they had both found it stressful but rewarding.

'Things should improve tomorrow, as we have obtained the services of two more nurses. Whilst I'm here, can you take me through the patients' database so I am familiar with it in your absence?'

Beth spent the next 20 minutes explaining each section of the database. Although there was still some patient's information missing, Shona was impressed with what had been achieved on the first day. Once Shona had understood the workings of the database, she suggested that they finished for the day, as no more patients were expected until tomorrow.

That suited both Beth and Ellis. Before departing they walked around the unit to familiarise themselves with the children that had been admitted that day. As they finished their tour, Ellis understood why Perla was so upset earlier that afternoon. Beth merely nodded in response, as there were tears in her eyes once more. Ellis said no more as he sensed Beth was digesting what they had just seen. The first thing Ellis did when he arrived back at the room was to pour himself a large gin and tonic, with a slice of lemon while Beth opted for a cup of tea.

Ellis turned the television on again just as Joanne Birch of *Star News* was going through the detail of the Prime Minister's visit tomorrow. She mentioned that after his meeting with the Italian Prime Minister he would be going elsewhere in the Naples region to view the aftermath of the eruption. There was no mention of Sorrento at this stage. As she came towards the end of this topic, Joanne revealed that the latest fatality figures were now officially approaching 50,000. As he watched the remainder of the bulletin unwind, Ellis wondered just what the final fatality numbers would be?

Chapter Twelve: Eruption plus 4

Both Beth and Ellis woke early that Wednesday morning, in anticipation of what lay ahead for both of them that day. Whilst Beth made them both a cup of tea, Ellis drew the curtains back and went through to the balcony, to see what mood Vesuvius was in that morning.

He looked across the bay. Although early, the sky was already forming to what looked like being another sun drenched day. Ellis noticed that there was a halo around the top of Vesuvius; it was in fact a thin wisp of light cloud forming an almost perfect circle. He wondered if that was an omen for the rest of the day.

Beth shouted to him, 'Any change with Vesuvius this morning?'

'Not really, it looks about the same as yesterday. I can still see lava slowly trickling down the mountainside, and the smoke emission is also similar to yesterday,' he responded.

'That's a good sign then,' said Beth with a definite optimistic tone to her reply.

Whilst he was still pondering the view, Beth came onto the balcony, placed two cups of tea down on the wicker table and sat down opposite Ellis. As they sat there drinking their tea, they discussed the day ahead. Both wondered what the Prime Minister would have to say; and perhaps more importantly what help he would give to the Italian people.

When Beth finished drinking her tea, she announced that she was going to dress for breakfast. Ellis agreed and said he would do the same shortly.

As with every other day since they had arrived at the Hotel Geranio, dress for the day was a pair of shorts, sneakers, and a cotton tea shirt for Ellis. Beth's was the same except for a loose cotton top and a pair of sandals.

On the way to the breakfast room they mulled over whether or not they would change into more formal clothing for the visit of the Prime Minister. Both were undecided, and agreed they would discuss it after breakfast once they were aware of the itinerary for the day.

Once in the breakfast room they selected their juice and starter, and then moved through onto the terrace and seated themselves at a table near to the perimeter fence.

Within a minute Augusto the waiter, was at their table side bidding them good morning and asking, with a familiar smile, if they wanted their regular tea for two with three tea bags. Beth smiled back and confirmed they did.

As they started to eat their breakfast, Beppe appeared on the terrace. He looked around spotted them and immediately hurried across to their table.

'Mr and Mrs Smeeth, may I 'ave a moment of your time?'

Ellis beckoned him to sit at the table. 'Of course you may,' Ellis replied. 'What can we do for you?'

'I thought you should know,' responded Beppe, 'Your Prime Minister will be arriving soon after lunch time.'

'I understand that he may wish to speak with you, Mr Smeeth, after he has made a statement on *Star News*.'

Beppe continued, 'He will be making his statement from the terrace here at the Hotel Geranio, to the people of this area. Also present will be the Mayor of Sorrento and other town officials.'

'Thanks for telling us,' said Ellis.

Beppe stood up and offered his hand to Ellis, saying as he did, 'Ciao I will see you later.' He then walked briskly towards the breakfast room.

As they continued with their breakfast, Ellis and Beth discussed the forthcoming visit. The first topic of conversation from Beth was what she should wear. This caused an initial titter from Ellis but, after some thought; he reluctantly agreed that perhaps they might want to consider an alternative to what they were wearing now.

They continued through breakfast to weigh up the 'pros and cons' of what to wear, and what they might say to the Prime Minister if given the chance. As they finished eating, they also agreed their course of action for the remainder of the morning. This included changing their clothes before lunch in readiness for the visit.

Once breakfast was finished, they bade cheerio to Augusto, and made their way from the terrace back into the breakfast room. As they walked through they saw William and Sandie coming towards them. They stopped for a quick chat, and briefly told them what Beppe had said, adding they would see them later to fill in the details.

As they parted company, they decided to go straight to the casualty unit to ask Shona what her plans were for the day.

On entering the unit they could see Shona was actively involved in a situation at the far end of the room. Not wishing to interrupt proceedings, they moved across the room to Shona's desk, sat down and waited patiently for her to finish her task.

They could see Shona was caring for a young girl, aged about five years old. Shona and another nurse were attempting to change a large surgical dressing on the girl's back. Clearly the action of removing the dressing was causing distress to the little girl. From where they were sitting Ellis and Beth, could see that the old dressing was sticking to the skin as a result of previous bleeding. To reduce the adhesion of the old dressing Shona was softening it with cotton wool and warm water. Although progress appeared to be slow, this method was generally successful, until occasionally a piece of the dressing stuck to her skin. When this happened the girl whimpered and cried louder. Gradually they succeeded in removing the dressing. After Shona had finished cleaning up the wound, she came across to where Ellis and Beth were sitting leaving the nurse to apply a new dressing.

Beth asked Shona if she was aware of the details of the Prime Minister's visit later that day. 'Yes I am,' she replied. 'I am expecting a visit early this afternoon, so we need to discuss our priorities for today. I will hold a meeting with everybody at 10 o'clock this morning. Would you please spread the word?'

As they left the unit, Ellis left a message at reception asking Gino to inform people of that meeting. He also found Gavin, the holiday rep., and asked him to pass on the information. Gavin agreed to do so and said he would do by printing some notices and displaying them in prominent positions.

Later, when Ellis and Beth returned to the unit, they found there were only a few people present. Beth went to the computer to get an update on the patient's situation. She noted that there were still only eighteen admissions. However, as she scrolled through the database, she could see where some patients' details had been updated.

It took Beth nearly an hour to read all eighteen records. By now the number of people in the unit had increased to about 30. She shut down the database and made her way over to Ellis. As she did so, William and Sandie came through the door, followed closely by Dene and Paula, together with Phillip and Bernice.

At precisely 10 o'clock Shona and three nurses came out from the cubicle in the far corner. All had folders in their hand; Ellis presumed that Shona had been debriefing them before this meeting. They made their way to the centre of the room.

Without any hesitation, Shona spoke. 'Good morning everybody, thank you for your attendance and for being so prompt. We are going to be very busy today, as we are expecting more patients. We are also expecting a visit from the UK Prime Minister later this afternoon. Most of you have probably already heard his statement following his meeting with the Italian Prime Minister.

'I can tell you that he will reveal more about the aid the Government intends to offer, when he makes a statement on *Star News* this afternoon.'

Shona continued, 'With the help of my nurses, we have developed a revised rota for the next 48 hours. For all of you who are already part of our care team, you will see your names and responsibilities listed there. Anybody who is reporting here to help for the first time, please see me after this meeting.'

Ellis and Beth listened as Shona discussed some activities in more detail. Ten minutes later all relevant information had been covered. Shona concluded by asking everyone to check the new rota and commence their duties after this meeting.

By now there was a steady droning of noise within the unit, as people milled around looking at the new rota and all seeming to talk at the same time. Some of the children were becoming restless and some of them had begun to sob and cry adding to the general noise.

Once Ellis and Beth had checked the rota, they moved towards Beth's workstation where Beth quickly tidied up her desk. Ellis asked her to run off a copy of the database for him.

As she gave him the copy, Beth asked Ellis what he wanted it for. 'I'm going to tell Shona that it might be worthwhile for me to pay a visit to the Sorrento hospital, and check out who has been admitted from the Naples area. It might be that there are some parents, relatives or other family members undergoing treatment there. I know it's a long shot but in any case I can establish contacts for a day to day exchange of new patient intake information.'

Beth warmed to that proposal straight away. 'That's a good idea. Maybe Sorrento hospital could be part of a missing person's network that could operate from Naples to the Campania region.'

Feeling enthusiastic about this idea Ellis went looking for Shona. He soon found her, and they spent the next ten minutes discussing his plans including the idea that all patients admitted to the unit should have their photograph taken as this could help reunite family members.

Shona told Ellis to instigate obtaining a camera and then to make an initial visit to the hospital for talks on this suggestion. Meanwhile Shona added that she would need to ensure that taking photographs would be an acceptable thing to do. She would need to obtain clearance from the authorities before they proceeded. They agreed to talk later that day to discuss what progress they had both made.

Ellis made his way over to Beth and told her of his latest idea. He debriefed Beth on what Shona had said. He was now going to seek advice about obtaining the right camera. He would visit the Sorrento hospital as soon as it was convenient to do so. Beth suggested that he talk to Beppe, to see if he had a contact that would assist in finding a photographer. Also ask him she added, if he knows who you should contact at the hospital, Ellis nodded in agreement.

'Right, I'm going to follow up your suggestion,' Ellis remarked to Beth, 'See you later.'

As Ellis entered the reception area he spotted Beppe going into his office. He quickly lengthened his stride and followed him. 'Ah, Mr Smeeth, what can I do for you?' Beppe enquired.

Ellis proceeded to tell Beppe about the need for a camera and contacting the Sorrento hospital. Beppe liked the idea and said he would find him a photographer. He beckoned Ellis to follow him as he walked out of his office and headed for the reception desk where Cirino was on duty. With a wave of his hands Beppe explained in Italian to Cirino what Ellis had just told him.

Once he had finished, he said, 'Cirino will organise somebody at the hospital to see you, Mr Smeeth. We also think you will need an interpreter, Cirino will organise that for you as well.'

Now this plan was in operation, Ellis decided to return to Beth, as he moved towards the casualty unit door, he heard the sound of wailing sirens. Within seconds he could see a flashing blue light through the hotel entrance doors, as an ambulance pulled up. Ellis immediately went into the unit to find Beth. As he entered, he saw her at her desk. She didn't see him approach as she was engrossed with something on the computer screen.

'How did you get on?' asked Beth.

'Okay,' replied Ellis. 'Beppe is going to talk to a photographer, and Cirino will be making contact with the hospital. He will also try and find an interpreter to assist me at the hospital.

'What I really came to tell you,' said Ellis, 'is that it looks as though you have some more patients. If Shona agrees, perhaps we should have an early lunch?'

'Good idea, I'll check with her now,' replied Beth.

Shona had no objections. Before they went for lunch, they went to their room for a wash and tidy up. It was just approaching noon as they walked onto the terrace; they were met by the smiling face of Carlos.

He beckoned them to a middle table by the perimeter fence, as he gave them both a menu. Ellis ordered a beer and a glass of orange for Beth. They both ordered a light meal. Ellis decided upon a ham and tomato omelette, whilst Beth stuck to her trusty tomato salad. As they were eating their meal, Ellis suggested that once they had finished they would have time to change their clothes, before the Prime Minister arrived.

Just as they were finishing their meal, Beppe came onto the terrace. He walked very briskly towards the centre, stopped and announced that the Prime Minister was arriving early. 'His helicopter will be here in five minutes.'

Ellis looked at Beth and said, 'We need to get our skates on then.'

Both rose from the table together just as a large whirring noise could be heard in the distance. Ellis looked across the bay; there in the sky coming from the direction of Naples were two helicopters. Within seconds the noise grew louder, and even more deafening as the first helicopter slowed as it flew directly over the Hotel Geranio.

Ellis shouted across to Beth, 'They are going to land on the football pitch across the road.'

The first helicopter disappeared out of sight behind the trees. The second one peeled away to the right. As it approached the Marine Grande, it arced round to the left and headed back towards the football pitch. They lost sight of it as it slowly descended behind the trees presumably to land.

As they moved back towards the casualty unit, they could see the *Star News* technicians and camera crew setting up their equipment at the corner entrance to the swimming pool. Inside the unit they were met by what might be described as organised chaos. There appeared to be four more admissions on the far side of the room. Two of them were crying. Carla, Shona's assistant, was trying to calm both of them. She appeared to be on her own so Beth went over and began soothing the child by stroking her forehead with one hand and holding the little girl's hand in the other.

It was then that Shona came into view; she had two other nurses with her. They all looked harassed as they looked around at the noise that was being generated by those children that were upset.

Within minutes the three of them had moved to the areas where other children were now becoming restless. More helpers then arrived so Shona met them and Ellis could see her giving them instructions. Shona's presence was restoring order.

The young girl that Beth had been pacifying now seemed to be settled. Beth spoke to Carla and went across to her workstation to check what needed to be inputted into the computer.

Shona now seemed to have everything under control. The additional helpers were all around the room ensuring that the unit was now looking efficient and tidy.

Word went quickly around that the Prime Minister was going to make a short statement on *Star News* in five minutes.

Once she heard that, Shona scurried around the unit with Carla checking everything was in order. When she spotted something she didn't like, she asked Carla to inform the nearest helper of the problem. Soon everything was 'ship-shape' and people began to inch towards the doors in an attempt to hear what the Prime Minister was going to say.

It was precisely 2 o'clock when he walked through the reception area and made his way outside towards the perimeter fence on the corner of the swimming pool. He was flanked by many people. To his surprise, Ellis noticed the Foreign Secretary was alongside him, together with bodyguards and some Whitehall officials. On his other side were notably Italian officials. One in particular had a chain of office around his neck; Ellis surmised that he was probably the Mayor of Sorrento.

Within a short time the *Star News* crew had positioned everybody they needed in shot with their backs to the perimeter fence, with Vesuvius sitting in the background behind them. To add to the drama there was still a trail of smoke winding its way into the atmosphere from the crater of Vesuvius.

Suddenly, everything went quiet, as a member of the television crew lifted his hand into the air. As he dropped it, the Prime Minister started to speak.

'Good afternoon ladies and gentlemen. I am going to make just a brief comment at this moment. After I have looked around the casualty unit and spoken to some of those involved, I will make a full statement regarding the aid that the United Kingdom Government is proposing to make to the Italian people.' (At this point an interpreter translates into Italian.).

'As I stand here I have on one side my Foreign Secretary, who joined me late last night after his ministerial meeting with EU members in Paris yesterday.' (Pause for translation.) 'On my left I have the Mayor of Sorrento.

'Last evening I met him for the first time, as he joined me and the Italian Prime Minister for dinner.' (Translation). 'I have to confess to you all, that listening to the Mayor of Sorrento's summary of the tragic events as they occurred over the past few days, hurt me greatly and left me initially with a feeling of despair and helplessness.' (Translation)

'Even as I watched the tragic events unfold, by courtesy of *Star News* back in London, it did not prepare me for what I saw on my brief tour around Naples yesterday.' (Translation).

'I know I speak for all the people of the United Kingdom, when I tell you how profoundly sorry we are for what has happened to this part of Italy. When I talk to you all again later I will, as I stated earlier, give you further details of our aid package.

'Thank you all very much.' (Translation).

***

Ellis began to retreat back into the casualty unit. As he did so he caught the eye of Shona. He waved to her and mouthed, 'They are on their way.' Shona gave him the thumbs up and moved further into the unit encouraging people to continue with their work.

Ellis had rejoined Beth as the group headed by the Prime Minister and the Mayor of Sorrento entered the unit. As they did so, Shona went over to greet them. As she approached, Beppe introduced her to the group. Once the formalities were over, Shona proceeded to guide them around the unit. When the visiting group reached Ellis and Beth, the Prime Minister spoke to Ellis.

'Well Ellis, how are you?' he said, offering his hand at the same time. 'I must congratulate you on your return performance for *Star News*, when you gave your eye witness account on the eruption of Vesuvius.'

As he was about to reply, one of the *Star News* team with a portable television camera mounted on his shoulder, and another one carrying a microphone boom came towards him. Not to be put off, Ellis replied, 'Thank you for your kind remarks. I am very well considering all that has happened. May I introduce you to my wife, Beth?' the Prime Minister leaned forward to shake her hand.

For a while they discussed the recent events surrounding the eruption of Vesuvius. The Foreign Secretary wanted to know whether they had considered packing their bags and going home and the politicians nodded with approval when Beth explained that they had wanted to help.

As the group made to move off, the Mayor also offered his hand to them both as he passed by them.

Once they had moved further along the room, Ellis and Beth relaxed.

'That went okay,' Beth remarked.

'Yes it did. Let's go outside, grab a drink and get a good position so that we can hear the Prime Minister's aid package,' replied Beth.

It was one hour since the arrival of the Prime Minister. As they walked into the swimming pool area, they could see Marco sitting in his cabin looking across the pool.

Ellis walked around the pool to him, and ordered two cappuccinos. They walked back around the pool to the spot where they used to sit before the eruption. It was four days since they had last sat there and they couldn't believe how much had happened during this time. More people began to arrive so they knew the Prime Minister's arrival was imminent so they moved to a more advantageous position. As they walked outside the pool area towards the perimeter fence, Ellis noticed that the corner table on the edge of the terrace dining area was empty. He nudged Beth and pointed as they walked quickly to the table and sat down.

They were just in time. Five minutes later the Prime Minister and his entourage arrived. The news crew positioned them as before, once ready the signal so familiar to Ellis a few days ago was given. 'Counting down, 10 seconds to broadcast, stand by 3, 2, 1, you're on.'

The Prime Minister began: 'I spent most of yesterday and last evening with the Prime Minister of Italy. Together we visited the devastation that the City of Naples and the surrounding area have suffered as a result of the eruption from Vesuvius.' (Translation given.)

'Although I had seen news coverage via *Star News* I was still not prepared for what I have seen in the last 24 hours.' (Translation)

'Yesterday I came prepared and ready to announce a broad package of aid from the people of the United Kingdom, for the help and relief of those people directly affected by the eruption.' (Translation)

'Last evening I gave the Italian Prime Minister a general indication of what that aid would be. I promised him I would announce the extent of that package in more detail this afternoon.' (Translation)

'As a direct result of the devastation I witnessed yesterday, I spoke at length with my aid minister last night. I instructed him to increase the original aid package and report back to me by noon today with details of the amendments. This I am pleased to say he and his team have done.' (Translation)

'I would now like to read out to the details of the aid package:'

'We will be donating along with the rest of other European countries, one hundred and fifty million Euros (E150, 000,000). This amount will be reviewed on a regular basis.

'As from 12:00 o'clock noon local time today, the RAF will be transporting by two Hercules aircraft transport carriers, emergency medical supplies, basic food, bottled water, canvas tents, sleeping bags, blankets, clothing and footwear.' (Translation)

'In addition to the above, the UK Ministry of Defence has within the last 24 hours been able to make the following Royal Navy ships available to assist the Italian Government.' (Translation)

'First is the aircraft carrier *HMS Illustrious*. She will be accompanied by the amphibious assault warship *HMS Bulwark*.' (Translation)

'Both vessels will have on board a number of Sea King helicopters, *HMS Bulwark* will in addition have on board a CH-47 heavy lift Chinook helicopter.' (Translation)

'Both ships will have only the minimum operating crew on board. This will make more personnel available to assist the authorities with their rescue work.' (Translation)

'*HMS Invincible* is to be set up as a hospital ship, it will have on board many doctors and surgeons, all accompanied by a full nursing staff.

'*HMS Bulwark* will have a full detachment of Royal Engineers on board. These will come with all the necessary equipment to carry out engineering work, and assist in the recovery of victims buried within Naples and the surrounding area.

'Also on board *HMS Bulwark* and reporting to the Royal Engineers, are a number of volunteer fire-fighters from many of the United Kingdom fire brigades. They will come fully equipped, and will be beneficial seeking people buried beneath the rubble, with their infra-red body heat detectors.' (Translation)

'Mr Mayor, that is all I have to say at this moment, except to confirm that both ships of the Royal Navy will be arriving in the Bay of Naples tomorrow morning.' (Translation)

'Before I finish I would like to take a few moments to say how impressed I am with what is being done here at the Hotel Geranio.   I think that Beppe Marcello   and Perla together with their staff are making a tremendous contribution to the welfare of those people who are victims of the eruption.' (Translation)

'In addition to those I have just mentioned, I must add that I admire those people who were here on holiday. They have now ceased to be on holiday but instead have been assisting in whatever ways they can.   In particular I must say how proud I am to see that at the forefront in the running of the casualty unit, are people of all persuasions from all over the United Kingdom and Ireland working all hours to help those children who need treatment, love and affection?' (Translation)

'Thank you all very much.' (Translation)

***

As he turned to shake the Mayor of Sorrento's hand, the audience that were assembled there, applauded loudly. Ellis could see many of the employees of the hotel had tears in their eyes, especially Carlos who was also clapping vigorously.

When the clapping had ceased, the Mayor of Sorrento stepped forward. As he started to speak, one could sense the emotion in his voice. Initially there was a slight tremble to his voice however this soon passed as he regained his composure and began his response to the Prime Minister.

His reply lasted about five minutes, and as expected was spoken in Italian. Although it was translated into English, people sensed what he was saying. It was as expected full of emotion. As he neared the end of his speech, he began singing the praises of all the helpers, particularly the British. He turned to the Prime Minister with his arms outstretched as he thanked him, and the United Kingdom Government for the aid package they were going to deliver. With tears running freely down his cheeks, he threw both his arms around him, saying as he did 'Molte Grazie' (thank you very much).

Ellis and Beth watched from their seats as the watching crowd clapped loudly, particularly, the hotel staff and the Italian holiday makers. The scenes were truly emotional. As the Prime Minister and the party of dignitaries moved away, Ellis and Beth made their way back towards the unit.

Once inside the unit Beth made her way across to Carla to see if any information was now available on the new casualties. Meanwhile Shona introduced Ellis to Vincenzo, a local photographer. As they shook hands, Shona explained that Vincenzo had been asked by Beppe to assist and advise us in the photographing of the patients.

'Perhaps Ellis,' Shona remarked, 'you and Vincenzo could go somewhere and discuss what we are trying to do. Oh and by the way, it will be okay to photograph the children providing we keep a tight control of the photographs and all the connecting personal information.'

'Will do,' replied Ellis. 'Come with me Vincenzo; let's find a quiet spot on the terrace.'

Whilst Ellis had been engaged with Shona, Beth had collected the information on the latest casualties. She had just inputted the last casualty name into the computer, when there was a sudden movement beneath her feet. A feeling of panic swept over her as she realised it was another tremor. As she was about to hold onto the desk, it stopped as suddenly as it had started.

Initially the unit was completely silent, then it was as if a conductor of an orchestra had waved his baton as children started to cry in unison. Shona and the other three nurses all rushed across the unit to where most of the crying was coming from. Beth moved to a bed close by, where a small boy was sitting up and sobbing. As she sat down on the bed trying to pacify him, Sandie, Paula and Bernice came out of the assessment cubicles. They went to the beds in the middle of the unit, each of them moving towards a crying child to comfort. Soon the panic was over leaving only one or two children either sobbing or just having a snuffle. The tremors seemed to have subsided, as the unit returned to normal.

Meanwhile, outside on the terrace, Ellis and Vincenzo were seated at the far end drinking a cappuccino. Ellis explained why the photographs were needed and Vincenzo agreed to show him how to use his digital camera.

Back in the unit all was now relatively quiet. Beth had finished inputting the latest information and she was showing Sandie and the rest of the girls what information was on the computer.

When Ellis and Vincenzo went back into the unit, Ellis attracted Shona's attention and explained that Vincenzo wanted to show them how to use the camera.

Shona was pleased with the quick response. She directed them to the first bed in the unit where a young boy was sitting up playing with a small plastic car. After a couple of minutes' tuition, Vincenzo handed the camera to Ellis and he took the boy's picture. The resulting image was very clear and Ellis felt confident that he would be able to take good photographs of the children.

'Okay,' Vincenzo said, 'you now take the camera, take your pictures, and when you need to I will print off the pictures for you to put in an album.'

'That's exactly what we want,' replied Ellis. 'I will start first thing tomorrow morning and let you have the memory card by tomorrow evening.'

Vincenzo shook both their hands, bade them goodbye and left them to discuss their next move.

Just as they had finished talking, Beth arrived. She explained to Shona that the database was now up to date. Ellis showed her the first picture image they had taken, and informed her of what their next moves would be.

Once the discussions were finished, they decided to finish for the day.

'Right,' replied Ellis, 'we'll see you tomorrow bright and early; I'd like to photograph all the children as soon as possible. If Vincenzo can print them tomorrow evening I can go to the

Sorrento hospital on Friday, to commence identification of the children.'

They were glad to relax with their friends later that evening as it had been a very busy day. Both Ellis and Beth enjoyed their meal, but felt as usual that they had eaten too much. Once they had finished they made their way to the terrace bar, where they ordered their usual two cappuccinos and one brandy. As Carlos served them, he told them how pleased he was with the Prime Minister's speech earlier that day.

He asked how soon the promised help would arrive. Ellis told him that he expected the two Royal Navy ships to arrive sometime tomorrow, with most of the personnel and necessary equipment on board.

On hearing this, Carlos broke into a smile. As he did so, he moved towards another couple who had just entered the terrace. Beth looked at Ellis saying, 'I hope you are right, otherwise Carlos will be upset tomorrow.'

It wasn't very long before their friends joined them. They pulled a table and more chairs across so they could all sit down together. They stayed on the terrace all evening discussing what they had all been doing that day. William and Dene explained how they had been up and down twice to the hospital collecting medical supplies and materials. En route they had stopped off at a waste disposal unit to discard used and soiled medical dressings etc. Sandie, Paula and Bernice had spent all of their time that day in the unit, doing general duties. Phillip had spent his time entertaining the children. Although there was a language barrier, he had a unique way of communicating with those children who were not suffering from being traumatised.

The evening passed quickly. Although the mood of the 'gang' remained downbeat, there were still fleeting moments when some humour was evident. Without it stress levels that were already high would have probably increased even more.

With another busy day promised tomorrow and most guests having already left the terrace the 'gang' decided it was time to retire. They bid good night to Carlos and the rest of the bar staff, before they all went their separate ways.

As they made their way back to the room, Beth said that she would like to telephone the girls. On arrival at the room she texted to check they were available. Within two minutes both of them confirmed they were at home and awake.

Beth picked up the telephone and dialled Jamie first. Whilst she did that, Ellis made his way to the mini bar to select a night cap. As he walked across the room towards the settee, he switched on the television and selected the *Star News* channel. His eyes were drawn to the 'Breaking News' headline that was scrolling across the bottom of the screen. He adjusted the sound downwards so as not to disturb Beth's telephone conversation. As he did, he read the script.

STAR SOURCES: HAVE INDICATED THAT THE NUMBER OF FATALITIES WITHIN THE NAPLES AREA HAS NOW RISEN TO OVER 150,000. THE SAME SOURCE HAS ALSO LEARNED THAT FOR THE FIRST TIME THE ITALIAN GOVERNMENT WERE ADMITTING THAT THE TOTAL NUMBER OF FATALITIES WOULD PROBABLY BE HUNDREDS OF THOUSANDS.

***

Ellis turned to Beth just as she said to Jamie, 'Dad sends his love, bye for now.'

As she acknowledged Ellis, she said 'I'll give Louise a ring now.'

'Before you do', Ellis said in a quiet voice, 'look at what they are now saying about fatalities, pointing towards the television.'

There was silence as Beth read the 'Breaking News' comment still scrolling across the bottom of the screen. She read it two or three times before turning to Ellis shaking her head as she did.

As Beth looked at Ellis, he could see the tears in her eyes. She wiped them away and said, 'I'll ring Louise now.'

She walked across the room picked up the telephone and dialled her number.

Ellis carried on watching the television in silence.

Chapter Thirteen - Eruption plus 5

Thursday July 13 was to be an eventful day for people living in the Bay of Naples region, particularly those areas suffering from the after effects of the eruption.

Ellis and Beth had risen early on that bright, sunny morning and were already sitting on the terrace having their breakfast. Across the bay Vesuvius was also awake. Smoke was still being emitted from the crater, albeit only a moderate wisp. Lava was still making its way down the mountainside, although you had to look hard and long to notice its movement.

As they sat there eating breakfast, Ellis and Beth were contemplating the day ahead. In their minds as in most other people's, was the promise by the Prime Minister that the two Royal Navy aid ships, namely *HMS Illustrious* and *HMS Bulwark* would arrive today.

'I wonder what time the ships will arrive?' enquired Beth.

'Don't know,' Ellis replied. 'However my instinct is that they will arrive around lunchtime.'

As soon as breakfast was finished, they visited their room to brush their teeth, and to pick up the camera. Once that was done they made their way upstairs to the casualty unit.

On arrival Carla was just entering the unit she spotted them and walked across.

'Ellis,' she said, 'I am going to help you photograph the children this morning, is that okay?'

'Yes that's fine,' said Ellis. 'I'll collect an up to date register print off and then we can get started.'

Once he had booted up the computer he printed off a copy of the register. He was ready to photograph the children. Carla was tidying up the hair and clothing of one of the children so he was the first to be photographed. Ellis took the camera from around his shoulders and began checking the position from which he would take the photo. As soon as he was satisfied, he pressed the shutter which released the flash at the same time. The boy blinked at first and looked a little startled, however, within seconds this passed as his face broke into a smile. Carla smiled back at him, saying something in Italian to him at the same time.

By mid morning they had photographed at least 50 per cent of the children. At that point Shona required Carla to assist her for half an hour, so Ellis took time out to see if Beth was ready for a break. After this, Carla helped Ellis again. They had just finished taking the last photograph when they heard a ship's siren tooting loudly, followed by an Italian voice exclaiming loudly, 'The Breetish Sheeps 'ave arrived.'

With that comment a number of people began moving towards the terrace. By now Beth had arrived alongside Ellis saying, 'Let's go and see.'

They walked together through the doors onto the terrace where many people had already gathered all looking south towards the Isle of Capri. At first nothing could be seen then Ellis spotted the bow of a ship coming around the peninsular from the direction of the small town Massa Lubrense. It was the *HMS Illustrious*.

As it progressed towards them, they could see that the ship's complement was all standing to attention, facing them along the outside of the flight deck. In the middle of the deck helicopters were clearly visible, together with masses of wooden crates filling every available space. The ship's siren tooted three times. In unison all the ratings raised their right arms and saluted the watching crowd from the shore and the hotel terraces.

Ellis looked at Beth whose eyes were moist and getting moister by the second. He glanced down the terrace just as Carlos came through the door carrying a huge Italian flag. He made his way to the perimeter fence and began waving the flag backwards and forwards.

A number of the Italian staff, who had now made their way alongside Carlos, started to clap and cheer. This was the signal for everybody else to join in; within minutes the whole of that small area of the coastline became noisy, as maroons were fired into the air from Marina Grande. This was immediately picked up from the Sant' Agnello side who responded with three maroons, one after the other.

Ellis nudged Beth and pointed her in the direction of Carlos who was still waving the flag. He appeared to be shouting, 'Thank you, thank you.' Ellis noticed that Carlos was showing his emotions as tears were cascading down both of his cheeks. Ellis turned away as he felt himself welling up.

The drama continued as another ship's siren sounded and into view appeared *HMS Bulwark*. What a sight this was. It was similar in size to *HMS Illustrious*. It too had a large flight deck designed specifically for the operation of large helicopters. Ellis immediately recognised a Chinook helicopter that was parked at the front of the deck. Further back were two smaller ones. He thought to himself, 'They are probably Sea Kings.'

In similar fashion to *HMS Illustrious*, the complement of Royal Engineers were all lined up in single file along the near side area of the flight deck. Once again, as the siren was sounded three times, all arms were raised as they saluted the watching crowds.

Ellis glanced over to Carlos who had stopped waving his flag and instead was looking through his binoculars and giving a running commentary to the people around him.

By now *HMS Illustrious* was past the hotel and seemed to be turning out to sea. As Ellis watched it manoeuvre for a few minutes, it was evident it was now coming back on itself. Turning to Beth, Ellis remarked, 'I think they are going to drop anchor and park up in line with the "Geranio".'

He was right. A few minutes later they heard and could see the anchor and its chain moving into the sea. 'How far out do you think that is?' asked Beth.

'About 500 metres I guess,' replied Ellis.

HMS Bulwark followed some distance behind and after passing *HMS Illustrious* it dropped its anchor, 200 metres further on towards the Isle of Capri.

'Well, the Prime Minister kept his word,' said Ellis.

'Yes he did indeed,' agreed Beth. 'The arrival of the two ships should give the people of Naples a big boost.'

They stayed on the terrace for a further 10 minutes, before deciding to return to the unit. On the way they saw Vincenzo coming out of Bruno's office. 'I've got something for you,' Ellis said smiling at Vincenzo. He handed him the card from the camera.

Vincenzo looked surprised, 'You've taken all the photographs already?' Ellis nodded.

'Right I'll take these and get them printed off for you by tomorrow morning,' Vincenzo promised. He took the card from Ellis and left through the main entrance door.

Ellis and Beth continued through the reception area into the casualty unit.

Once there they went their separate ways, agreeing to break off for lunch at 12.30.

As Ellis was about to go and find Shona, he heard a voice calling his name. It was Colin from the *Star News* production team.

'What are you doing here?' Ellis asked?'

'Can we have a word?' Colin replied. Ellis nodded and beckoned Colin to follow him.

They went out onto the far end of the terrace and found a suitable quiet position. As they sat down, Ellis asked, 'What can I do for you?'

Colin went on to explain that *Star News* had been given permission to take a small team into the Naples area to report the devastation and personal tragedies caused by the eruption. The production team back in the London studio wanted Ellis to be part of that team.

Ellis paused for a while before replying, 'I would, however need to talk to Beth first, and then see if it is okay with Shona.'

'That's fine,' replied Colin. 'At the moment we are hoping to go over this weekend. I'll get back to you.' With that they shook hands and made his way to the hotel car park.

Ellis also left the terrace and went in search of Beth. She was at her workstation talking to Carla. 'I expect you're ready for lunch,' she said as Ellis approached her.

'How did you guess? Let's go to the tennis club today.'

Ellis wandered out of the unit into the reception area to wait for Beth. As he did so, Beppe came through the main entrance and waved. Ellis went across to him, 'Ah just the man,' Ellis said, 'I'm hoping to get the photographs from Vincenzo tonight. If I do I will need an interpreter to accompany me to the hospital tomorrow. Can you get me one?'

'Leave that with me, Mr Smeeth,' replied Beppe. 'I will make enquiries.' He went into his office and began to make a telephone call.

As soon as Beth joined him, they set off for the tennis club. As they walked out onto the road outside the hotel, Dene and William pulled up in the van. Dene was driving and stopped alongside them opening his door as he did. They spent a few minutes listening to Dene and William's antics with the van that morning, before bringing them up to date with their situation. Once the small talk was completed they made their farewells and confirmed they were lunching at the tennis club.

Maura and her family were as usual pleased to see them. This meant plenty of hugs and kisses in the way only the Italians can do. Once that was over Maura appeared with a glass of fresh orange juice and a large bottle of Peroni beer.

As they studied the menu, Ellis told Beth of Colin's offer from *Star News*.

'What do you think?' he asked. 'Go for it,' Beth said.

At that point Maura arrived to take their order.

Over lunch they discussed further the *Star News* visit to the Naples area.

Once lunch was finished, they said goodbye to Maura and her family and headed back to the casualty unit. On approaching the hotel they watched as two ambulances crossed outside the hotel entrance. As one came out the other went down the slope pulling up outside the hotel entrance.

Beth remarked, 'Looks like more patients. I'd better get myself into the unit.'

Beth made her way swiftly to the casualty unit where Carla updated her on the latest situation. Four of the children were now ready to be discharged as their injuries had healed so they were being taken to a holding area within the Naples region whilst family or relatives were traced. Just arriving were another four children with trauma problems and various types of minor to medium injuries.

Carla gave Beth the information on the four discharged children. They agreed that any children leaving the unit without confirmation of reunion with family or relatives would stay on the database and be annotated accordingly. This they hoped would ensure that a cross check with family or relatives being treated in the Sorrento Hospital would not be overlooked. Beth assured Carla that she would debrief Ellis on this latest database modification. As she continued the discussion with Carla, Beth inputted the information onto the database.

Meanwhile Ellis had wandered into the reception area to see if Beppe was in the hotel. He could not have timed it better as Beppe was just pulling up on his scooter just outside the entrance doors. He saw Ellis and beckoned him over. 'Mr Smeeth, come into my office please. I tell you about an interpreter.'

Ellis followed him into the office to hear the good news that Beppe had found an interpreter. 'She is a very nice lady, Mr Smeeth. Her name is Cristina. She will come to the hotel tomorrow morning, and drive you to the hospital.' Ellis nodded and thanked Beppe with an exaggerated 'Grazie' and then returned to the casualty unit to receive an up-to-date summary prior to his hospital visit.

'Good', said Ellis glancing at the paperwork. 'Now, if you're finished, let's go to our room.'

As they entered the reception area, they spotted Vincenzo talking to Gino at the desk. Before they could say anything, Gino waved his hand towards them. They went over and Vincenzo offered Ellis a large blue folder and said. 'I have the photographs for you.'

Ellis and Beth sat down and opened up the folder. As they turned the pages over, both their faces showed an expression of delight. Their smiles grew even larger when they noticed that against each photograph, there was a blank identity label with headings for a person's name, age, sex, address etc. Each label had the appropriate identity number that had been allocated to every patient on the database. Ellis turned to Vincenzo smiling as he did. He shook him by the hand and at the same time told him what an excellent job he had made of the photographs.

Vincenzo also broke into a beaming smile, obviously pleased at the accolade he had just received. 'I ave to go now,' he said still smiling. 'I will see you tomorrow or the day after, Ciao for now.' With that he rose from the chair and left.

As he disappeared through the hotel doors, Ellis and Beth picked up their belongings including the photograph folder, and made their way to their room.

Ellis sat on the bed and trawled through the photographs again, remarking as he did so about the quality and workmanship that Vincenzo had put into the production of the identification folder.

Once he had finished looking through the photographs he lay back on the bed contemplating his task at the Sorrento Hospital tomorrow. Within minutes he was fast asleep, his heavy breathing soon noticed by Beth.

Just as she was wondering what to do, Beth's phone bleeped twice. She picked it up and read the message. It read. 'Good News RING ME. LOUISE.'

Without hesitating, Beth dialled Louise's number. Before she could say anything Louise said. 'I got my exam results today; they are brilliant I'm so chuffed.' Beth joined Louise in sharing her joy, saying as she did. 'Dad's asleep but I'll tell him as soon as he wakes up.' They spent a few more minutes chatting excitedly to one another before saying their goodbyes. Elizabeth replaced the phone, she then went over to Ellis and gently shook him saying at the same time, 'Wake up, good news from Louise.' Ellis stirred; 'Louise has just told me that her exam results are excellent.' 'That's great news,' replied Ellis.

Chapter Fourteen - Eruption plus 6

When Ellis woke on Friday morning he got straight out of bed, not needing prompting as his mind was already focussing on his visit to the Sorrento Hospital. Beth soon followed him and within an hour they were making their way upstairs for breakfast. Once there they collected their fruit juice and cereals, and walked through to the terrace where they had the choice of many tables.

During breakfast they discussed the day ahead. Beth planned to spend most of it in the casualty unit. Ellis' intentions once he had met his interpreter Cristina were to go straight to the hospital and make a start on trying to identify at least some of the children currently in the casualty unit.

As they made their way through the breakfast room, they met William and Sandie coming towards them. They stopped for a few minutes to discuss each other's events for the day, before moving on to their initial destinations.

On reaching the reception area Ellis told Beth to carry on down to the room as he was going to inform Gino about the visit of Cristina. As he approached the reception desk, Gino looked up and greeted Ellis with, 'Good Morning, Mr Smeeth, what can I do for you?'

Ellis explained about his visitor and asked Gino if he would call room 505 when she arrived. With that Ellis thanked him and set off to his room, preparing himself for the hospital visit by collecting everything he needed and placing it on the sofa. Whilst he was doing this Beth was getting herself ready for her day at the casualty unit.

As they went about their different tasks, Beth asked how long Ellis thought he would be at the hospital. 'I'm not really sure,' responded Ellis. 'It will depend on how many victims of the eruption they are treating.'

'I'm off to the casualty unit now,' said Beth, 'I'll see you later.'

Shortly after 9.30 the telephone suddenly burst into life. Ellis immediately moved across the room and answered it. A voice spoke saying, 'Mr Smeeth, Cristina has just arrived in reception.'

It was easy to recognise Cristina as she was the only woman waiting at reception. With an outstretched hand Ellis walked towards her. 'You must be Cristina,' he said.

She smiled and shook his hand, 'And you must be Ellis. I have heard so much about you.'

'I hope it was all good,' said Ellis with a smile. He added, before we head off to the hospital, I suggest we have a cappuccino and discuss the purpose of the visit.'

Cristina agreed and they made their way to the terrace. As they walked Ellis studied Cristina and surmised that she was about 35 years of age and five feet six inches in height. Her long dark hair and olive skin gave her the classic Italian look.

On reaching the terrace they were soon spotted by Carlos who ushered them to a table by the perimeter fence. Ellis noticed Carlos giving Cristina an admiring look. Ellis smiled as he introduced them to each other. Carlos turned on his Latin charm by kissing Cristina's hand, speaking quietly in Italian to her. Cristina smiled back politely. Whatever Carlos had said to her, Cristina had dealt with it in her own way.

Within a few minutes Ellis and Cristina were sipping their cappuccinos and planning the day ahead.

Ellis showed Cristina the folder of photographs and explained what they were hoping to achieve that day. After thirty minutes of discussion and the time approaching 10 o'clock, they decided it was time to go to the hospital. They bid Carlos farewell and walked out through the reception area towards the car park where Cristina stopped by a black and white Smart car. She turned to Ellis smiling as she said, 'This is your taxi for today, sir.' Ellis wondered how he was going to fold his long legs into such a small car.

Back in the casualty unit Beth was going through the intended work schedule with Shona and Carla. The number of patients now stood at 35, although Shona identified two children who were going to be discharged later that day. They had both been confirmed with minor fractures and were to be sent to an Orthopaedic Hospital for remedial treatment.

So far that morning there had been no indications of any further intake. With that in mind Beth suggested to Shona that her first task for the day would be to update each patient's record on the computer. After that, if time allowed, she suggested that she could assist Carla in treating or helping patients, as and where her skills were suitable. Both Shona and Carla were happy with that suggestion.

Beth switched the computer on to update the patient's records. However, before she could start Sandie and Paula appeared. Once they had cleared the formalities out of the way, they moved on to ask each other what their tasks for the day were. This together with a bit of chatter lasted about 10 minutes. After that Sandie and Paula moved off to start their daily chores.

Beth was now able to commence her first task of updating the computer records. She picked up the small pile of cards that were in the basket marked 'Patients Update' and began sorting them into numerical order. That done she opened up the relevant database and proceeded to insert the updates. In all Beth had counted 22 cards out of the total 35 patients currently within the casualty unit that required updating. At five minutes per card Beth calculated it would take about one and three quarter hours to complete this task, providing there were no interruptions. Her estimate proved reasonably accurate as it took just two hours to complete the task. It would have been less but for one small interruption. With the patients' database updated Beth printed off two copies. One was inserted in the folder on her desk, the other she kept for Ellis.

Before she could move away from the desk, Shona appeared and said, 'We have two more children arriving within the next hour, will you be around?'

'Yes I'll wait,' Beth replied.

As the car stopped outside the hotel entrance to allow vehicles to pass, Ellis was pleasantly surprised at the amount of leg-room he had. He looked across at Cristina and commented to her about it. She smiled at him, at the same time releasing the clutch and turning right along the one way street leading towards the centre of Sorrento.

Although the traffic was very busy at that time, within five minutes they were on the outskirts of the town centre. Once they had negotiated the congestion within the Piazza Tasso area they headed along the main road Corso Italia. This road started from the Sant' Angello side and ran directly through the centre of Sorrento. It then joined up with the cliff side road that eventually became the road known as the Almafi Drive.

As they made their way along the Corso Italia, Ellis questioned Cristina about the hospital, which he understood to be only an Accident and Emergency Casualty Unit. He also commented that he had seen it referred to as 'Santa Maria della Misericordia'.

She confirmed that the hospital was only small and was mainly a Casualty Unit. Serious cases were normally transferred to Naples by road or helicopter. The name 'Santa Maria Della Misericordia', she did not recognise. Cristina said she would let him know what the significance of the name was later.

Towards the end of the Corso Italia, they saw the sign for the hospital. Cristina indicated a right turn and slowed down waiting for a break in the oncoming traffic. Once a gap appeared, Cristina took the opportunity and turned across the traffic into the short road leading into the hospital. As they cruised into the hospital grounds, Ellis spotted a car reversing out from a parking bay right alongside the entrance. Once the car had moved away Ellis looked to see if there was any sign of a reserved notice. They were in luck as no sign could be seen. No sooner seen than done, Cristina reversed the black and white Smart car into the vacant spot. With the car parked they made their way towards the entrance. Ellis stayed a short space behind Cristina as they entered the hospital. 'Did you say the Administrator's name was Rosa Maresca?' Cristina asked. Ellis nodded.

On reaching the reception area they stood for a few moments wondering where to go, Ellis then saw someone he believed to be a hospital worker. Cristina moved towards the woman, speaking to her in Italian as she did. As soon as the name Rosa was mentioned, she raised her arms and nodded to Cristina. She then walked away and disappeared into a side office.

Two minutes later a smartly dressed middle aged woman appeared. She walked towards them. Speaking very good English, she said, 'I am Rosa Maresca. I have been expecting you; please let us go to my office.' They did so and then introduced themselves in more detail, describing what they were trying to achieve. Ellis showed her the photographs explaining at the same time what was happening back at the Hotel Geranio.

Since the eruption and the urgent need for hospital beds, Rosa outlined what the hospital had achieved in the few days since the eruption. Their first priority had been to create a main ward for non serious injuries and a few side wards for trauma cases. This action had created beds for forty patients, all of which were currently occupied.

She continued by confirming what types of injuries could be treated at this hospital, and also explained that any complicated injuries were transferred elsewhere. The patients were mostly adults; however in three cases where injured children had been found with one or more parent they were being kept together.

Once Rosa had finished summarising the situation she suggested that they made their way to the main ward and begin showing the children's photographs.

Both Ellis and Cristina nodded in agreement. With that they all moved out of the office and began walking along the corridor towards the general ward.

As they entered the ward, Rosa asked them to wait whilst she spoke to the Sister in charge. They both watched and presumed that Rosa was telling her the purpose of their visit. During the conversation, she turned and pointed to them both. After a few minutes she turned and beckoned them over.

As they approached, Rosa informed them that all was okay and that a junior nurse was available to assist them around the ward if required. As soon as the introductions were over, they began their task, and all four of them moved towards the first bed that was situated in the corner of the ward.

Meanwhile, back at the Hotel Geranio, an ambulance had brought two more arrivals to the casualty unit. The first child through the doors was a boy of about eight years of age who had a bandaged head and one arm in a sling. He had clearly been given some form of pain inhibitor as he seemed reasonably relaxed, although his eyes showed a certain amount of anxiety. Once he had been helped from his wheelchair the two paramedics departed to fetch the other casualty.

A few minutes later the doors opened again. This time Beth saw a young girl of about four years of age clutching what looked like a comfort blanket and sobbing gently. As the wheelchair approached, Carla went over and helped the paramedic lift the young girl onto the bed. Beth could see from her position that the girl had sustained injuries to both her knees and face; both looking badly lacerated.

At this point Shona joined Carla and, after a short conversation, they began preparing their treatment for both children. The paramedic handed Shona some paperwork and then departed, taking the wheelchair with him. As he did so, Beth went over to Carla to see if she could assist in any way. Carla was grateful for the offer and asked Beth if she would help her remove the girl's clothing.

Although they managed to remove the clothes, it did cause the young girl some discomfort, particularly when removing her jeans. To prevent the lacerated knees coming into contact with the material, they cut the legs off the jeans. Once they had done this, the remainder of the clothing was removed without too much difficulty.

Beth prepared a bowl of warm water and added a small amount of antiseptic and spent a few minutes cleaning the girl's knees. On completion of that task Beth commandeered the wheelchair and decided to take the girl to the room that had been allocated for showering and bathing purposes.

So far at the hospital Ellis, Cristina, and Rosa had already visited ten patients, all had drawn a blank. No one had yet recognised any of the children portrayed in the photograph folder. They continued on with their task until lunchtime. With over half the patients visited they had still not identified anybody.

For lunch they sat at a corner table in the small dining room. The meal consisted of various Italian snacks laid out on two large oval silver styled plates. There was bruschetta topped with cheese and tomato, a pizza marguerite, slices of Italian bread, salami and other meats. Added to this were a large bowl consisting of a mixed salad and two jugs of various fruit juices.

After lunch they returned to the ward and continued to visit the patients. Initially the success rate was no better than the morning, until they reached their twenty eighth patient, a woman called Francesca married to Michael Maschella. Ellis guessed she was in her mid thirties. When they arrived at her bedside Rosa explained who Ellis and Cristina were, and what they were trying to accomplish. Rosa asked her where she was from and did she have any children.

'Yes,' she said. 'I have two children, both girls aged seven and ten years. I do not know where they are or even what's happened to my husband. We were separated when the avalanche from the eruption buried us in the outskirts of Naples.'

Ellis handed her the photograph folder. She began to look through it turning each page over slowly as she did so. It was when she reached the middle pages that she suddenly let out a loud shriek. Rosa said, 'Francesca what is it? Do you recognise anybody?'

'Yes, yes, my bambino Enrica,' she shrieked.

Francesca burst into tears kissing the photograph as she did. 'Il mio bambino,' she kept saying over and over again.

Rosa tried to comfort her, but to no avail as Francesca continued sobbing. Nobody seemed able to appease her and they began wondering what could be done to settle her. It was Cristina who first realised why Francesca was so inconsolable. She heard her utter the word 'Morto'. She turned to Rosa speaking in Italian as she did telling her that, 'She thinks Enrica is dead'. Similarly she reported her comment to Ellis.

Rosa immediately spoke to Francesca explaining to her that Enrica was alive and well. The look on Francesca's face had to been seen to be believed; she looked completely bewildered. She said nothing for some seconds then her look turned to joy as she started crying again. Although this time they were tears of joy.

After a few minutes Francesca had settled down, Cristina spoke to her and explained where Enrica was and what injuries she had. It was whilst Cristina was explaining to Francesca about Enrica that Ellis suddenly remembered that two girls were brought into the casualty unit together. This had been during the second day of admissions. He recalled Beth saying that there were two girls next to each other in the unit. They appeared to know each other.

Ellis picked up the photograph folder, and turned to the photograph of Enrica. It was the last one on that page; he turned to the next page and showed the first photograph to Cristina. He said, 'Tell Francesca that this little girl is also alive; does she recognise her?'

As soon as Francesca saw the photograph, the shrieking and the tears started again. She put the photograph to her mouth and kissed it over and over again, repeating the words, 'Anna il mio Anna.'

It was clear that Francesca had identified both of her children. Cristina asked Rosa to get full details of all the family. Rosa called the junior nurse over. Once Rosa had obtained all the relevant family details, they moved on to the next patient. They had no success there or at either of the next few patients.

When they had finished showing the last patients the photographs, they decided to have a cappuccino break before visiting the side wards. Rosa joined them for the break and took the opportunity to give Ellis all the family details she had obtained from Francesca. As Ellis filed it away in his briefcase, he commented that Beth would now be able to complete her first patient record. Before they had finished their break Ellis realised that he had the camera with him. He suggested that perhaps it would be a good idea to take a photograph of Francesca to show both her daughters back at the hotel. They all agreed. Cristina also commented that it would also be confirmation that Francesca was the mother of the two girls. With that in mind Ellis and Rosa went back to the ward while Cristina made her way to the first of the side wards.

Friday went very quickly for Ellis and Beth, as they both went about completing their tasks for the afternoon.

Once Ellis had completed photographing Francesca he went to assist Cristina. She had already visited three side wards. She had drawn a blank with all of those.

Beth had by now almost completed her afternoon. She had finished showering the latest admission - a young girl with badly lacerated knees and face. Since she had been treated, the girl was now showing signs of settling down. As Beth finished putting cream on her lacerations, she dabbed a little on the girl's nose. This brought a smile to the girl's face for the first time since her admission.

Back at the hospital, Ellis and Cristina had finished showing all the casualties the photographs. Unfortunately they did not identify anyone. They said their goodbyes to Rosa and, after making sure they had all the paperwork on Francesca Maschella, they left the hospital shortly after 5 o'clock, and headed back to the hotel.

Beth meanwhile had also finished and was now tidying up her desk. She was about to say goodbye to Shona and Carla when Ellis came into the unit.

'How did you get on?' Beth asked. With a look of joy on his face Ellis explained that they had identified two sisters. He walked to the desk and began opening the photograph folder. As Shona and Carla came up to the desk, Ellis, with a look of triumph, turned to the two photographs. 'Let me introduce Enrica and Anna!' They all leant across the desk to get a better view.

'I have all the necessary details here,' said Ellis, showing them a form he had just taken from his briefcase. 'I also have a photograph of their mother Francesca. Who is going to tell the girls the good news?' Ellis asked.

'I think Carla and I should do that,' Shona replied. They all agreed.

Ellis handed Shona the photographs and Carla the camera. Everybody watched as the two of them made their way across the unit to the girls. Shona called Anna across to Enrica's bed. Once they were all seated, Shona started to tell the two girls what had been discovered that morning. As soon as Carla showed them the photograph of their mother, there were shrieks of delight followed by tears of relief from both girls.

Ellis looked around at all those who were watching this bedside drama. There wasn't a dry eye to be seen.

Once normality had been restored people began drifting away or returning to their tasks.

Suddenly Beth spoke, 'That reminds me. Colin from the *Star News* production team needs to discuss the weekend visit to Naples with you. He said he will see us this evening after dinner.'

'Right,' replied Ellis. 'I'll inform reception of our movements tonight so we don't miss him.'

Before they left, Beth updated the patient database to include the details of the two girls now firmly identified.

Whilst Beth started to prepare herself for the evening, Ellis went onto the balcony and watched the activities on and around *HMS Bulwark* and *Illustrious*. Both ships seemed to be fully operational now. Ellis watched closely as a helicopter came into view from the direction of Naples. It circled once and then slowly hovered over its designated landing area before setting down on *HMS Illustrious*.

Whilst this was happening two large amphibious troop carriers were casting off from *HMS Bulwark*. Ellis leaned over the balcony rails to get a closer view. Both vessels appeared to be carrying troops; Ellis guessed it was the Royal Engineers. As they moved away from the ship, a Sea King helicopter was preparing to take off from *HMS Bulwark* as well.

It took off very slowly and Ellis soon realised why. As it rose slowly into the air, it began to lift a large wooden crate from the deck. Ellis could now see a cable attached to the underside of the helicopter, from it were suspended four other cables which were connected to all corners of the crate.

As it rose slowly into the sky, his attention was drawn once more to the helicopter on the *Illustrious*. He could see two stretchers with people strapped in being taken from the exit door at the back of the helicopter. He watched as both stretchers were carried by four people across the flight deck, and through a door and out of view. Ellis assumed that *Illustrious* was now a fully operational hospital ship.

He was still mulling it over in his mind when Beth shouted through that she had finished in the bathroom. As Ellis acknowledged her, he moved from the balcony towards the bathroom, telling Beth as he did what he had just seen.

Later, that evening, they had just ordered from the sweet trolley when Angioletto, the maitre d', came across to inform Ellis that Colin from *Star News* was asking for him. Ellis thanked Angioletto and asked if he would inform Colin that they would meet him in fifteen minutes on the terrace balcony.

True to their word they walked onto the terrace some fifteen minutes later. They spotted Colin immediately as he was seated at the middle table adjacent to the perimeter fence. As they sat down, Carlos appeared with two cappuccinos and one brandy. 'I've taken the liberty of ordering your drinks,' Colin said looking at Carlos. Ellis raised his glass and then he and Colin started to discuss the details of their visit to Naples on Saturday.

For the next ten uninterrupted minutes Colin went through the itinerary for Saturday. He began by identifying an early start from the Marina Piccola where they would catch a Seacat ferry at 7.30am. On arriving at Naples, they would dock in the 'Vio Nuova Marina.' Once ashore they would meet up with representatives from the *Italian TV Station TG5*, who were going to assist them during their visit. If for any reason they were unable to dock in the main Marina, the ferry would divert south to Santa Lucia on the outskirts of Naples. The plan was to make their way into Naples with the *TG5* personnel. This was dependent on there being any suitable vehicle access, or no restrictions imposed by the authorities. If they were successful in reaching any stricken areas within Naples they would set up their transmission camp and attempt to produce a live feed to the *Star News* studio in London.

Colin then detailed what type of programme content they required, and he confirmed that Ellis was to present the link in the same way that he did when Vesuvius first erupted.

'Right, I think that's everything; any questions?' Colin asked.

'Yes, I have one,' Ellis replied. 'What do we need to take with us?'

'That's all taken care of,' was Colin's reply. 'We will have our own water, food rations, boots and additional protective clothing etc, dress initially as you wish.

Okay if that's all I'll see you in reception at 7.00am tomorrow. Cheerio for now.'

Beth and Ellis stayed on the terrace waiting for the rest of the 'gang' to appear. Within half an hour all were present. Once Ellis had ordered drinks for them all, he informed them they were all invited to dinner with himself and Beth in the hotel next Thursday to celebrate their Golden Wedding. He apologised for not taking them to a restaurant in town but had decided in view of the current situation to keep any celebrations at a low level.

Everybody was in full agreement with the last statement, and all decided it was an excellent way to end the holiday. At that point Dene called Carlos over for another round of drinks.

Chapter Fifteen - Eruption plus 7

Shortly after Ellis rose on Saturday morning, the door bell rang. Ellis answered it clad only in his dressing gown. It was room service delivering their breakfast that Ellis had ordered the night before.

'This looks nice,' Beth commented.

'It certainly does,' replied Ellis, as he poured himself a glass of fruit juice. It was all there as ordered; fruit juice, tea for two, cereals, prunes, croissants, toast butter and preserves.

Over breakfast they discussed the visit to Naples, and in particular what Ellis would take with him. 'That reminds me,' said Ellis, 'I'd better put my mobile on charge. I suggest you do the same, and whilst I think about it make sure you leave it on all the time, so I can contact you if I need to.'

'Will do,' replied Beth.

Whilst he finished his breakfast, Beth started to pack the small rucksack that Colin had given Ellis. Although Colin had suggested that he had organised everything they might need, Ellis decided to be on the safe side and pack a few additional items. The items he had selected were all laid out on the bed: spare shorts, tee shirt, socks, a bottle of water, packet of plasters, a bottle of surgical spirit, box of tissues, some paracetamol tablets, toothpaste and brush, plus a bag of mixed sweets.

By the time Beth had finished packing; Ellis had just drunk the last of the tea and was applying a good measure of sun lotion to his face arms and legs. 'That should keep the sun at bay until lunch time,' he said to Beth. As he was saying that he screwed the cap back on to the tube of sun lotion and slipped it into the rucksack.

'Right,' he said. 'It's time I wasn't here.' With that he leant over and kissed Beth and said, 'I'll ring you as soon as I can. ' He picked up his rucksack, checked that his mobile was in his pocket and set off to meet Colin.

As he arrived in the reception area just before 6.50am, Colin was already waiting there for him. Within five minutes their taxi arrived outside the main entrance. Once they had stowed their rucksacks in the boot, Ellis and Colin climbed into the back seat of the taxi.

The journey to the harbour took about fifteen minutes. As they pulled into the taxi rank, Colin spotted the other two members of the *Star* team; one was a camera operator, the other a sound technician.

Both men were from England, Pete the camera operator came from Hertford in Hertfordshire, whilst Steve the sound technician originated from Croydon. Once the introductions were complete, they headed for the departure dock.

On arrival, they soon identified the Seacat ferry that was destined for Naples. As they approached it, Colin handed Ellis a 'Press Pass'. As Ellis took it from him, he noticed his photograph emblazoned on the front of it.

'Just show that as we board,' said Colin. 'That saves us having to buy a ticket.'

Ellis did as he was told. As he approached the man in uniform standing by the gangway entrance to the ferry, Ellis raised his hand with the pass in it and showed it to the official. After a cursory glance, the official nodded and waved him straight through. Ellis acknowledged the nod and made his way into the ferry.

Once all four of them were onboard, they made their way to the back of the Seacat. Ellis in particular was glad of this as he had previous experience of a bumpy ride when sitting at the front of this type of craft, when the sea swell was above average. They managed to find a row of four seats together in the last but one row. After placing their rucksacks and equipment in a storage void alongside where they were sitting, they were able to stretch out and relax.

Within minutes they heard the sound of the two doors being closed and shortly afterwards the diesel engines burst into life. Almost straightaway they started to move towards the harbour exit. They were soon outside and when they were about one hundred metres away from the entrance the throttles were opened. Immediately the Seacat rose up on its front skids and began moving swiftly across the top of the water.

As they picked up speed, Ellis was relieved to notice that the craft was skimming smoothly across the top of the water. That indicated to him that the sea was calm; unlike his previous experience onboard a Seacat.

The journey time across the Bay of Naples was officially twenty minutes. Ellis laid his head back onto the head rest and glanced out of the window just as the Hotel Geranio sitting proudly on top of the cliffs came into view.

Although the journey was expected to take twenty minutes, Colin suddenly said, 'It looks like we are here already.' Ellis looked towards the front of the craft; sure enough he could see quite clearly some small buildings and what appeared to be a harbour wall.

At that point the intensity of the engines subsided somewhat and the front of the craft dipped slightly. This was a sure sign that they were at their destination.

The craft reduced its speed again and this time the front of the craft settled fully down, as it turned towards their docking berth. As they slowly made their way towards shore, Ellis wondered if they were entering the official Naples Marina or elsewhere?

No sooner had he raised that question to himself, when he saw the answer. Attached to the harbour wall was sign saying, 'Vio Nuova Marina'.

Once the craft had stopped at its docking berth, Ellis and the other three began to collect their baggage and equipment. Very soon both exit doors were opened and a voice speaking in Italian came over the tannoy system. Ellis assumed that the voice was telling the passengers that they could now embark from the craft. All four of them moved towards the nearest door and made their way down the gangway and out onto the dockside.

Once there Colin started looking around for his contacts from *TG5*. He need not have worried as he heard his name called out by someone with an Italian accent waving to him from some thirty metres away.

'Okay, lads, it looks as though we are in business!' Colin exclaimed.

With that they all picked up their belongings and headed towards the voice.

Colin was the first to reach his Italian counterpart. As he did, they embraced each other, not forgetting the traditional kiss on each cheek.

'Gentlemen', said Colin. 'Let me introduce you to Ottavio Caggiano, better known as Otto.' With that he introduced Otto to his colleagues one by one.

Once the formalities were over Otto took them all to one side to explain what he had laid on for them. He began his briefing by explaining that the original plan was to take them around parts of Naples in a 4 x 4 vehicle but, as the roads were so impassable, he had now managed to acquire a helicopter instead.

The programme he had in mind was as follows:

1. The helicopter would transport them to a vantage point overlooking a   devastated area where the pyroclastic flow first struck. From there they would fly around Vesuvius to see what was left of the volcano following the eruption.

2. Once that was completed he suggested that they then begin moving back towards the Marina where they are now standing, but stopping off en route to show different aspects of the avalanche, including if possible interviewing people affected by the avalanche and those working for the rescue services.

3. Otto then concluded his programme by saying that if all went well they could then catch the last Seacat back to Sorrento at 7 o'clock tonight. If not he knew where there was accommodation for the night.

'Does anyone have any questions?' Otto enquired.

'That sounds perfect, let's give it a go,' said Colin.

With that they followed Otto out of the harbour area and began walking to a flat area that lay to the left-hand side of where they had disembarked. Parked two hundred metres away Ellis could see a helicopter. On the way, Ellis managed to give Beth a quick ring to let her know what was happening; he was missing her already.

On arriving at the helicopter with the exception of the camera, they stowed all their baggage and equipment in the rear storage area. They then proceeded to board.

First on was the camera technician who settled in a seat up front of the passenger section and next to a window. Situated below the window was a shelf which would assist him in supporting the camera. There was room for eight passengers, so with the *Star News* team consisting of three plus Otto and Ellis, space was no problem.

Once they were all seated, Otto asked them to put on the helmets and earphones that were hanging at the side of their seats and he did the same. He then clipped a microphone to his helmet which located itself across the front of his mouth. All was silent in the cabin then suddenly they all heard Otto speaking, 'Gentlemen, this is a sound check. If you can hear my voice, please raise your hand.' Ellis looked around all hands including his were raised.

Otto continued, 'Good, as we commence this trip I will be your guide. I will describe where we are and I will also translate to you what the pilot is saying. The route we intend to take unless advised differently by the authorities is the one I mentioned at the Marina. We will be commencing our journey shortly; we are going to travel north towards Vesuvius to seek the first area that was struck by the pyroclastic flow. We will if possible stop en route to film and interview any newsworthy events.' Otto concluded with, 'That is all for now, prepare for take-off.'

Within seconds of Otto talking to the pilot, an engine burst into life. This was shortly followed by a low whining noise as the rotor blades began to rotate. Once up to speed the helicopter began to gently lift from the ground. As it did so, Ellis sensed the front of the helicopter dip slightly. As the revolutions of the rotor blades increased the helicopter gained height, quickly moving forward at the same time.

The first thirty seconds of the flight Ellis found quite strange as the helicopter rose and banked slightly to the left at the same time. However once the pilot had levelled off and was satisfied with the course he had set, the flight stabilised and became more enjoyable, if somewhat noisy.

Now he was settled, Ellis looked out of the window. As he did so, his earphones burst into life as Otto told them that they would be flying between 2000 and 3000 feet. As they gained height, he started to explain what they could see below.

Although Ellis had seen similar views over the past six days on all of the news channels, it still did not prepare him for what he was witnessing. He heard Otto's voice in his ear once again. 'Our intended flight plan is to head towards Vesuvius so that we can map the route that the pyroclastic flow took.'

He continued, 'If you look to your left now, you can see the Castel Nuovo, which fortunately was untouched as the pyroclastic avalanche passed by some 200 metres away.' Otto paused at this moment as their first sighting of the effect of the avalanche came into view.

It was just as Ellis remembered it from the first viewing on *Star News*. All that he could see in front of the helicopter was a landscape that was reminiscent of the surface of the moon. He looked to his left to try and gauge how wide the avalanche had been at this point and he estimated it had been at least one mile.

They continued on, trying to identify what remained of this the capital city of Campania. In his earphones Ellis heard a grimace from Otto; this was followed by a pause. Otto then explained that the large building with the roof partially caved in on the left of the helicopter with the remains of an orange and green type facade was the Museo Nationale. He told them that it was one of the best Roman Empire museums in the world. Many of the treasures from Pompeii and Herculaneum were housed there.

Ellis looked hard and long at what remained of the building. He estimated that half of its original height remained above the debris of the avalanche. Unfortunately when it was struck by what must have been a raging torrent of force the building had partially collapsed. Ellis wondered just how many of the priceless items had been destroyed forever.

The building soon passed them by and Ellis began to notice the activity on the ground below. He spotted a gang of workman with what looked like dumper trucks, being filled with rubble by a large JCB type digger. Further along there were more workmen all wearing bright orange bibs and red hard hats. They could be seen using their hands to throw debris and rubble into more trucks.

Whilst he was studying the scene below, Ellis realised that a large number of buildings had collapsed roofs, even though the rest of the building appeared to be secure.   As he reflected on this, his memory recalled the *BBC* documentary on the 79 A.D. eruption that devastated the Roman City of Pompeii.   He remembered vividly the scene where the volcanic ash fell from the sky and landed on the roofs of the houses and other buildings.   The amount of ash that collected on the roofs was such that many of them buckled under the weight. It was reported that Pompeii was buried under seven metres of ash and debris. That, said Ellis to himself, is probably what has happened here.

As his eyes scanned the ground below, he suddenly realised that he had not seen any normal civilian adults or children. This sent a cold chill right through his body. Surely he thought to himself, there were some survivors? If so where are they now? Before he could dwell any more Otto came on air again. To his amazement he started to answer the question Ellis had just imposed on himself.

'Gentlemen, I can tell from the expressions on your face that you are bemused by the lack of civilians on the ground below. It is true that many people have not survived the eruption. However, there have been many that have survived with or without injuries. They have all been moved away from the areas of destruction and are now housed in either temporary accommodation, or with people who have spare living capacity within their own homes.'

Otto continued. 'If you look through the front window you will now see Vesuvius on the horizon. We are not allowed to fly within 100 metres of the crater; however our pilot is going to circle around it from east to west. I think what you are about to see will remain with you for the rest of your lives.'

As the pilot adjusted his course, the helicopter started to turn eastwards. Whilst this was happening, Steve the sound technician gave Ellis a microphone, and said,   'Make a good job of your commentary and this could be an exclusive for *Star News*.'

Ellis replied, 'No pressure then?' Steve just smiled.

The helicopter started to turn back towards the west gaining height as it did so. They were now getting increasingly close to Vesuvius. Because of the height they were at, Ellis was beginning to see the changes the eruption had made to the mountain.

With no further thoughts Ellis gave Steve the thumbs up and after a ten second count down went straight into his commentary.

'We're here flying over Vesuvius so you, the viewers at home, can see what it look like today. Vesuvius, or as it is known the Somma-Vesuvius range, is a volcano of 1281 metres above sea level. This range comprised of Somma the older volcano whose summit collapsed, creating what we call a Caldera. This is a large crater caused by the violent explosion of a volcano that collapses and then forms a depression. From inside this a younger volcano now known as Vesuvius was created.

'The mountain range of Mount Somma and its associate volcano Vesuvius prior to the eruption could be seen from miles around. Its distinguishing features were two humps with a shallow depression between them. These two humps have now been obliterated leaving a gigantic, flat crater situated on the top of what was left of the mountain.

'The original crater had a diameter of 700 metres. By my estimation it is now double this. As you can see, it does look like a gigantic lake without any water.'

As they continued to circle around Vesuvius, Pete continued filming.

On the second circuit as they approached the eastern side Ellis wondered what had happened to the Observatory. He posed the question as part of his commentary; just as he did this, he spotted it on the side of the mountain. Its original position he knew to be about half way up the mountain (600 metres). Now there was only about 100 metres remaining between the Observatory and what was left of the cone of Vesuvius.

Ellis studied the Observatory looking to see if it had received any structural damage. All he could see was what looked like ash and debris lying all around and on top of the building. Other than that the building seemed untouched. Ellis surmised that thankfully the full force of the eruption had discharged itself in the opposite direction.

Whilst he continued with his commentary, he calculated that almost half the height of the original mountain had been destroyed. Once he had confirmed that in his own mind, he added into his commentary that almost 600 metres of mountain rock along with millions of tonnes of ash and billions of fragments of pumice had been hurled with tremendous force in the direction of Naples.

As they approached the completion of the second circuit, Otto came on air again. 'Gentleman we are going to change course now and head towards the airport. Fortunately the location of the airport was outside the path of the eruption avalanche. It did sustain some ash and debris fall out which has caused some minor damage. This has caused closure for most commercial flights; however rescue and aid flights have now began to operate.'

Although Pete continued filming as the helicopter changed direction away from Vesuvius, Ellis signed off his commentary. He would add any further comments to the film once it had been edited.

At this point the helicopter banked right to put it on course for the airport. In doing so it crossed the route that the pyroclastic flow had taken following its discharge from Vesuvius. Ellis was mesmerised by what he saw. For as far as the eye could see, and that seemed to be about a mile or so either side of the helicopter, was the sight of a grey/black undulating mass dominating the landscape.

With the whirring of the helicopter rotor blades in the background, Ellis studied the view below. Everywhere he looked he could see the orange bibs and red hats that identified the rescue services. Accompanying these were diggers, lorries and dumpers of all shapes and sizes.

It was difficult to imagine how anyone could prioritise the devastation that Ellis could see from above. Where once there were buildings there were now just piles of rubble, or parts of structures still standing. Vehicles of all types; cars, lorries, buses, could be seen strewn all over, some on their side, others upside down. Ellis wondered how many people escaped if any from these vehicles. His attention had now turned to blocks of high rise apartments that were coming into view. They must have originally been at least twenty storeys high; many were still standing even though the bottom few storeys were buried in debris and ash. In between those that were still standing, there were others that appeared to have just collapsed under the impact.

Otto spoke again. 'Gentlemen we have the airport in view.' Ellis looked straight ahead.

The change in the landscape was dramatic. Ellis could now see in front of him a scene of normality. Suddenly the scene of mass destruction below him ended as they flew away from the path that the pyroclastic flow avalanche had taken. He looked around; he could see ordinary buildings, vehicles and people moving about their daily business. The change was incredible and a little eerie. Life really does go on! Ellis thought to himself. He continued looking below for the next few minutes, until they reached the outskirts of the airport.

At that point the helicopter banked to the right and began flying around the perimeter of the airport. As Ellis looked below at the landing and parking areas, he could see many planes. Most of them appeared to be carrying freight. The rear doors were open; people and vehicles including fork lift trucks were all scurrying about.

As Ellis wondered what they would see next his thoughts were interrupted as Otto asked for their attention.

He continued, 'Our pilot has been speaking to the airport controller, in the hope of persuading the authorities to allow us to land at the airport. We are still awaiting confirmation or otherwise. If we are successful, with your agreement we will land and stay for one to two hours. This will give the pilot chance to refuel, and we can all have a comfort break and perhaps some lunch. If we are lucky we might be allowed to film and interview. Do you all agree?' They all answered in the affirmative.

As they continued to circle, word came through that permission had been granted to land. The authorities also confirmed they could stay for lunch if they wished. Filming and interviews had yet to be decided; Otto would visit the appropriate person to discuss these points after they had landed.

The time was approaching 9.30am as the pilot began his landing procedures.

They descended slowly towards a large white circle; Ellis assumed this was the standard landing area for helicopters and two minutes later they touched down.

After a few minutes delay whilst the pilot completed the engine shut down, they left the helicopter and got into a small, twelve-seater airport bus which was waiting to drive them to the airport building.

As they arrived at the airport building, they were met by the chief security officer. He introduced himself, apologising for his English as he did so, and then asked them to accompany him to the office. Once there they signed in and were issued with a security pass. Not long afterwards, a security officer informed them that the airport director wanted to see them so they were taken through a small hanger and up two flights of stairs until they reached a reception area where they were met by a tall, grey-haired distinguished looking man. Ellis guessed he must have been in his middle to late fifties.

The security officer stepped forward and guided him towards Otto. 'Mr Baldini may I introduce Ottavio Caggiano from the *TG5* News Channel.' Otto responded to the introduction by taking hold of Mr Baldini's hand and shaking it. They exchanged pleasantries in Italian before Otto then proceeded to introduce the rest of the team.

After the introductions were completed, the security officer bid them farewell as Mr Baldini led them into his office asking them to take a seat. 'Would you all like refreshments?' Mr Baldini enquired. Ellis was impressed with his excellent English. When the refreshments arrived a few minutes later, Mr Baldini again formally welcomed them thanking them at the same time for the sensitive way they were showing the world the catastrophe that had devastated Naples.

'Before I ask you what is the purpose of your visit to the airport. I will briefly explain to you the operating status of the airport,' he said. 'Firstly, I think we all appreciate how fortunate the airport was in being spared the full wrath of the eruption. Some superficial damage was done, and a certain amount of ash did affect us for the first two days. That has all been resolved and we are now more or less restored to full operating capability. However, because of the urgent need for all that is required for such an emergency as Naples is experiencing, the operating role of this airport has changed.'

Mr Baldini told them that the numbers of passenger and freight traffic had been reversed. Freight traffic was now the priority; while incoming passenger traffic was negligible. With the need to repatriate tourists who had been trapped within the Campania area, an outgoing passenger service was planned, albeit on a slightly reduced service than normal. It was hoped that the backlog would be cleared within seven days.

As he spoke, Mr Baldini's voice faltered slightly. 'Not many people are aware of what I am about to tell you. We have chosen not to advertise this information for obvious reasons, but the authorities believe that we now need to release it in a controlled way. Your visit today gives us an opportunity to do this.'

Ellis wondered what he was about to hear.

Mr Baldini then went on to explain that the latest official fatalities, to be released later this week were estimated at nearly two hundred thousand. 'When a disaster like this happens, the largest and most difficult problem that the authorities face is where to keep all the bodies of the deceased.'

With that he paused. It appeared from everybody's expressions they had not considered this.

'Here at Naples airport we have a number of large hangers. These have been designated as emergency mortuaries and for the last few days we have been bringing the deceased here as and when they have been recovered.'

The room remained silent. Mr Baldini continued by explaining that whilst the hangers they were using were not ideal, there were few alternatives. He briefly explained that they were sealing the hangers as and where they could, in preparation for the installation of mobile cooling air blowers. This he said would enable the temperature within the hangers to remain at a level suitable for the retention of bodies.

He also stated that the accommodation space at the airport would not be sufficient for the number of fatalities forecast. Other areas outside of Naples were being sought to facilitate the anticipated requirements.

'I am sure that you all have many questions,' Mr Baldini said. 'However, the time is now 11.30. Can I suggest we go for an early lunch? Afterwards I will show you the mortuaries if you are comfortable with that, and then feel free to talk and interview staff and any of the rescue services that are here.' Otto looked around the room and everybody nodded in agreement.

Mr Baldini rose from his chair and gestured for the others to follow him. Whilst they were making their way down the iron staircase, Ellis rang Beth. Once she answered, Ellis explained where they were, and what they intended to do that afternoon. Beth had a few things to say before Ellis confirmed he would call later to inform her if they were staying overnight. Within five minutes they had reached the canteen. With the official lunch starting time still thirty minutes away the canteen was almost empty. They were soon served.

Ellis didn't feel particularly hungry, although he managed to eat something. During the meal they discussed the various options that were open to them that afternoon. As they did it became clear to them that staying overnight would allow them to cover everything they wished to do. Otto therefore arranged an overnight stay at the main rescue centre accommodation a short distance from the airport.

When they had finished their lunch, Mr Baldini led them from the canteen. Once outside he stopped and announced that he was now going to take them to the first temporary mortuary. Within a short time they arrived outside a very large hanger. As they stopped outside the entrance, Mr Baldini briefed them on what to expect inside.

'One final comment gentlemen, please no filming. Can I suggest that you film a summary of what you have witnessed instead? Thank you.'

One by one they went through the entrance door. Inside the immediate area was surrounded by screens, all were about two metres high. They were met by two female attendants who were fully dressed in what looked like hospital scrubs. Both had their faces covered with a mask.

As he walked through the door, Ellis noticed a change in temperature. Compared to outside it was very cool. He also detected a whirring sound that he thought might be from cooling fans.

The attendants took them over to a side area where they were told they could leave any coats or baggage. They were then each given a face mask and were told to keep it on at all times.

Prior to entering the main hall, a male attendant also dressed in green scrubs and a face mask introduced himself. He spoke in English and he spent a few minutes explaining what they were about to see. 'If at any time you feel you need to leave, please do so. Will you now come with me?' he said, very solemnly.

Otto was the first to move. As he did so, they all followed him around the last screen and into the main area of the hanger. There they found row after row of light brown, wooden coffins. Ellis glanced at the others. Colin caught his eye and slowly shook his head. Ellis returned the gesture.

The attendant turned around saying as he did. 'Gentlemen if you are all okay we will proceed to move further into the hanger.' They all nodded.

As they moved down the central aisle, he explained that no bodies were visible. The coffin lids had been placed in position but not fixed. Attached to the front of each coffin was a small file; both had a corresponding number attached.

After walking down the middle aisle for ten minutes, Ellis asked the attendant how many bodies were stored in the hanger and how many had been identified. The attendant answered. 'About 20 per cent of the bodies have so far been identified. Currently there are almost 5000 bodies being stored here. In the other hanger there are another 3000.'

Ellis asked, 'Where are all the other bodies going to be stored which at present is estimated at two hundred thousand?'

The attendant replied by identifying numerous sites within the Campania area and also many further afield. He went on to say that they were looking at the possibility of installing a temporary metal flooring system about six feet above the present one. This would then increase the storage place to place coffins and their occupants.

When they reached the first of the many walkway crossover points, they turned right and gradually began moving back to the reception area. As they did so, Ellis stopped and looked at a file on one of the coffins. The person in this coffin had been identified as a teenage boy aged 15 years. The date of when he had arrived at the hangar was logged, and there was a signature presumably of the person who had identified him clearly visible. He assumed that there was more information inside the file, however he had seen enough and he quickly moved on not wishing to probe any more.

Whilst they were moving along, for the first time Ellis noticed a slightly perfumed smell within the building. As he looked around he could see high up on the girder work and around the inside of the walls what appeared to be canisters. From some of them he detected little puffs of mist coming from a spout like protrusion at the top of the canisters, in an attempt to make the atmosphere more palatable.

It wasn't many more minutes before they reached the screened area. After giving back their masks and collecting any belongings, they made their way outside after Mr Baldini thanked the attendants for their assistance. It was a few minutes before anybody spoke. Clearly everyone had been affected by what they had just seen.

Before they moved away, Colin asked Mr Baldini if it would be okay to film a short summary of the visit to the mortuary. Mr Baldini agreed. Within minutes Steve and Pete had everything set up. Once Ellis had run through a brief outline with Colin what he was going to say, they got into position for the first take.

Ellis heard the familiar '3, 2, 1 action', as Colin cued him in. He went straight into his introduction by informing viewers that he was reporting from Naples airport where two temporary mortuaries had been set up there and that he along with the *Star News* team had just visited them. Ellis then went on to describe what they had all just witnessed.

This took him only a few minutes as his commentary was brief and to the point, however his voice showed emotion. Colin who was listening to every word, knew that this short report would be all that was required to inform those who did not know already, that this was a disaster of a size never before witnessed in modern times.

Once Ellis had started his final summary Colin lifted his hand giving the thumbs up as he did. He then drew his hand across his throat to indicate time was up; Ellis took the cue and at the first opportunity signed off with the customary. 'This is Ellis Smith for *Star News* reporting from Naples Airport.'

As Steve and Pete began to pack up the equipment, Mr Baldini came across to Otto asking him whether they wanted to go to the other mortuary. The team agreed with Otto that they had seen enough. After a brief discussion, it was agreed that their visit could now be concluded as it had been very fruitful. With that Otto conveyed the team's views to Mr Baldini, and suggested that they made their way back to the helicopter.

'Of course,' said Mr Baldini. 'Tell me,' he said, turning to Colin, 'when will your report be screened on *Star*?' Colin explained that the first showing would be at 6 o'clock UK time.

Before long the helicopter came into view. As they walked towards it, Otto's mobile phone rang. He excused himself and answered it, the call only lasted a minute.

'Good news,' he said as he put the mobile in his pocket. 'Headquarters have arranged for us to spend this evening at the central rescue centre accommodation, which is only three kilometres north of the airport. I suggest we go there now and get ourselves settled, then you can if you wish collect more newsworthy stories, from the people who are directly involved on the ground.'

Before they boarded the helicopter, Ellis rang Beth to tell her he would be staying overnight. He also reminded her to watch *Star News* at 6 o'clock.

They all said their goodbyes to Mr Baldini as they climbed aboard the helicopter. Within ten minutes they were airborne and on their way to the central rescue centre.

As they rose into the sky, Ellis looked back at the airport. He spotted the large black hanger they had just visited. To the east of that and about two hundred metres away he saw what looked like another hanger that was also black but not as big. Ellis assumed that was the second mortuary.

With the rescue centre being only three kilometres away, it soon came into view. From the air it looked like a sprawling mass of wooden, single storey constructions housed in a field about the size of a football pitch. Alongside in another field adjacent to that one was all the mechanised equipment that the rescue services would be using. Ellis was able to identify JCBs, dumper trucks, large lorries, mobile cranes, and numerous other vehicles.

Just as Ellis was wondering where they would land, Otto's voice came alive in his headphones. 'Gentlemen, we will be landing shortly in a nearby school playing field. If you look ahead you will see two storey building complex with a large tarmac playground and a sports field attached.'

The pilot kept the helicopter heading on a straight course for the playing field. It swooped low over the school building and hovered slowly above the landing area before gently touching down. Otto was the first to disembark. He was met by a short stocky man who offered his hand to Otto speaking in Italian as he did. When he had finished speaking Otto translated saying that this was Alberto Donini, the superintendent of the site.

Once they had collected their baggage, they moved off in the direction of the site, approximately 300 metres away. On arrival they were taken to a hut at the far end of the compound. Mr

Donini spent a few minutes talking to Otto, and then introduced him to someone else who had joined them. Although they spoke in Italian, Ellis thought he caught the name Eduardo. He was right, as Mr Donini moved away raising his hand to them as he did, Otto said 'Eduardo' to them all.

Once introductions were over, they climbed the few steps that lead them into the hut. As they arrived inside, Eduardo spent a few minutes talking to Otto. When he had finished, he bade everybody goodbye leaving Otto to debrief everybody on what he had been told.

Otto pointed out the area they had been allocated within the hut; this consisted of five single bunks in the far corner each with a small cupboard alongside. He told them in which direction the canteen, toilets and shower block were, and the times meals were available. That said everybody made their way to the far end of the hut and selected themselves a bunk. Within fifteen minutes all five of them had sorted themselves in their temporary accommodation. They all agreed they would go for a shower, watch the *Star News* at six o'clock if available, and have a beer before trying the local cuisine.

They found their way to the recreation hall just before 6 o'clock. When they walked inside to the main room, twenty pairs of eyes turned to look at them. As Ellis looked around the room, he judged by the clothes they were wearing they must be part of the rescue teams.

Otto took it upon himself to walk forward and speaking in Italian he introduced himself. He then turned towards the rest of them and informed the listening audience who they were and what they were doing in Naples. Ellis heard him mention *Star News*. As he did so, some of those listening turned and pointed to the television. As it happened *Star News* was at that moment being screened.

As Otto finished talking a large man dressed in overalls and brown boots, rose from his chair and walked over to Otto. On reaching him he put his hand out grasping Otto's at the same time shaking it vigorously. He then gestured to Otto and the rest of them by raising his fist up to his face and then he tilted it in the direction of his mouth. He spoke as he did it. Otto leant forward and asked the man something. He then said, 'This man's name is Dino. He would like to buy you all a drink.'

In unison they all said 'Grazie'. A big smile broke on Dino's face.

As they stood by the bar collecting their drinks, the *Star News* bulletin began. The room went silent as Charles Small summarised what was to be seen. Ellis wondered how these people would understand what he was saying. He soon found out the answer as a streamer in Italian began to run across the bottom of the screen.

Ellis was surprised to see that their item was the first up. As Charles Small began the introduction, Pete's film showing them flying over Naples came into view.

At that moment all the workmen in the room moved towards the television to look at the view from the helicopter of a devastated Naples. There was complete silence except for Charles Small's description of the view. The film continued for a further minute or two showing the route that the pyroclastic avalanche had taken. Then the scenery changed as Vesuvius came into view. At this point Charles Small mentioned that the commentary was now being taken over by Ellis Smith (he mentioned who he was), who was on board the helicopter when it flew across Naples and around Vesuvius. There were gasps from the watching audience as the helicopter banked around what was left of Vesuvius. Particularly when they realised how little of the volcano cone was left.

After a short time the scenery changed as the helicopter flew towards the airport. Pete had continued running the film right up to where the helicopter landed at the airport. Ellis had forgotten that after landing Pete had set the camera on a tripod and had automatically filmed a short piece of them all beside the helicopter, at that point the film ended.

Charles Small came back onto the screen. He announced to the viewers that during the 10 o'clock news bulletin, the same *Star News* team had another story to tell. This report would feature another side to Naples airport. He concluded by warning that the topic to be shown might be upsetting to some viewers. As Charles Small moved on to another story, all the workmen turned to the five of them and applauded. When they had stopped, Otto thanked them and offered them all a drink, which was received very well.

Chapter Sixteen - Eruption plus 8

Ellis was the last of the group to wake on Sunday morning. As he sat on the side of his bunk, the others were already getting dressed.

'Hey, Ellis,' said Colin. 'Before I fell asleep last night I had an idea for today. Can I run it past you?'

'Carry on I'm listening,' replied Ellis.

'Right, here goes,' Colin said. 'I suggest we get a lift to the nearest rescue site, and spend one hour there filming and interviewing the workmen as they continue their rescue work then we come back to camp and prepare to fly back to Sorrento. What I also had in mind was to phone London and see if they could arrange for us to land on *HMS Illustrious* and interview the captain.'

'Sounds good,' said Ellis. 'I'm willing as long as that's what everyone wants to do.' All the team were in agreement with that proposal so Ellis picked up his toilet bag and went for a shower. When he arrived back, all the team were ready and dressed. Colin informed Ellis that he had spoken to his contacts in London, who promised to ring back as soon as they had any news.

Otto was going to stay on in the camp, as a news team from *TG5* were going to join him later.

As soon as Ellis was dressed they all departed for breakfast. On arrival at the canteen they met some of the workmen they had drank with last night. While they chatted and ate breakfast, Colin's phone rang to tell them that they had permission to land on *HMS Illustrious*.

Once breakfast was over they made their back to their hut to prepare for the trip outside the camp. Otto had arranged road transport with the site supervisor to be available by 9.30am. Right on time a large four-wheeled vehicle drew up outside their hut. All five of them scrambled aboard with their equipment; already seated were four workmen all kitted out for a day's work. They were to travel about five kilometres south to the outskirts of Naples so that they could see one of the areas that had been hit soon after the eruption.

As they moved off, Ellis rang Beth and told her of their movements for the day. He promised to phone her when they left for *HMS Illustrious*.

The journey took longer than expected due to the number of detours they were forced to make down minor roads. By the time they had reached their destination one and a half hours had passed.

After the equipment was unloaded from the vehicle, the driver bid them farewell and he arranged to collect them around 1 o'clock. This gave them only two hours to prepare a short recording on the effect of the eruption in this area.

Whilst Otto, Colin, and Ellis went looking for people to interview, Pete and Steve sought out a high spot so they could film some views of the devastated area.

It took Otto twenty minutes to find an Italian supervisor who also spoke some English. His name was Alberto Barretti; his home was in a small town not very far from this site. Otto explained that they were looking for someone familiar with this area to do an interview for *Star News*. When asked if he would be willing to be that person he agreed.

Otto and Colin then explained what they expected of him, telling him they would do a practise run first. After two practice runs, Colin decided that they would go for a filmed interview. Ellis and Mr Barretti positioned themselves ready for the signal to commence the interview.

It wasn't long in coming, Colin lifted his hand and counted down; '3, 2, 1, action'.

With that Ellis commenced the interview. He started by introducing Mr Barretti and asked him where he was and what his reaction had been when Vesuvius erupted. Mr Barretti began by explaining that he and his family lived just a short distance away from where they were now standing. He stated that he was at home with his family on that Saturday when the eruption occurred. When he heard the initial explosion he was unsure what had caused it. But within a few minutes he and his family witnessed what he now knows was a pyroclastic flow. It took the form of a large, grey cloud many metres high travelling at a very high speed over the ground less than a kilometre away from their apartment. They were on the tenth floor of the apartment block and they had a bird's eye view of the avalanche.

At this point Mr Barretti paused and composed himself before continuing. 'When we saw the power of this avalanche as it destroyed anything in its path, we realised that we were witnessing one of the largest catastrophic events in the history of Naples. We were powerless to do anything; all we could do was pray.'

Ellis could see that Mr Barretti was becoming increasingly emotional so he moved on from the eruption and asked him how he had got involved with the rescue services.

Mr Barretti explained that he worked in the construction industry. With his knowledge and experience of the equipment now being used by the rescue services, he had been seconded by the local authorities.

Ellis moved on to question Mr Barretti about how he and the rescue services were coping with the distressing task of retrieving bodies, and the trauma associated with that. Mr Barretti replied by saying that initially they all found it very difficult to cope with, but felt they had to do their bit to help. What really helped them was the discovery of people still alive beneath the rubble. This always gave them a boost to continue digging no matter what else they found.

As Ellis glanced towards Colin, he was given the sign to finish the interview. He turned to Mr Barretti and thanked him on behalf of *Star News* for sharing his thoughts with them. Mr Barretti smiled and with a breaking voice wanted to thank everybody on behalf of the people from the Naples area, for all the help that had been forthcoming over the past few days. Ellis turned to the camera and signed off with the familiar comment. 'This is Ellis Smith for *Star News* from the outskirts of Naples.'

As he finished, Colin was finishing a call on his mobile phone. He turned to the crew and said, 'That was the London News Office, congratulating everybody on this morning's work. Once edited it would be shown on the first available news bulletin.'

'Okay, let's get the equipment packed up and head back to the camp,' said Colin. 'I'm looking forward to a good lunch.'

As they departed from their vehicle back at the camp, Otto bade them farewell and told them that they would be leaving at 3.30. He was staying on at the camp to await the arrival of his own television network crew. They were going to spend a few days reporting on the rescue work in that area.

For the rest of the team, it was a quick break before they returned to the helicopter to go to *HMS Illustrious*. As the helicopter began its journey, Ellis opened a note that Otto had given him before they departed. It read, 'Ask the pilot to go back via the Naples Football Stadium.' This comment was also written in Italian. Ellis passed the note to the pilot who read it, passed it back and gave the thumbs up. Ellis paused before passing the note to the others. They all read it and nodded. Within a few minutes the 'San Paulo Stadium' came into view. The pilot changed direction and began circling the stadium. As they looked into the stadium, there was no sign of a football pitch. In its place was row after row of different colour canvas tents. They all realised that they were looking at one of the emergency housing camps that the authorities had said they were going to set up.

Ellis looked across at Pete the camera technician; he had already positioned his camera against the window. He was recording as much footage as possible. After the third circuit of the stadium the pilot looked across at Ellis to see if they had seen enough. After checking with Pete first Ellis gave the thumbs up sign to the pilot. He nodded back and immediately changed direction away from the stadium.

It was at this point that Ellis decided to ring Beth and let her know of their imminent arrival. Shortly after pressing the ring button he heard her voice. He had to speak loudly to overcome the noisy whirring of the rotor blades. 'Just a quick call,' he said, 'to let you know we are in the helicopter on our way to *HMS Illustrious*. We should be there in a few minutes.'

'Okay, I'll keep a look out for you; bye see you soon,' replied Beth.

Ellis switched off his phone and looked out of the window at the activity below. He said nothing for the next minute or so, as he reflected on what he had seen and heard over the last thirty six hours. His thoughts were abruptly interrupted as he heard Colin say. 'We're over the sea now, only a short distance to *HMS Illustrious.*' Ellis looked out of the window again. They were just passing over the marina they sailed into yesterday morning.

As the pilot adjusted the helicopter's course, Ellis could not prevent himself feeling excited at the thought of landing on an aircraft carrier despite the circumstances. He did not have to wait long. Within a minute it was in sight. The pilot took a course between the cliffs of Sorrento and the carrier at sea, giving Ellis a clear view of his hotel. He looked towards the perimeter rail by the swimming pool and could clearly see Beth and the rest of the 'gang'. He lifted his hand towards the window and waved. He managed to see their response before the pilot banked and headed directly towards the deck of *HMS Illustrious.*

The carrier came closer as the pilot adjusted the speed and height of the helicopter. On deck someone in a fluorescent jacket and a semaphore bat in each hand, was directing the pilot to a marked landing spot. The pilot followed him. Within seconds of hovering over the deck the pilot landed the helicopter in the middle of a white circle. They felt nothing more than a slight jolt as the helicopter made contact with the deck.

They sat there for a short time with the rotor blades still whirring. Then, as he looked out of the front window, Ellis saw the arms of the naval rating cross in front of his chest. Ellis assumed that all was okay; straightaway the pilot cut the engines the loud whirring sound of the rotor blades began to cease.

Shortly afterwards they disembarked. As they stepped out of the helicopter, they were met by a naval officer. He greeted each one of them by shaking their hands. He then turned and led them to a small group of officers who were waiting a little way from the helicopter.

'Gentlemen,' he said, as they approached the group. 'May I introduce you to our Commanding Officer, Captain Donald Ward?'

After being introduced to the Captain and the other two escorting officers, they were invited to accompany them to the wardroom. On arrival at the wardroom they were offered refreshments by the on duty steward. Tea, coffee, wine or beer was all on offer. After their long day in the sun everyone except the helicopter pilot chose a small beer.

After their refreshments, Captain Ward asked them to follow him. He took them through a door that was held open by a rating. As they stepped into the space beyond the door, they were directed into a lift. Once inside and secure the lift moved swiftly upwards before stopping at the programmed floor with a jolt.

As they stepped out of the lift, they realised they were in a hanger directly below the flight deck. They were amazed by what they saw. This was a space normally occupied by aircraft, forklift trucks, crates, boxes etc, but this hanger had been transformed. For a start the decor was white and bright; all round the outside structure was row upon row of metal frames with white plastic curtains hanging from them.

As they looked down the length of the hanger all they could see was row upon row of beds. Most of the beds seemed occupied; there were doctors and nurses all scurrying about. They all stood looking, amazed at a scene they had never seen before.

Ellis moved alongside Captain Ward and asked him if it was okay to do a short summary for *Star News*. The Captain agreed. Ellis signalled to Pete who quickly placed the microphone boom into position. Once Pete had given Ellis the thumbs up, Ellis went straight into his introduction, and then asked the Captain to summarise the role *HMS Illustrious* had been given by the British Government.

There was a moment of silence before Captain Ward spoke. 'Gentlemen, if you look behind me you will see our version of a field hospital. This is one of the roles we have been asked to fulfil. On board *HMS Illustrious* we have the full capability of dealing with many forms of injuries. We have two fully operational operating theatres that are manned by some of the finest medical specialists and nurses. As you can see the temporary wards we have set up are already 75 per cent occupied.

'Our other task is to use our helicopter fleet in any way that will assist the Italian Authorities in their quest to overcome the terrible disaster that has overwhelmed Naples and the surrounding area. The fleet is there to airlift injured personnel to the nearest suitable medical centre or take supplies to wherever they are required.' On that note Ellis thanked Captain Ward and terminated the interview.

At that point they all moved towards the lift where they would descend to a lower deck in readiness for their departure. Before they departed, the Captain suggested they came on board one evening with their partners for dinner. This he said would give them more time to continue their discussion on the current situation. He asked his first officer to make a note and to organise an evening.

As they all said their farewells to the Captain, his first lieutenant departed to organise a tender to take Ellis and the *Star* team to Marina Piccola. Whilst he did that, Ellis excused himself and rang Beth to organise a taxi to meet them.

On their way to board the tender the helicopter pilot bid them farewell. Before he left Colin, with his small knowledge of the Italian language, managed to make the pilot smile, and at the same time understand that they were all grateful to him for the last forty eight hours.

The ride on board the tender took only a few minutes. As they stepped ashore, Ellis spotted his name on a board being held aloft, he assumed by their taxi driver. They walked across to him. As they reached him Ellis held out his hand, before he could say anything, the man said.

'Mr Smeeth.'

'Si' replied Ellis.

The driver continued. 'I take you to Hotel Geranio.'

'Si, Si, please' said Ellis.

With that they loaded their bags and equipment into the people carrier and set off for the hotel. It only took a few minutes to reach the hotel. On arrival Ellis could see Beth sitting in one of the seats positioned by the hotel entrance. As they unloaded their baggage, Colin explained to the driver that the rest of the team were staying at the Hotel Pleassuro. 'No problem,' he replied. As the driver reorganised the baggage in the taxi, they bid farewell to each other and promised they would meet each other again at the dinner on board *HMS Illustrious*.

After they greeted one another, Beth helped Ellis with his bags. Together they walked through reception waving to Cirino as they went on their way to room 505 where Ellis relaxed in a large, bubble bath which he felt he deserved after his hectic couple of days. As he walked out of the bathroom into the main room, Beth had just finished putting a slice of lemon into a glass already half filled with gin and tonic. 'There you are, sir,' she said, with a smile on her face. 'I'm off for my bath, see you in a while.'

Soon they were both dressed and ready for the evening. During their meal Ellis mentioned the Captain's invitation for dinner and asked Beth to remind him to tell their friends later.

After dinner they joined the other six on the terrace. William informed them that some commercial flights would be operating out of Naples airport later this week. He added that he had heard, via Gino, that the holiday rep., Gavin, was going to discuss with everybody their preferential dates for travelling back to the UK.

Ellis mentioned the invitation for dinner on board *HMS Illustrious*. He said that it would probably be confirmed tomorrow. The invitation was for them all and the *Star Te*am. All the 'gang' enthused at the invitation.

Chapter Seventeen - Eruption plus 9

After breakfast on Monday morning Gavin, the holiday rep, and Beppe assembled all the guests for a ten o'clock meeting. Gavin placed a large folder on the highly polished top of the grand piano. Without hesitation he started to talk. 'Ladies and Gentlemen, I have invited you here this morning to inform you that some commercial flights will be operating again from Naples airport towards the end of this week. However, unfortunately it seems that there will be insufficient flights to ensure that all those people who were due to fly back to the UK this week can be accommodated.'

'What I need to do before I can identify those people who can fly back this week is to ask for volunteers to delay their return. Once I have that information I can draw up a schedule of departure dates and the people it will affect. Anybody who wishes to delay their return will be able to stay at the hotel. Any additional costs will be met by the holiday company.'

Gavin picked up the large folder from the top of the piano and pulled out a form. He held it in the air and asked that everyone should take one on the way out and fill it in before lunchtime tomorrow morning and then hand it in at the reception desk.

'That's all I have to say at the moment, thank you all for coming. I will be at one of the tables in reception for the next hour. If you have any further questions you wish to ask me, please see me there.' With that he and Beppe walked towards the lounge door.

Once they had collected their form, Ellis and Beth made their way to the pool. They decided they would have a cappuccino, and talk to the 'gang' about Gavin's proposal before continuing with their various tasks for the day. They didn't have long to wait and soon all their friends had joined them and they began discussing who wanted to go home and who wanted to stay. After much discussion, everyone seemed to have made a decision. Phillip and Bernice needed to return because of Bernice's aunt. Dene and Paula needed to return because of previously arranged family commitments. William and Sandie said they could stay but preferred to go if possible. Ellis and Beth were flexible; they said they would not take up the offer of a seat at the expense of any of the other six.

Once they had all completed their forms, they all went their separate ways. Beth went to the casualty unit to see Shona. Meanwhile Ellis visited reception to ask Gino if he would check with Rosa at the hospital to see if any more children had been identified from the photograph album. Gino made a note and promised to get back to Ellis as soon as he had any information.

With this still in mind Ellis went back to the room to collect the camera. He decided it was time to update the photograph album with any more new additions into the casualty unit. As he came back through reception, Gino called him to the desk to tell him that an officer from *HMS Illustrious* had called to confirm the dinner date which was for Tuesday evening. The message gave the time that a boat would pick them up at the Marina Piccola. After Ellis had read the message, he gave Colin's mobile number to Gino and asked him to give Colin the same details and confirm who was coming.

With that sorted, Ellis went through into the casualty unit. Beth was already working on the computer. Ellis headed for Shona and asked her for an update on new admissions, explaining that he wanted to update the photograph album. 'I'll get Carla to show you,' she said. Ellis followed her as she walked across the unit towards Carla.

'We have only had six new admissions since your last update,' reported Carla, after Shona had asked her the question.

'Okay', replied Ellis, 'let's go and take some pictures.' With that Carla took him to the first of the six.

In less than an hour Ellis had finished. 'Right I'll get the memory card to Vincenzo as soon as I can.' With that he set off to reception to give Gino the card to pass to Vincenzo when he next visited.

With that task accomplished, Ellis went back to the casualty unit to see Beth. She had just finished updating the database records. As they were talking, Shona came over. 'I'm glad I've got you both together. You have probably noticed that the activity has slowed down somewhat over the weekend.' They both nodded.

Shona went on to explain, that the majority of minor case injuries had now been identified and were being treated throughout the region. The number of those now being reported nine days after the eruption was very minimal. This would mean they would be receiving very few, if any new admissions. Consequently, the current workload of the unit was reducing.

'However,' she said, 'it has been suggested that once beds become available, we can use them to facilitate other children who have lost contact with their parents, relatives or friends. We will be used as a holding unit whilst efforts to trace the next of kin etc are in progress. We will continue to use the database to record these children, plus the photograph album as both will be invaluable. 'Finally, until that happens, you will probably find you do not need to spend as much time in the unit as you currently do, although the choice is yours and you are more than welcome.'

'That's fine by us', replied Ellis. Beth nodded. 'I suggest we visit you each morning for an update on your workload. We can then both plan the day ahead.'

They both bid Shona farewell and made for the pool area. On arrival they found their deck chairs positioned as normal on the shady side of the pool. Even with all the problems Marco the pool attendant had consistently ensured they were available for them.

Of the 'gang' only Phillip and Bernice were there at that moment so, after they had off-loaded their bits and pieces, they went across for a chat. Ellis asked the whereabouts of the others. Phillip explained that the others had no chores today so they had decided to go into town for the morning.

They sat talking to Phillip and Bernice. During this time Ellis confirmed that dinner on board *HMS Illustrious* would be tomorrow night. A naval launch would arrive at Marina Piccola at 7.30pm to take them to the carrier. The thought of that excited both Phillip and Bernice, 'As you have mentioned food,' Phillip said, 'we are going for lunch shortly. Would you care to join us?'

Ellis looked at his watch. 'Is that the time?' he said, and then looking at Beth, 'I think we could be up for that.'

Phillip and Bernice went ahead and found a suitable table as Ellis and Beth said they would freshen up and join them shortly. As they walked onto the terrace, Carlos welcomed them and escorted them to the table, leaving them the lunch-time menu.

When Carlos came back over to take their orders, they had all decided on more than a lunch-time snack. Phillip and Bernice both ordered king prawns, whilst Ellis went for the chicken l'orange Beth decided to forego her usual toasty, for a Capri Salad.

Halfway through lunch the other four entered the terrace. First came Dene and Paula followed closely by William and Sandie. Phillip beckoned them over as soon as he saw them to tell them about their dinner date aboard *HMS Illustrious.* Dene was delighted about the invite. 'You know,' he said. 'This has been the most extraordinary week.' 'Yes I agree replied Ellis, 'so let's ensure we enjoy this evening.'

Chapter Eighteen - Eruption plus 10

It was another clear blue sky that greeted Ellis and Beth when they rose from their beds on Tuesday morning. Normally they would have been up for at least an hour by then. However, after a leisurely day yesterday, they were both very relaxed and for once overslept.

Normally this would bother them. Not now, after what they had witnessed over the past few days, their keenness to always be punctual had been moved lower down their list of priorities. They had become more laid back than ever they had before.

After breakfast, they checked in at the casualty unit to see if Shona required any help. All was under control and very quiet so they were not needed. Shona did comment that she was expecting maybe four or five children tomorrow. These were to be the first of the children who had become separated from their parents or relatives. The unit when room permitted would be used to house these children until family relatives or friends could be found. Ellis and Beth left Shona telling her that they were at the pool if required.

They were the last to arrive at the pool and the other six were all either engrossed in reading their newspaper or a book. Once sorted Ellis started on the *Daily Mail* small crossword. This was it for the day as far as Ellis and Beth was concerned - sun, peace and good company.

Midway through the afternoon William ordered cappuccinos and ice creams for them all. This kept them going until they all decided at 5 o'clock it was time to retire to their rooms to prepare for their evening out. Whilst they were preparing to leave the pool, the ladies began discussing what they would wear that evening. They decided on dresses or long skirts and tops.

On hearing this, the gents discussed what they should wear. Dene jokingly suggested that they wore semi formal dark trousers a white short sleeved shirt and a black bow tie. Those who wanted to wear a jacket could. The rest of them laughed at first but then agreed it would be fun, until they realised that they did not have a bow tie. William said he would speak to the head waiter about obtaining bow ties for everyone. Ellis said he would speak to Colin about their plans.

With that settled they all made their way to their rooms.

Shortly after Beth went into the bathroom, the doorbell rang. Ellis opened the door. It was Oddjob, the house porter, he smiled at Ellis and handed him a black bow tie. 'Just in time, Grazie,' said Ellis smiling back. As he closed the door, he turned and held the bow tie up for Beth to see it. 'What will you all look like?' She said with a broad smile on her face.

On the stroke of 7 o'clock, Ellis and Beth reached the top of the stairs, arm in arm they walked towards the reception area. The other six were already there. The men were all wearing white shirts and black bow ties. Phillip and William, as expected, were wearing jackets. Not to be outdone the ladies stood alongside them dressed in all their finery.

As Ellis and Beth joined them, Beppe came out of his office. When he saw them, he raised both arms in the air and a large smile appeared on his face stretching from ear to ear. 'My friends,' he said, 'you all look so beautiful. I think the captain will like how you look. I hope you all enjoy your evening.'

'Mr Smeeth,' Ellis heard Gino calling, 'your taxi is here.'

With that they all moved towards the hotel entrance where parked outside was a large, white Mercedes people carrier. Once aboard the driver inched his way up the slope towards the hotel exit.

The evening traffic into Sorrento was just beginning to get congested. However, even with a few delays, they pulled into the Marina Piccola with eight minutes to spare. As they walked towards the departure area, they saw the *Star Team* waiting for them. They went over to them; all were smartly dressed and wore bow ties. Ellis introduced Colin, Pete and Steve to the rest of the 'gang' before they moved on.

As they walked forward, Dene pointed out a launch coming through the harbour entrance towards the docking area they were heading for. 'I think that's our transport,' said Dene joyfully.

They watched as the naval ratings skilfully manoeuvred the 30 feet launch alongside the jetty. Once they were satisfied two of them jumped onto the jetty, and each with a long pole held the front and rear of the launch steady whilst they all stepped onboard.

They were met by an officer who introduced himself as Lieutenant Clarkson. He beckoned them to take a seat. As they sat down, they all remarked at the red leather padding that covered the seats and were impressed by the highly polished wood of the interior.

The concern of all of them before boarding the launch was how comfortable a ride they would have en route to *HMS Illustrious*. Fortunately the sea was very calm with very little swell. Within ten minutes they were coming alongside the massive carrier, the launch headed towards a large opening half way along the ship's side. As with the jetty the two ratings manoeuvred the launch alongside the disembarking platform.

First off were the two ratings that again held the launch steady. They were followed by Lieutenant Clarkson who stood at the side of the platform and assisted everybody as they stepped from the launch.

'Ladies and Gentlemen, would you please follow me?' he said in a very imposing voice. They all followed on through a door being held open by a rating. As they stepped into the space beyond the door, they realised they were in the bottom of an enormous deck hanger. It was three quarters full, mainly containing large crates and boxes.

After a short ride in the lift, they were surprised to see four naval officers all dressed in their white uniforms waiting for them. Ellis immediately recognised Captain Donald Ward as he stepped forward and introduced himself; he followed this by introducing the other three officers. When he had finished, Ellis took it upon himself to do the honours on behalf of the guests. He quickly introduced the rest of the 'gang' and the *Star Team*.

With the formalities over the Captain, pointed out that they were on the main flight deck of the carrier. 'Before we go to the wardroom, let me show you where you are.' With that he walked across the flight deck to the rails on the other side. They all followed behind, on reaching the rails he pointed to the shore. 'Do you recognise that white building?' he asked. They all looked. It was the Hotel Geranio standing proudly on the edge of the cliff; Ellis immediately took out his camera and took a photograph. As he did so, the captain suggested they made their way to the wardroom.

After using another lift, and a short walk, they arrived at the wardroom. They were met inside by a wardroom attendant who offered them a drink from a silver tray. There were two choices - champagne or fresh orange juice. Once everybody had a drink, another attendant came in carrying a large tray of canapés. Very soon everybody was relaxed and beginning to enjoy the surroundings.

As they all stood there sipping their champagne and nibbling their canapès, the Captain gave them a guided tour of this part of the wardroom, explaining the history behind wardrooms and showing them much of the memorabilia that was positioned on shelves and walls.

When he had finished his impromptu guided tour, Captain Ward mentioned that on the side tables there were copies of the dinner menu. He asked if they would spend a few moments looking at them, so that the attendant could take their orders before they went through into the dining room. Ellis picked up a menu. He was very impressed by the wide selection of the dishes.

It didn't take Ellis long to choose. He went for the grilled parcels of Mozzarella cheese wrapped in Parma ham, served with a mixed Italian salad. He chose the Sea Bass with new potatoes and fresh vegetables, as his main course. Beth's starter was to be Leek and Potato soup with croutons, followed by English lamb new potatoes, and fresh vegetables. Dessert would be from the sweet trolley.

Once orders had been taken the other attendant came to take orders for aperitifs. Ellis opted for a gin and tonic whilst Beth stayed with an orange juice. By now everybody was beginning to relax and enjoy themselves. The chattering noise level within the wardroom had definitely increased by a decibel or two. This was also accompanied by occasional laughter.

Suddenly without warning there was a double bang, as one of the officers struck the table with a gavel. In a loud voice he then pronounced dinner would now be served and the double doors to the dining room opened. They were escorted into the dining room by one of the officers and guided to their table by an attendant. Everybody stood behind their chair as the Captain and his first officer entered last and made their way to the middle of the table. They paused for a few seconds behind their chairs before the Captain said, 'Ladies and Gentlemen, I am very pleased to see you all here this evening. Please be seated and let us all enjoy ourselves.'

No sooner had they sat down than the wine waiter appeared asking each person their preference for red or white wine. Once that was completed the starters were served, by two waiters. Once the last dish was set down on the table, Captain Ward raised his glass and proposed a happy evening.

All was quiet for the first few minutes as everybody began to eat. Within minutes a gentle buzz began to emanate through the room as people began to comment on their food. As they moved on to the main course and their wine glasses began to empty a more jovial atmosphere started to take over. Ellis in particular was beginning to cause a few laughs with some of the stories he was telling.

The evening progressed well; all were enjoying the meal immensely. When everybody thought their meal was over, the waiters brought out two large cheeseboards and decanters of port. At the appropriate moment, the Captain tapped his glass with a spoon and stood up. 'Ladies and Gentlemen, may I ask you to stand for the loyal toast.' Everybody stood, at which point the Captain turned to a portrait of Queen Elizabeth II and holding his glass in the air he proposed the Queen. In unison they all replied, 'The Queen.'

'Whilst I am on my feet,' Captain Ward said, 'I would just like to say a few words to you all. I have invited you all this evening so that I could show you how much your work over the last 10 days has been appreciated. Not only have you all been at the forefront of helping children who had been injured and separated from family and friends, some of you went further afield and with the aid of *Star News* brought the effect of the Vesuvius eruption into millions of homes throughout the world. I would like to pass on to you all the thanks of the British Government who has called you "true ambassadors of your country".'

As he sat down, there was a tapping of hands on the table and a response of thank you from those seated. Ellis went a little further because he stood to reply to Captain Ward's speech. After thanking the captain for his kind words, he summarised briefly the events of the last 10 days, particularly the tasks where they had played a role. Some of those tasks had not been pleasant. However, when looking at the wider picture, Ellis stated they were insignificant compared to what the people in the Naples area had suffered. He concluded by thanking Captain Ward, his officers and crew for this evening and in particular the chefs for such a wonderful meal.

They spent another hour in the wardroom before making their way up onto the flight deck to view the Naples and Sorrento coastline by night.

It was after 11 o'clock as they prepared to board the launch. Captain Ward and his immediate officers were there to see them off. Once the farewells were complete the launch pulled slowly away from the carrier. As the launch picked up speed, Ellis called the night porter Benigno on his mobile phone to ask him to organise a taxi.

As they stepped off the launch at Marina Piccola, they could see that the white Mercedes was already waiting for them. Soon they were all walking through the entrance to the Hotel Geranio. As they walked through into the reception area, the night porter, was on duty and he bade them all 'Buona Notta' as they filed past en route to their rooms.

'Well,' said Dene, as they all arrived at the foot of the stairs. 'That's a night to remember, and tell our grandchildren about.' They all agreed with that, and bid each other goodnight.

Once inside their room Ellis and Beth changed straight into their night attire. Beth put the kettle on, and Ellis helped himself to a nightcap. Before retiring for the evening, they went out on to the balcony to have another look at *HMS Illustrious*. She was out there sitting in the middle of the Bay of Naples, as Ellis looked at her he understood why she was the flagship of the Royal Navy.

As they climbed into bed he looked at his watch; it was just after midnight.

Chapter Nineteen - Eruption plus 11

Ellis and Beth were late arriving at the pool on Wednesday morning. They had called in on the casualty unit to check Shona's workload. She was pleased to see them as they had received three new patients late on Tuesday afternoon. These children were not physically injured but the whereabouts of their parents or relatives was currently unknown. Whilst there was room at the casualty unit, it had been decided it would also serve as a refuge for displaced children.

Before they left the unit Beth updated the database. Whilst she was doing this Ellis fetched the camera and took photographs of the three children. As they left, Ellis informed Shona that he would take the memory card to reception for Vincenzo to pick up later. Hopefully he could update the photograph album by Friday.

As Ellis and Beth arrived at the pool, the main topic of conversation amongst the rest of the 'gang' was last evening's visit to *HMS Illustrious*. Once they had finished discussing the visit it was time for cappuccinos. After their drinks Ellis rang Peter back in Rugby to inform him that they were planning to fly back on Monday barring any last minute hitches. Before he rang off he advised he would ring on Sunday to confirm the flight times.

Between their cappuccinos and lunch time, Ellis and Beth lounged around the pool, swimming and perusing the *Daily Mail* small crossword.

They decided to lunch at the hotel, and when Carlos signalled that tables were becoming occupied they made their way to the terrace. They spent the next one and a half hours eating drinking and talking to anybody who would listen to them.

Once they were back at the pool and seated in their deck chairs, both Ellis and Beth were soon fast asleep. It was late afternoon before they awoke. Soon after they collected their belongings and departed to their room.

Whilst they were sitting in their room Beth reminded Ellis that he needed to speak to Angioletto that evening to clarify tomorrow night's anniversary meal. Ellis nodded and agreed he would take care of it tonight.

Chapter Twenty - Eruption plus 12

Thursday was the last day that the whole 'gang' would spend together that holiday. It started like all other days. Breakfast first, then down to the pool to set up the sun beds and deck chairs, before each couple decided what they were going to do.

Ellis and Beth had decided on a day by the pool, whilst the other six at different times were going to do some last minute shopping. Before they all departed, Ellis reminded them of their anniversary meal that night. With the day sorted they all went their separate ways, agreeing to meet again at lunch time.

Whilst their friends were away from the hotel that morning, Ellis and Beth enjoyed their time around the pool swimming and taking in the warm sunshine. Ellis as usual had found a young couple with a small child to talk to. When Beth saw him talking to them she smiled to herself, thinking that if they did not know their way around the hotel or Sorrento, they soon would.

Phillip and Bernice were the first to arrive back shortly after 11 o'clock. They were just in time to catch Ellis who was about to order cappuccinos from Marco.

William and Sandie were next, followed ten minutes later by Dene and Paula. They all congregated around Ellis and Beth and spent the next fifteen minutes displaying what they had bought.

Once that was completed, they all agreed it was time for lunch. Couple by couple they made their way to the terrace to be met by Carlos and Dario. As Carlos pulled Beth's chair away from the table, he asked if they required their normal drinks. Ellis confirmed they did.

After lunch they made their way back to the pool, they were soon joined by the others. Shortly afterwards Bebbe appeared by the pool with a number of people. On seeing the 'gang' all together, he walked across to them, and said, 'my friends may I introduce you to the Mayor of Sorrento, his wife and some of our local council officials. They have come to speak with you all before you go back home.'

The Mayor started to speak, shaking each one of their hands as he did. For the next thirty minutes with the aid of some translation by Beppe, they all thanked the 'gang' for their help to the children and people of Naples. They wished them all well and hoped they would come back to Sorrento next year. Ellis assured them that they all would.

After Beppe and his guests moved away to the other side of the pool the 'gang' decided it was time for cappuccinos or ice cream. William gave Marco the signal.

The eight of them stayed around the pool all afternoon before departing to their rooms. They agreed to meet in reception at 7.30pm en route to the dining room.

Back in their room Beth decided on a cup of tea and half an hour on the balcony with a book. Ellis also decided on the balcony but went for a bottle of beer in preference to a cup of tea.

An hour later, Beth stirred herself from the balcony and announced she was going to use the bathroom. 'Call me when you have finished, please?' Ellis asked.

Whilst he was waiting, Ellis switched on the television for a news update. He was just in time, as Charles Small handed over to a *Star News* reporter in Naples. The reporter was just announcing the release of the latest video footage, showing the route the pyroclastic flow took through Naples and the surrounding district.

Ellis was still contemplating the scenes being shown when Beth came out of the bathroom announcing that she had finished.

Ellis picked up his electric razor and made for the bathroom. Twenty five minutes later he emerged in his white bathrobe. Both were soon ready and dressed waiting to go upstairs, at twenty five past seven they decided it was time to go. They were the first to arrive in the reception area but within two minutes everyone else was there.

They made their way downstairs into the dining room where they were met by Angioletto. He led them to a large round table that was set for eight people.

As they sat down, Giraldo, the head waiter, appeared with a silver bucket of ice and a large bottle of champagne. As he filled each glass, he told them that the champagne was from Beppe and Perla.

Whilst Giraldo was doing this, Angioletto handed everybody the evening menu. Everybody was silent for the next few minutes as they studied the menu.

Once their orders had been taken, William picked up his glass of champagne and announced. 'I would like you all to raise your glass to Ellis and Beth on their achievement in reaching 50 years of marriage.' With a smile on his face he said. 'I think Beth deserves a medal.' He nodded to Angioletto who came across and handed Beth a gift wrapped box. William continued, 'On behalf of all of your friends around the table please accept this gift from us in celebration of your anniversary, and of our friendship. May you both enjoy each other's company for many years to come.' With that they all stood raising their glasses and said in unison. 'To Beth and Ellis.'

Before Ellis responded, Beth was persuaded to open the parcel. On doing so she revealed a Capodimonte statuette of a fine female figure. Once she had brushed away the tears Beth thanked everybody.

It was now Ellis' turn. He thanked them for the present, and for making the evening so memorable, adding that it was something Beth and he would always treasure. Thanking Angioletto and his staff for a wonderful evening in such difficult circumstances, he concluded by wishing all their friends a safe journey home and looked forward to seeing them all again next year if not before.

They all sat around the table till after 10 o'clock. Afterwards they departed to the terrace where Carlos served them more drinks until midnight. By then they decided with an early start to the airport tomorrow morning it was time to retire. Those leaving queued up to say their goodbyes to a tearful Carlos.

Chapter Twenty One - Eruption plus 13

Friday July 21 2012 was a day that Ellis and Beth would remember for a long time. That was the day that the other six members of the 'gang' were going home, whilst they stayed until Monday.

It was 8 o'clock when they arrived in the reception area to see the others depart. They had not yet had breakfast so they decided to eat after they had said farewell to the others. All six of them were leaving by taxi at 08.30; their flights all departed within one and a half hours of each other.

As they sat there waiting for them to emerge, Beppe entered the hotel removing his scooter crash helmet as he did. After he put his belongings into his office he came over and spoke to them, 'It weel be your turn on Monday.' They both smiled.

Before they could continue the conversation, Beth spotted all six coming from the direction of the breakfast room. They came over to where Ellis, Beppe and Beth were sitting. As they arrived, Beppe excused himself, saying as he left he would see them before they departed.

Whilst they waited for the taxis to arrive, they discussed the past fourteen days, and the dramas they had witnessed. Dene commented that to wait another year before seeing each other again was too long. He suggested they organised a weekend together before Xmas. Everybody was in agreement.

Very soon the taxis started to arrive and Gino began calling their names out. William and Sandie were the first, soon to be followed by the other four. Beppe and Perla came out of their office and began hugging each one of them in turn.

As they finished, Ellis and Beth went over to say their farewells. It was Beth that started the tears rolling, as soon as she kissed and hugged Dene and Paula. Tears rolled down her cheeks soon to be followed by everybody else, even Beppe and Perla could be seen wiping their eyes. They followed their cases out through the hotel entrance, then turned and gave one last wave. Ellis and Beth waved back and watched as the taxis moved slowly up the slope and out through the gates of the hotel en route to the airport.

As Ellis and Beth turned to go to the breakfast terrace they saw Gino wiping his eyes with a handkerchief. He saw them looking at him, and quickly removed the handkerchief and put it in his pocket. 'Mr and Mrs Smeeth you are very unhappy to see your friends go?'

'Yes we are,' replied Ellis, 'but thankfully we are all going home safe and well, unlike many people from Naples.'

They left Gino, who nodded in understanding, and made their way through to the terrace for breakfast. It was probably their quietest breakfast in the two weeks since they had been there. Neither of them spoke very much. When they did it was mostly about their friends who had just departed.

Once they finished their cappuccino, Ellis suggested they checked with Shona on her workload for today, adding. 'If we are not required let's spend the morning in town and do some shopping.'

Beth perked up at that suggestion. 'Good idea, let's go and see Shona.'

Shona confirmed that everything was under control and that they were not required today. With that they departed to their room to freshen up before making their way upstairs to reception. Cirino was now on duty, as they arrived at the reception desk, he called to them. 'Mr Smeeth, Gino has left a message for you. Vincenzo will pick up the photo card this afternoon.'

'Grazie', Ellis replied and then said to Beth, 'That's all sorted then. Let's go shopping.' She nodded in agreement and they headed out of the hotel. An orange bus came into view, and they moved quickly to the bus stop, and boarded it. Once inside Ellis inserted their tickets into the ticket machine. There was a double click as the tickets were clipped and date stamped.

They soon arrived at Piazza Tasso and, after a little thought, they decided they would wander away from the centre, and head into the small cobbled streets of the 'drain'. Particularly at this time as not many people ventured into town so early.

The first shop they encountered was one that sold all leather products, particularly hand bags. Beth made that her first port of call as she had been asked by a friend to purchase one for her.

Once inside she made straight for the racks of handbags. Ellis left her to it whilst he looked at the numerous leather belts that ranged from three euros to thirty euros.

Within a few minutes he had bought two belts. It was another fifteen minutes before Beth emerged with two designer type bags. Under interrogation she confessed that one was for her friend and one for herself.

They wandered down the narrow cobbled street. The proprietors of the shops were all washing down their piece of walkway. The fruit and vegetable stores were being topped up with the fresh produce of the day. Ellis never got tired of the smell of fresh fruit and those large Italian tomatoes.

It took them over one hour to reach the end of the 'drain'. Once there they turned left and walked onto the main street, the Corso Italia. They immediately felt the effect of the bright sunlight, so they crossed over the road onto the shadier side. The pharmacy thermometer was already indicating 25 degrees centigrade. They decided to walk back towards the Piazza Tasso; in the back of their minds was the Fauna Bar, where they anticipated they would stop for a cappuccino.

On reaching the Fauno bar two people vacated a roadside table. Moving quickly they claimed it before anyone else. They sat there whilst a waiter removed the existing table cloth and replaced it with a newly laundered one. This procedure took place every time a new customer sat at a previously occupied table.

Once he had completed that task the waiter took their order. The order was tapped into a small hand held electronic device that sent it directly to the bar. Before he left the waiter enquired when they were going home. 'Monday,' Beth replied. As they finished the conversation with the waiter, their cappuccinos arrived. He smiled and started to move away saying as he did. 'Enjoy the rest of your holiday.'

They spent an enjoyable thirty minutes people watching, as they drank their cappuccinos whilst nibbling the cookie biscuits that were served with every order.

Before they left the bar, they decided to look in at the jeweller's shop less than one hundred metres from where they were sitting. Beth had seen a pair of gold earrings that had taken her fancy. Ellis wasn't over keen as he had noticed the price tag. Ellis paid the waiter and gave him a small tip as they left the table and headed for the jeweller's shop.

It didn't take Beth many minutes to make up her mind on her choice of earrings. Ellis coughed when he saw the price. Even though he haggled with the proprietor and reduced the price, he still felt he had been mugged. Beth wasn't too bothered as she put her latest purchase carefully into her handbag. The proprietor opened the door for them, wishing them well and saying with a broad smile. 'I see you again.' Ellis muttered under his breath, 'Not if I have anything to do with it.' He received a little kick on his shin from Beth as he said it.

As they left the shop, Ellis asked, 'Shall we lunch at the tennis club today?'

'Yes,' Beth replied. 'That's fine by me.' With that they crossed the road and began heading back.

Fifteen minutes later they were walking up the slope to the entrance of the tennis club. As they sat down at a table, Maura saw them and came over. They were given her customary hug before she gave them a menu. Shortly afterwards Fernando came across to take their order. Ellis ordered a large Peroni beer and a chicken salad; Beth went for an orange juice and the tomato salad.

When they arrived back at the pool, Beth commented how strange it was that none of their friends were there. It was strange to see other people sitting in the places normally occupied by William, Sandie, Phillip and Bernice. The two deck chairs to the left of them were also empty; Marco had put them out for Dene and Paula not aware that they were leaving that morning.

They both had an empty feeling as they sat down in their deck chairs. However, they soon put their feelings to one side as a couple they had seen around the hotel asked them if the deck chairs were taken. Ellis confirmed they were available and began telling them that the normal occupants had flown home that morning.

Beth shook her head and smiled to herself, thinking if they start to ask Ellis about Dene and Paula they will get the history of Sorrento holidays going back over the past years. She listened intently to try and hear what their next question would be.

Fortunately it was the other way round; this was their first holiday in Sorrento so it was Ellis who had to listen to their experiences. Thank goodness for that Beth said to herself. Whilst Ellis spoke to the couple, Beth became engrossed in her book.

They spent the rest of the afternoon by the pool Beth all but finished reading her book, whilst Ellis became engrossed in the *Daily Mail* crossword. They stayed till he had finished the crossword before going back to their room. On arrival Beth headed straight for the balcony to finish her book before preparing herself for the evening.

Ellis decided to catch up with the events of the day and switched *Star News* on. The first item was the latest official fatality figures for the Vesuvius eruption; these were standing at 320,000. The Newsreader stated that *Star* sources close to the Italian Government believed that the final number dead would be around half a million people. Ellis shook his head and went to the mini bar to get a drink.

When Beth came in from the balcony thirty minutes later, Ellis told her about the latest fatality figures. She reacted the same way that Ellis had.

They were both still feeling down after the departure of their friends. So after dinner they went for a short walk into Piazzo Lauro and did some window shopping.

As they dawdled their way back to the hotel via the Corso Italia, Ellis mentioned to Beth that he had given a lot of thought to her comments about Jamie and the children. Without fully committing himself he agreed that when they got back home they would discuss it with all the family.

'What made you come to that decision?' enquired Beth. 'There are disadvantages and advantages,' replied Ellis, 'however; living with us at our present home is a non starter. Firstly there would be insufficient sleeping room, and we would be always be on top of one another. With Emily approaching the age of 16 and Matthew 12, both of them are going to require their own bedrooms. Jamie really needs her own bedsitter type room. Just those few areas identify to me that the only option would be for both of us to sell up and purchase a larger property bearing those requirements in mind.'

Okay,' Beth said, with a slightly surprised tone to her voice. 'I suggest we say no more about it till we get home.' Ellis nodded in agreement and they both crossed the road with a brisk step in their walk.

Chapter Twenty Two - Eruption plus 14

With two days left before they were to depart for home, Ellis and Beth spent Saturday and Sunday trying to fully occupy themselves rather than just sitting around the pool. Over breakfast on Saturday morning they decided they would walk down to the Marina Grande, spend the morning there and have lunch before returning.

Thirty five minutes later they arrived by the side of the jetty at the Marina Grande. As they passed by the small Catholic Church that served that community, they heard singing so they decided to look inside. They entered through the large wooden door and sat down in the last row of pews. In front of the altar were a number of young children who were singing. Ellis and Beth sat there quietly listening. It continued for at least another five minutes. As it finished, they were both tempted to applaud but decided against it.

They quietly left the church and wandered around looking at the souvenir shops and reading the menus of the sea front restaurants.

Reading the menus made them feel hungry, with the time approaching noon they decided to lunch early. As they walked onto the pontoon of the small restaurant they had chosen, they were met by the proprietor. He led them to a table and they ordered their drinks and meal. Two hours later they finished their last drinks paid their bill, and decided to head back towards town.

It was after 4 o'clock when they walked through the entrance to the hotel. They decided to go straight to their room and relax before preparing for the evening; Beth decided to spend some time relaxing on the balcony with a book and a cup of tea. Ellis switched on the television to catch up on the day's news.

Joanne Birch the Star Newscaster was talking about Italy and the London Olympics' due to be held during August. Wondering what that was about, Ellis' eyes was drawn to the 'Breaking News' at the bottom of the screen. It read:

THE ITALIAN GOVERNMENT HAS JUST ANNOUNCED THE WITHDRAWAL OF THE NATIONAL TEAM FROM

THE OLYMPIC GAMES TO BE HELD IN LONDON
DURING AUGUST.

As he was reading that a further statement followed, it read:
'THE ITALIAN GOVERNMENT HAS JUST ANNOUNCED
THAT FATALITIES HAVE NOW REACHED 400,000.'

***

That evening they decided to make their last visit to town rather
than the following night. They spent two hours browsing around
the shops, and then decided on a last stop at the Fauna Bar. They
spent some time there before heading back to the hotel. They
arrived back shortly after midnight. They made straight for their
room, once there they prepared themselves for bed and retired.

Chapter Twenty Three - Eruption plus 15

When Ellis awoke on Sunday morning Beth was already up. She was out on the balcony with a cup of tea and a book in her hand. 'What is the time now?' she enquired.

'Coming up to 6.30,' Ellis replied.

'I'll finish this chapter then I'll get ready,' said Beth.

'Okay, I'll use the bathroom first you can follow me, then we'll go for breakfast,' commented Ellis.

After breakfast they headed for the casualty unit to see if Shona needed any help.

On entering the unit they noticed a young boy in the far corner of the room sobbing; both Shona and Carla were with him. They went over towards his bed. Once he came into view they realised that he was one of the new admissions. He was not injured but was separated from his parents.

They were about to ask Shona why he was crying when they noticed he had the album open at his photograph. Beth asked what the problem was.

Shona explained that shortly after Ellis gave her the updated photograph album on Saturday morning, Carla was about to pay a visit to the Sorrento Hospital so she had taken the photographs with her to show to any new admissions. Once her business was concluded Carla began showing the photographs.

It was when she showed it to a third person there was a reaction very similar to the one they had during their first visit to the hospital. It was from a woman in her mid thirties. She recognised the boy in the photograph whom they were now looking at. Unfortunately Carla was not able to take a photograph of the woman as she did not have a camera. However, after explaining to the woman that he was in good health and he was being looked after at the Hotel Geranio, the woman calmed down. Carla explained what they were trying to do, and asked if she had anything they could borrow to show the boy she claimed was her son. The woman took a locket from around her neck. She opened it. Inside were pictures of two very young children. The woman indicated one of those was the boy in the photograph that Rosa had showed her.

The woman gave Carla the locket saying that her boy would recognise that.

As they stood by the bed, Shona told them that they had held back showing the locket to the boy on Saturday afternoon as he had become agitated, so they gave him a mild sedative. She said he slept well through the night and seemed more relaxed so they had showed him the locket only a few minutes ago.

After a discussion between the four of them, it was decided that Carla would take the boy to see his mother that afternoon. When Shona told him of the planned visit, he started to cry again. However, this time they were tears of joy. He threw his arms around Shona and hugged her so tightly that she thought he would never let go. As he began to settle down, Ellis and Beth left the unit. They told Shona and Carla they would call back that afternoon to say their farewells to them.

They lunched at the tennis club that afternoon saying their goodbyes to Maura and Fernando. It was a very emotional farewell and when the hugging and kissing had finished Ellis and Beth walked away with tears in their eyes.

That was just the start of an emotional afternoon that was to follow them right through the evening as they bid farewell to many people. They began with going to the casualty unit to see Shona and Carla. They arrived there just as Carla arrived back from the hospital. As they went inside and met Shona, Carla confirmed that the woman at the hospital was the mother of the boy who they had shown the locket to that morning.

They walked around the unit and the four of them chatted and reminisced about the last two weeks. Shona and Carla told them that they had been asked to stay on and operate the unit until all the children had been reunited with relatives or friends. Both said they had agreed.

On reaching the door to the reception area, they stopped. Ellis turned to both of them, saying as he did. 'Well this is where we have to say our goodbyes.' With that he kissed and hugged both

Shona and Carla in turn, doing his utmost not to show too much emotion. When it came to Beth's turn she found it very difficult. Initially everything was okay but as soon as she turned to Carla and saw her facial expression Beth could contain herself no longer.

Once the farewells were over, they left the unit quickly. Both were visibly upset as they walked out through the reception area. Ellis suggested they went to the pool and bid farewell to Marco.

As they walked up the steps to the pool area they could see Marco in his cabin at the far end of the pool.

'Mr and Mrs Smeeth, how are you?' he asked, as they came towards him. 'We have come to say goodbye,' Ellis said. 'We fly home tomorrow.' Marco came out of his cabin and shook both of them by the hand. As he shook his hand, Ellis gave him a ten euro note.

With that the last farewell of the afternoon they headed back to their room.

Whilst Beth sorted out more items for packing, Ellis sat on the balcony enjoying the afternoon sunshine. He looked across the bay towards Naples visualising the scene less than 20 kilometres away from where he was sitting.

He came back to life with a jolt when he heard Beth suddenly calling him. 'Shall we go for an early dinner this evening?'

'Yes, let's,' replied Ellis.

As they entered the dining room, Angioletto the maitre d' was there waiting to greet them as he had done every evening. They spent a few minutes talking to him before they moved on towards their table.

As on previous nights, the waiters were standing together to form two lines. They were then ready to bid anybody who walked between them, Buona Sera, (good evening). Tonight, as they approached them, Ellis sensed something was different. He was right, as they walked between the waiters Giraldo the head waiter was waiting to greet them. He led them to their table. There was a large box of chocolates and a bottle of wine sitting on it. 'Mr and Mrs Smeeth, these are for you from all of us in the restaurant. We thank you for your help during the terrible times of the past two weeks.'

Ellis and Beth choked up for a few seconds. Ellis turned to the waiters saying as he did Molte Grazie (thank you very much).

That evening seemed very special to them. They took longer than normal over their meal. Before saying their farewells to all the staff, they shook hands with the maitre d' Angioletto Ellis handed him an envelope. 'This is a little something for you and your staff for looking after us so well once again,' Ellis said. Angioletto nodded.

'Only Carlos to see now,' said Ellis, as they made their way to the terrace. On arrival Carlos saw them and took them to a table, 'Last night for you and your wife, Mr Smeeth.'

'Afraid so,' Ellis replied.

As they waited for Carlos to return with their drinks, Ellis decided to ring Peter in Rugby to confirm flight details for tomorrow. Carlos arrived with the drinks just as he finished the call.

They stayed on the terrace all evening where they spent some time with people they had met during the last two weeks. Towards the latter part of the evening Carlos spent some time talking to them. As the time approached 11 o'clock, they decided it was time to leave.

Ellis went through the protocol of giving Carlos some euros in an envelope. Carlos responded by hugging them both and with sadness in his voice he bid them farewell. 'I will miss you and your lovely wife next week,' he said.

'And we will miss you,' Ellis replied, giving Carlos a hug back.

They made one more stop at reception to say cheerio to Benigno the night porter as they made their way down the staircase to their room. Once there they put on their night clothes and spent the next thirty minutes relaxing before retiring for the evening.

Chapter Twenty Four - Eruption plus 16

Neither Ellis nor Beth needed waking on Monday morning; both were up and ready for breakfast by 6.30. Once Beth had finished packing leaving out only their toothpaste and brushes, they set off for breakfast.

With blue skies and the sun shining they were again able to eat outside on the terrace. With a long day ahead they enjoyed a full breakfast complimented with a cappuccino.

Although they had said their farewells to the dining room staff the previous night, as they made their way out of the dining room they spoke briefly to Giraldo and the two waiters who were on duty that morning.

With the taxi due at 8.30 they had thirty minutes to tidy themselves up, clean their teeth and get a porter to take their cases upstairs. This was soon accomplished and by 8.15 they were upstairs ready to say their farewells to the reception staff.

They were all there: Gino, Cirino and Saverio. As they arrived, they came from behind the reception desk to give Ellis and Beth the traditional Italian kiss on both cheeks. It was quite an emotional scene that became even more moving, when co-owners Beppe and Perla emerged from the office to say their farewells to Ellis and Beth.

Although both Ellis and Beth's eyes were watering, it was Beppe who seemed to be more emotional than anybody. There was a definite sob in Beppe's voice as he shook them both by the hand, saying as he did. 'Mr and Mrs Smeeth, you did not expect the activities of the last two weeks when you arrived. I thank you both for the help you gave us. I wish you a safe journey home. Pleese come and visit us again next year.'

With that he turned away, just as Gino called out. 'Mr Smeeth, your taxi is here.'

As they made their way towards the exit, Ellis recognised the driver. It was Giuseppe the same driver who had brought them from the airport just over two weeks ago. On reaching the exit they turned and gave a last wave to the remaining staff. As they did, Oddjob passed them with their cases stacked on his sack barrow.

Within two minutes the cases were placed in the boot of the white Mercedes. Ellis and Beth got into the rear seats fastening their seat belts as they did.

Giuseppe took his place behind the wheel started the engine and the taxi moved slowly up the slope and through the entrance gates of the hotel.

Neither, Ellis and Beth looked back. They knew that to do so would stir the emotions again.

The taxi glided away from the hotel. At the first junction Giuseppe turned left. He was taking the back way towards 'Sant'Agnello' before picking up the coast road towards Naples. In less than ten minutes they were through 'Sant'Agnello' and turning on to the coast road. As they did, Ellis noticed the road sign which showed 45 kilometres to Naples.

Soon they arrived at Bikini Beach. As always the green plastic palm tree was sitting in the middle of the small bay. 'I'll text Louise and tell her where we are,' Ellis said. Beth nodded as she heard him.

As he finished the text, Ellis looked at Beth and saw that her eyes were closed and her head was resting on the back of the seat. Ellis said nothing.

Giuseppe drove the Mercedes at a sensible speed and ignored the temptation to sound his horn at other drivers who contemptuously overtook on blind bends.

All through the journey what was left of Vesuvius could be seen still sitting on Mount Somma. Whilst Beth dozed, Ellis sat looking out through the car window at Vesuvius thinking about all the terrible devastation that it had caused.

The taxi continued with the journey. Soon they had gone through the last of the three tunnels. After that they were soon to join the dual carriageway to Naples.

On joining the dual carriageway Beth stirred and woke up. They moved with the flow of the traffic, and Ellis saw the first sign for the airport. A few minutes later Giuseppe manoeuvred the Mercedes into the right hand lane, heading for the airport entrance. Ellis noted that the journey so far had taken only 55 minutes.

Soon the taxi had pulled up outside the departures entrance. Giuseppe lifted their cases from the boot of the Mercedes. As they shook hands, Ellis gave him a ten euro note, thanking him as he did. Once inside the departures building they saw the holiday rep who beckoned them into a short queue.

The check-in desks were operating very efficiently. Before many minutes had passed Ellis and Beth were handing their passports and flight tickets to the attendant. Once that was completed they made their way up the escalator and then through the security checkpoint and onto passport control.

On arrival they were waved straight through by the official who only glanced at their passports. That took them directly towards the departure lounge seating area where they soon found two seats adjacent to the loading gate 12B. As they sat down all they wanted to happen now, was to hear flight ITAL 5254 for Birmingham Airport to be called.

The digital wall clock had just moved to 10:45, when the tannoy system asked passengers flying to Birmingham Airport on ITAL 5254 to proceed to gate 12B. Ellis and Beth rose from their seats and walked the few metres towards their gate.

Within a few minutes the airport staff were checking tickets and recording passengers into their computer. Once they were checked in Ellis and Beth walked through the outside door and boarded the airport bus waiting to take them to the aircraft. It took only a few minutes for passengers to fill the bus. The driver climbed into his cab closing the hydraulically operated doors. After a short pause, the bus moved away from the terminal and headed across the airfield.

They had plenty of time to find their seats and stow their hand luggage. It would be many minutes before the next batch of passengers arrived.

By 11.20 Naples time it seemed that all passengers were onboard. This was confirmed five minutes later when the aircraft stewards began closing the doors.

The cabin intercom system crackled into life once the plane had reached the beginning of the runway. A voice spoke saying, 'Good

Morning, this is Captain Clarke speaking. We will be shortly taking off for Birmingham Airport. Our flight time is estimated at two and three quarters hours, we should arrive at Birmingham at 1.15pm local time thank you.'

Ellis turned to Beth. 'That is the same Captain that flew us here 17 days ago.'

Beth smiled, thinking to herself, 'What a memory for detail.'

Very soon after the announcement the engine revs of the Boeing 757 increased as the aircraft began moving swiftly down the runway. Within a short time the aircraft lifted off the runway and began climbing into the sky. They continued to climb whilst the aircraft banked slightly to the right as the pilot adjusted its position. After three more minutes of climbing and the aircraft in a level position, the cabin intercom 'ping ponged' at the same time that the 'Fasten your seat belt sign' went off.

Ellis leant back onto the head rest. As he did he said to himself, 'If I wrote a novel about what we have experienced over the last seventeen days, critics would say it was too far-fetched.'

As the aircraft engines droned on, Ellis thought of home. He felt his eyes closing and blinked in an attempt to stay awake. Within a few minutes he was sound asleep. Beth turned to say something to him. She looked at him and smiling to herself thought, 'He'll earn a few drinks back home reliving what we have experienced during this holiday. If only the members of his local Golf Club knew what was in store for them.'

And with that Beth leant back and was soon in a deep sleep.

Lightning Source UK Ltd.
Milton Keynes UK
171321UK00001B/45/P